PARAS OVER
THE BARRAS

To Mary
Best wishes
James Barclay

By James Barclay

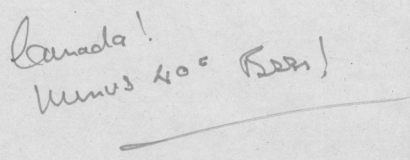

Canada!
Minus 40° Beer!

LANG SYNE PUBLISHERS LTD.

GLASGOW

Published in 1995 by Lang Syne Publishers Ltd.
Clydeway Centre, 45 Finnieston Street, Glasgow G3 8JU.
Distributed exclusively by Lomond Books, Edinburgh.
Origination by Newtext Composition Ltd, Glasgow.
Printed by Dave Barr Print, Glasgow.

© JAMES BARCLAY 1995
No part of this book may be reproduced by any means without the
publishers' permission other than for purposes of review.

I.S.B.N. 185 217 0131

CHAPTER ONE

Wullie McSorley pulled himself up from his easy chair, ambled over to the window and gingerly pulled back the curtain...just an inch.

He peered into the night. A large yellow moon glinted off the wet, grey slates on the tenement roofs of Well Street, in the Calton. The rain had stopped, leaving the asphalt streets shimmering like ochred ribbons.

Wullie sighed! They would be over tonight, that's for sure, he thought! The Luftwaffe had been saying their prayers for this was a 'Bomber's Moon'. Wullie let his eyes sweep down the street, up towards busy London Road where the clatter of the 'caurs' rumbled on - to the left and to the right. To Auchenshuggle and Dalmuir West, Burnside and Scotstoun. Their windows dimmed, showing only the silhouettes of their passengers, like black 'dabbities' stuck against the panes.

The darkness was no foe to the sturdy, reliable tramcars. Motor cars, with yellow slits for headlamps, crawled along warily —some,cautiously keeping in the wake of the tram in front.

Wullie pulled the curtain back a little further. Bombers or not, life was still going on behind those shuttered windows. Laughter and crying, fighting and moaning...and loving! Hitler's Bombers could go to Hell!Glasgow was ready, as always.The angry blast of a whistle pierced the night. An alert air-raid warden had spotted a chink of light coming from a careless window.

The city had its first night visit from Goering's squadrons back in September,1940 and, to Wullie, that seemed like a couple of other wars ago. People got blasè ..but not all of them!. The brick shelters, in back-courts, still had their regulars and there were always the deep down, dug-out sanctuaries at Glasgow Green where many a love blossomed and a rising star with tuneful tonsils would be discovered.

Wullie turned away from the window and shuffled back to the comfort of his easy chair. He flopped down by the grate where a roaring fire crackled and spat cinders and enveloped the room in a cosy warmth. He lit his pipe and watched the blue smoke curl up towards the whitewashed ceiling. His eyes fell on the framed photographs on the mantleshelf — lined up neatly between two wally dugs, snooty looking Cavalier King Charles spaniels that were Annie, his sister's, pride and joy.

There was the picture of Annie and Big Sammy on their wedding day. And then there was Rita, their daughter, standing proudly in her clippie's green uniform. Wullie reckoned that his niece was the smartest tram conductress in the Dalmarnock Depot fleet. And there was the picture of himself, resplendent in his Highland Light Infantry uniform....the famous H.L.I., called The Bantams because of their small, stocky, stature,and they were the scourge of the Kaiser, these proud Scottish soldiers! He stood straight and erect...but that was before a German sniper's bullet clipped his thigh on a Great War foreign field. He cursed that German soldier for the wound...and thanked him for the repatriation.

Wullie, small and dapper, was in his fifties now and lived with Annie in her three room and kitchen home in the Calton, just a few streets from the city's famous open-air market,' The Barras'.

Big Sammy was away in the army and had not been heard of in months, much to the consternation of Annie.

Wullie switched on the wireless and settled back once more with his briar, now going at full blast. Annie tolerated Wullie's pipe...but likened it to Dixon's Blazes, on the south side.

He picked up his Daily Record and perused the front page war news.The soft music of the Glenn Miller Orchestra playing 'Moonlight Serenade' wafted across the room.Wullie turned the paper to the back page and the Sports section as the music stopped suddenly and a familiar voice came over the air.

"Germany Calling...Germany Calling....Good Evening England..." Wullie threw his arms up in despair and slammed his paper down on top of the oil-clothed table top as the gutteral voice of 'Lord Haw-Haw', the derogatory title the Nazi radio presenter had been dubbed with by the people,droned on. "Are you still starving?" the voice asked in a flat monotone. "Poor souls," he went on, "are things too quiet for you, eh? Never mind, our Fuehrer will liven things up a bit for you tonight..Our magnificent Luftwaffe just maybe paying you a visit in Glasgow tonight ...or maybe you in Edinburgh...or Sheffield. You will know soon enough!"

The monotonous voice went on..and on. Wullie was about to switch the propagandist off but was beaten by Annie, who stormed in and, angrily, turned the radio off.

"Switch that aff!" she bellowed, "Who wants tae listen tae that yin?"

Annie did not like Lord Haw-Haw. She felt that maybe HE was behind Big Sammy's silence.

Wullie nodded: "Aye, he's a bit of a blawhard, int he, eh?" he said, picking up his paper again.

Annie agreed.

She was ten years younger than Wullie and still an attractive woman...and kept herself so! She could never tell when Big Sammy might walk in on her. But when he did, SHE would be ready!

She had looked after Wullie most of his life and was glad to have a man about the house. She could cope with Wullie and Rita doted on her uncle who was always there ready with his worldly advice.

Yes, Annie thought, it was nice to have Wullie about the house....sometimes!

Annie's one great wish was that her brother would have met a nice girl and married. But Wullie was a confirmed bachelor! Still, Annie thought, there was still time. Big Ina McLatchie, from next door, had made it plain that she was available. Often she had knocked on Annie's door on some pretence, but Annie knew that it was Wullie the heavy, roly-poly Ina really wanted to see.She had a great affection for Ina.

Annie switched the wireless on again and once more the mellow tones of the Glenn Miller band drifted from the speaker.

She took the brass poker from the fireside companion stand and jabbed the coals.The fire roared louder.

"Y'know," she said, turning to Wullie, "that Lord Haw-Haw seems tae know everythin' that's goin' on in Glesca! Last week he knew there was a sale at the Polly. How did he know that, eh? Wa's have ears, Wullie, "Wa's have ears!"

Wullie shrugged.

"Have ye heard frae Big Sammy recently?" he asked, not looking up.

Annie shook her head and sighed.

"Naw," she said, her eyes taking on a faraway look, "Ah only wish Ah knew where he was!"

"He's probably away fightin' for his country. "Poor Sammy — probably somewhere in England, trainin' hard and up tae his neck in muck an' grime.

A loud, authoritive rapping at the door brought the Sammy conversation to an abrupt end. Annie hurried to answer.

Special Constable Erchie McPherson stood on the threshold. His blue tin hat glinted from the stairhead gas lamp. The tall, thin, hawkish man was a plumber by day but when night came, the dungarees were discarded and the black uniform with the chromium buttons was ceremoniously put on...and Erchie became a dictator.

Special Constable Erchie McPherson, number seven, two, six zero, was somebody to be reckoned with.

Erchie McPherson ALWAYS strutted back to headquarters every night with a full notebook. God help anyone who so much as struck a match in the street during the blackout! It was said that McPherson had booked his grandmother when he found her with a pound of black-market butter in her pantry.

His one weak spot was Annie. He savoured her and never stopped trying to attract her with a lustful eye. But Annie was having none of it. She would be faithful and true to her Sammy...even if it did mean missing out on little perks that went around at the time.

Erchie did not wait to be invited into the house.He strode in, patting Annie on the cheek as he passed.

Wullie looked up as Erchie swaggered into the room. Wullie grimaced.

"Oh, it's yersel'!" he exclaimed.

Erchie ignored him and turned to Annie, who had hurried in after him.

"Ye're lookin' lovely the night, Annie! he said, his face beaming broadly.

"As usual," he added.

Annie gave him a contemptuous look.

"That's enough o' that,Erchie," she snapped,"Ma man might be away for a long time, fightin' for his king an' country, but Ah will be here waitin' for him...FAITHFULLY AND FOREVER!" Annie tightened her lips .

Erchie was not discouraged.

"He might be away a long time, hen," he said, patting her bottom. Annie rounded on him. Slapping his hand, she snarled: "That's enough o' that."
-Erchie laughed.

"Ah'll just be checkin' yer blackout blind while Ah'm here," he said in his most authoritative voice.

"Ye canny be too careful y'know," he went on, running his finger up the outer edges of the blind. He coughed and turned.

"They say Jerry can see a chink o' light at ten-thousand feet— can even see a match being struck in the street." Erchie spoke as a man who knew.

"There could well be a raid the night, Ah just..er..thought Ah'd pop up and see that yer blackout blind was a'right, he added."

Annie opened the outside door.

"Aye, well we're a'right," she said quickly, standing hand on hip with the door wide open."Just you get aboot yer business, Erchie"her voice was flat and commanding.

Erchie turned at the door.

"Make sure ye get tae the shelter if the siren goes," he ordered.

Annie nodded. "We wull," she said.

Wullie had been thinking about the probable air-raid.

"Ye know," he said, stroking his chin, "it's a wonder they've got the bloody gall tae mess aboot wi' us efter the tankin' we gave them the last time, int it?"

Erchie nodded.

He removed his tin hat and wiped his brow with the cuff of his sleeve.

"Aye, right enough," he said. "Ah'll away and get on wi' ma duties....checkin' the windaes an' doors. Ye canny be too careful y'know. They say that Jerry can see a match bein' struck."

"Aye, ye telt us that," Annie said, steering him out.

"We've a' got tae dae oor bit," Erchie said, hesitating at the door.

"Ah only wish that the army would have taken me." He sounded genuinely hurt.

Wullie raised his brows.

"So dae Ah," he said, "even the bloody German army. "Whit would they no' take ye for?"

"Flat feet," Erchie said, almost apologetically and not without embarrassment.

"Ach away," Wullie scoffed. "FLAT FEET? That would not have stopped US in the last war. When Ah was servin' the colours, we had a wee bloke, Dumpy Johnstone, in the trenches — just four-feet wan...and wi' TWO WIDDEN LEGS...it's a fact!"

Erchie looked incredulously at Annie who shrugged.

"Life and soul o' the trench, wee Dumpy was," Wullie reminisced, "He was oor observer and jist used tae staun' there and peer ower the tap o' the trench wi' his binoculars and many a time it was his timely warnin' that saved us frae disaster. They widden legs didnae stop HIM frae daein' his bit!"

Erchie dismissed the narrative with a wave of his hand.

"Whit a load o' rubbish!" he exclaimed. "How could he possibly see ower the top o' the trench a wee bloke like him?

"His legs were telescopic," Wullie said. "On wash days he screwed them aff and used them as claeths poles."

Annie threw up her arms.

"Right, Wullie," she cried, "that's enough. We canny a' be heroes. Be Erchie whit he is, he DID volunteer and it wisnae his fault that he was turned doon because he had a flat heid."

"Flat feet," Erchie corrected.

Annie flushed.

"Aye, well, heid or feet, they didnae take him...and maybe it was jist as we'll — he's got his auld maw tae look efter."Wullie gave out a hilarious cry. "Auld Boozy Bella?" he groaned. "She disnae need ANYBODY tae look efter her. She's the only wan in the street that can find her wey hame frae the pub in the blackout. Bounces aff every baffle wa', she does. Wan wa' tae the next. If ye want hame safely frae the pub, jist follow Bella. Ye might get a couple o' keekers, right enough, but ye'll get hame."

Erchie flushed with anger. Annie noted that his face was turning every shade of crimson, that his lips tightened into a thin red line and the whites of his knuckles stood out on his clenched fists. She stepped in immediately.

"Right, she snapped, "nae mair. That's enough o' that. We wull have nae violence in this hoose."

Erchie stepped back and, with a shaking hand, pointed at Wullie.

"He...he...suggested that MA maw drank too much...MA maw," he said, his voice trembling.

"He didnae mean it," Annie said. "tell him ye didnae mean it, Wullie," she said, glowering at her brother.

But Wullie was delighting in pricking Erchie's authority. Drawing himself up to his full five-feet two inches and puffing out his chest, he said: "Listen, wan dark night Ah bumped intae Boozy Bella at the coarner an' she was that stotious that she didnae know where she was, an' Ah struck a match tae see who it was that Ah had bumped intae....thinkin' it might have been a barrage balloon that had come doon. Well, Ah held that lighted match up tae her face and when she breathed on it, a ten-feet long flame shot oot and took the fur right aff Granny Black's tomcat." Wullie smugly folded his arms.

"Ah don't believe it,"Annie said coldly.

"Believe it if ye like," Wullie said, "but it's the only baldy cat in the street."

Erchie's nails dug deeper into his palms.

He grunted, straightened his tin hat and stormed down the stairs.

Annie turned to Wullie.

"Ye were a bit hard on him there, d'ye no' think so?" Wullie shrugged.

"He's faur too highfalutin and his haun's are over active," he said, adding, "an' that bloody tin hat's gone tae his heid!"

Annie had to agree. Erchie WAS 'the man wi' the hat'...but he was handy to know and he was well in with Auld McPhee, the grocer. Not that Annie had ever received anything she was not entitled to from McPhee...known as Auld Dirty McPhee!

And it was not without cause that the provision merchant had earned his tag. He was known as a more prolific patter of bahookeys than Erchie was. Naturally, he had his favourite customers who did not mind having their posteriors nipped now and then if it meant an extra half-pound of ham falling into the basket. Annie had managed to evade McPhee's wandering hand and administered the household culinary requirements with the rations available.

Annie sighed.

"Ah know Erchie can be a bore," she said, "but he means well...and he IS well in wi' Auld McPhee!"

"Watters his milk," Wullie said, without looking up.

"Who does?"

"Auld McPhee," Wullie said, knowingly.

Annie did not believe THAT. She shook her head.

"Naw, McPhee might be an auld reprobate," she said, "but he widnae dae that. He widnee do his customers...no' in these days of austerity. Ah think he does the best he can...under the circumstances."

Wullie laughed.

"Under the blankets ye mean, " he chuckled. "Ye see them comin' oot his shoap wi' big grins on their faces — the happy wans that have got a wee bit...and a wee bit extra. Their bags are bulgin'. He's a randy wee skelf so he is!"

Annie smiled:

"You're just jealous," she said, a twinkle in her eye, "cos you're past it and nae wumman will look at you."

"Ye're forgettin' aboot sex-mad Ina frae next door, "Wullie growled. "She canny keep her mitts aff me."

Annie dismissed his comment with a wave of the hand.

"Away ye go," she said, "Ina is a lovely person. Look how she looks efter her auld faither! She could've been married years ago only for her devotion tae the auld sowel and, believe me, when HE goes, she'll make a good wife tae some lucky man."

"Well, Ah'll tell ye somethin'," Wullie snarled, "It'll no' be me ye can bet yer life on that!"

Annie said nothing but wondered if Wullie was really as hostile to Ina as he made out? She had nothing but affection for Ina who had nursed her ailing father for twenty years, ever since her mother passed away.

Old Jake McLatchie had been an actor — not a profession prevalent in Calton. He had appeared many times in the Glasgow Queens' Theatre, in

Watson Street, near Glasgow Cross, reciting monologues and, so it was said, had once performed with Rin Tin Tin, the famous canine actor, during, a trip to Hollywood.

He always swore that this episode in his thespianic life was the beginning of his health problems, when rheumatics took hold of his left leg, due to Rin Tin Tin's detestable toilet manners. He hated all dogs from then on and never passed one in the street, be it an affectionate spaniel or growling rottweiler, that did not connect with his size-eight toe-cap. Now, as they say in showbusiness, he was 'resting' and he did this mostly in bed with the faithful Ina waiting on him hand and foot.

Annie ran a damp cloth over the oil-cloth table top.

"Aye," she said, "Ina hisnae had much of a life — you just don't appreciate whit ye've got, a sister like me tae look efter ye!"

Wullie knew well just how fortunate he was to have Annie as a sister, but would never admit it.

"And YOU'RE lucky that it's ME you're lookin' efter and no' Auld Shakespeare next door you've got on yer plate," he said dryly.

Annie swung round and slapped the wiping cloth on the table. Wullie turned his eyes away...knowing what was coming. Annie stood silent for a moment, her hands on her hips.

"Is that so?" Annie retorted "Well Ah think that Mr McLatchie is a proper auld gentleman. Anytime Ah meet him on the stairs when he's goin' doon tae the lavvy, he always tips his hat tae me."

Wullie shrugged.

"That disnae make him a gentleman," he said.

"Oh, aye it does," Annie replied adamantly, "and it is NOT a bunnet he wears, either...it is a soft hat!"

Annie spoke reverently as though Mr McLatchie's headgear was a golden crown.

Wullie threw up his arms.

"It's a soft heid he's got." he cried, "Over ninety-years-auld and he wears a saft hat just tae go doon a few stairs tae the cludge! And by the time he gets there it's usually too late. He should forget the saft hat and invest in a rubber bloody suit."

"The auld sowel never did YOU any herm, did he?" Annie snapped. Wullie stabbed his forefinger on the table top.

"Oh, naw? He has only kept me waitin', freezin cauld, on that stairheid blawin' intae ma hauns for hauf-an'-'oor — waitin' tae get intae that lavvy. Ah steyed there because Ah was too frightened tae move in case he came oot and Ah was beaten to it by another wan of oor frustrated neigh-bours. How Ah sigh wi' relief when Ah hear that chain gettin' pulled, the door openin' and him steppin' oot...only tae turn aboot sometimes and go straight back in again."

Annie dismissed Wullie's outburst with a contemptuous wave of her hand.

"Well, he's an auld man," she said, "you've got tae come and go!"

"He comes and goes a' the bloody time," Wullie said scornfully.

Annie ignored him. Giving the tabletop a final wipe, she strode towards the door, took down her coat from the hook and took her message bag from the top of the sideboard. Turning, she said. "Ah'm goin'. doon tae the shoaps. Ah just want tae make sure that Auld McPhee's been gettin' ma messages organised for oor Rita's engagement party a week on Setturday."

Wullie's jaw fell open but before he could utter a word, Annie was gone.

Rita's engagement party? He had forgotten about that. It had come around so quickly. And yet he wondered how he could have let it slip his mind? He knew how worried Annie was. Provisions for the celebration was the problem in this time of rationing. He knew Annie had been saving up her food coupons with McPhee. She had also managed to acquire two bot-tles of Johnny Walker whisky by altering the hem of a coat for Aggie Duffy, wife of the popular Seamus Duffy, owner and head barman of the 'Come Inn' pub, in Stevenston Street.

Wullie was not too sure of Rita's intended. While his niece thought the sun rose and set on her fiance-to-be, Wullie was not sure he was the 'Full Shullin'.

Rasputin Plunkett was a lanky, bespectled genius....or so he gave the impression.His long, thin nose was never out of a heavy volume and he could, undoubtedly, talk in equal terms with whoever was present in any company. Annie liked him very much and Rita stood by every word that came from his over generous mouth. Wullie, too, had a sneaking admira-tion for him although he would never admit to it. Besides, geniuses some-times are not the 'full shullin' anyway, he reckoned.

Rasputin was awaiting his call-up and was keen to get into uniform. God help Hitler then!

Wullie had asked him why, in God's name his mother had labelled him with a name like 'Rasputin'?"

"She is a very religious wumman,ma maw," Rasputin replied, "and want-ed tae call me efter a monk." The lad was proud of his name.

"But RASPUTIN?" Wullie cried, "Ah mean there is monks and there is monks. There's Francis of Ah-Sees-Ye, and there's good old Saint Benny Dick, whose followers make smashin' bevvy! But RASPUTIN!!!" He thought of the Horace Broon lookalike's mother leaning over her three-storey window yelling:"

"Rasputin...Rasputin...come up for yer dinner." Wullie winced!

Still, Wullie thought, Rasputin was Rita's choice and Rita was nobody's fool!

Wullie dozed off and Annie was back in no time. She put on the kettle and made a cup of tea. Placing a cup on the table in front of her snoozing brother, she poured one for herself and sat down by the table. Wullie woke with a start.

"Oh, Ah didnae hear ye come in!" he yawned. His eyes fell on the steaming cup of tea.

"Aw, ye're a pal," he said, reaching over and taking the cup.

"McPhee's got things well in hand," Annie said happily. "He's got a nice joint o' ham put aside and has promised some sausage rolls and coarned mutton....not to mention a couple o' tins of salmon." Annie placed her two hands around the cup and leaned back contentedly. "He never even tried tae pinch yer erse?" Wullie asked, his eyebrows shooting up.

Annie shook her head.

"He was the perfect gentleman," she said. "In fact he is gonny send up a boax of stuff on Setturday or Sunday...just tae get it oot the shoap."

Wullie frowned.

"Never even pinched yer bum? His wife must've been in the back shoap," he said in amazement..

Annie's thoughts were disturbed by a loud, frantic knocking at the door. She glanced at Wullie who leapt from his chair, a worried expression on his face.Ina McLatchie's hysterical voice was crying out ..."Annie....Annie, come quick....!"

Wullie threw the door open and Ina, clutching her chest and gasping, stumbled in and flopped on to a chair.

"Whit is it...whit's up?" Annie asked anxiously. "Whit's happened?" Wullie demanded. Ina , her chest heaving, took a deep breath and gasped: "It's ma faither," she blurted...

"He's loacked himsel' in the lavvy?" Wullie sighed. Ina dabbed her eyes with a handkerchief. "Ah...Ah think he's deid!" she sobbed. Annie's jaw dropped open. "Ar...are ye sure?" she stammered. Ina shook her head.

"Naw, Ah canny be sure," she sobbed. "Ah thought he was maybe havin' a long lie."

"A LONG LIE?" Wullie interrupted, "Gawd he's never oot his bed."

Annie drew him a look and turned back to Ina.

"Whit's happened, Ina," she asked, now more composed.

Ina blew her nose, examined her handkerchief and went on...

"Well," she said, "Ah noticed he hadnae got up this moarnin', no even tae go doon the stairs "

"Nae cludge? He definitely IS deid," Wullie said snidely.

Ina let out a loud wail. Annie scowled at Wullie and frantically fanned Ina with her apron.

Turning, she took Wullie by the arm and ushered him towards the door.

"Come on," she said curtly, "we'll see for oorselves. C'mon Ina."

Ina rose hesitantly and followed Annie still holding tightly on to Wullie. They crossed the stairhead landing and Annie shoved Wullie through the McLatchie's open door. The women hesitated for a moment in the small lobby but Wullie, impatient, pushed his way into the bedroom. He stopped at the door.

Old McLatchie lay on the bed, his toothless mouth gaping and his face the colour of slate.

Ina squeezed past Wullie and weeping loudly, hurried over and took the old man's frail shoulders and began to shake him uncontrollably.

"Da'...Da'...speak tae me, faither," she wailed.

The old man did not respond. He lay still, staring at the ceiling. Ina thrust her knuckles into her mouth and turned to Wullie.

"Dae...dae ye think he's deid, Wullie?" she asked, her eyes hoping that Wullie would say that the old man was just in a deep slumber. But Wullie was not known for his diplomacy.

"If he's no' deid," he said coldly, "he's daein' a bloody good audition. If he is actin', he should get an Oscar. Personally masel' Ah hiv never seen anybody mair deid than him!"

Ina wailed louder, Annie glared at Wullie, and put a comforting arm around Ina's shoulder.

"There, there," Annie soothed, "ye knew it had tae happen wan day, Ina."

Annie led Ina back across the landing into her own house and sat the shaking Ina at the table.

Wullie shuffled in and sat opposite. There was a long silence as Ina and Annie sipped their tea.

"Er....good auld age, yer faither," Wullie said at last, breaking the ice.

Ina nodded.

"Ninety- Four," she answered.

Wullie clicked his tongue.

"Nearly a hunner, eh! No' many of us wull live that long!"

Ina nodded and tried to smile. There was another long pause as they sat in silence sipping their tea.

It was Ina who broke the uneasy quietness.

"He had a good life. He had seen the world and was devoted tae the stage...tae the performin' arts," she said. "He would've loved tae have died wi' his make-up on!"

Wullie brows went up. "Even jist his teeth in would've been a bloody improvement!," he sniped.

Annie glowered and Ina gasped.

Wullie shrugged nonchalantly.

"We'd better get yer faither's doactor up," Annie said. Ina nodded.

"It's Doctor McGregor, in Claythorn Street," she said, dabbing her eyes once more.

"Right!" Annie said, rising and taking her coat from the door hook. "We'll go doon and see him." Then, turning, to Wullie,

"You go in and keep Mr McLatchie company till we get back," she ordered. "We'll no' be long." Ina fumbled in her bag and handed him the keys of her house.

Wullie suddenly thought of Ina. She was alone now. He would have to watch his step. One word of kindness and she may well misconstrue. He suddenly felt a pang of compassion for her but quickly suppressed it.

Wullie was too set in his ways. There was no place in his life for romance...with Big Ina or anybody else. There would have to be something very redeeming, some compensating factor, that would make him change his mind.

Annie and Ina arrived back in no time, accompanied by Doctor Angus McGregor, an elderly gentleman who was well liked.

He gave Mr McLatchie a cursory examination and had no hesitation in signing the death certificate. He handed it to Ina, who burst into tears.

"There, there, noo, hen, "he said, giving her arm a comforting squeeze. "He was an auld man, y'know. He had a good life."

Ina wailed and Dr. McGregor nodded to Annie and Wullie and departed as quickly as some of old man McLatchie's audiences.

Annie stepped in and took the piece of paper from Ina's shaking hand.

"Well, that's that!" Annie said, perusing the certificate.

Ina sighed and flopped down on a chair.

"Whit dae we dae noo?" she said.

Wullie gave a slight, nervous cough.

"You'll...er...have tae go tae Martha Street Registry Oaffice and then tae the undertaker," he said with authority."Ye canny leave him lyin' in there a' night. It's no' healthy," he added.

Annie glowered at him.

"Whit dae ye mean it's no healthy?" she snapped. Wullie shrugged..
"Well, it's jist no." he said.

Annie took Ina by the arm and steered her towards Wullie's room.

"Come on, Ina. It's been a terrible day for ye. Ye can stey here the night and we'll get things organised the morra."

Wullie watched the two women depart into HIS bedroom. But he felt no animosity towards Ina. In fact he was quite surprised to find himself sniffle and blow his nose. He sat down and lit his pipe. He could hear Annie's consoling voice and Ina's soft whimper coming from the room. Yes, he was lucky to have Annie, he thought.

Annie came back in and sat wearily down.

"She's quietened doon," she said, relief in her voice. "Ah've put her in YOUR bed."

Wullie smiled.

"She's been tryin' tae get in there for a while," he said.

Annie did not appreciate Wullie's facetious remark.

"That's enough o' that!" she snapped. "the lassie's been through a trauma."

Annie was right Wullie thought.His flippancy was uncalled for. "Ye're right," he said ashamedly.

He rose, walked over to the window and pulled the blind back a fraction of an inch.

"Jerry's late the night!" he said, looking up at the cloudless sky.

"Aye, he is!" Annie said, closing her eyes.

Wullie turned and walked slowly over to the sideboard, bent down and put his slighly quivering hand on the handle. He stopped and pulled his hand quickly away. The golden liquid was in there for Rita's big night. He wiped his lips with the back of his hand and went over to the window.

Annie's eye closed quickly and she smiled.

Wullie drew the blind back.

"Aye, Jerry's late the night," he murmured to himself.

The Glenn Miller Band played on....Moonlight Serenade. A Bomber's moon!

CHAPTER TWO

The number nine red tramcar from Dalmuir West to Auchenshuggle was trundling towards the Fare Stage in Trongate, near Glasgow Cross. It had been a busy car with workers spilling on from the city centre shops and offices. Under the Central Bridge was always a headache for Rita. It was there that she became more vociferous as the tired workers clamoured and clambered aboard in a hurry to get home.

Rita glanced at her small, chromium-plated pocket watch that was pinned to her tunic. She, too, was weary to get home. She was glad that this was her last run of the day. The car would drop her at Bridgeton Cross, where Wee Tilly McFadyen would be waiting, punctual as usual, to take over. Rita would hop on another tram going east, up Dalmarnock Road, and check in her cash at the Ruby Street Depot. Then home to a warm fire and a basin of hot, mustard water to steep her aching feet in. The thought made her sigh.She would soak her feet until new life revived them and they were back in prime condition for the night ahead. For this was Barrowland night! She suddenly felt excited and was transported to the floor of that famous ballroom in the Gallowgate. Rasputin would be there. They would have a wonderful time and the war and the crowds under the Central Bridge would be forgotten.

Small and blonde, Rita had inherited some of her mother's traits.

She had the same soft centre but was nobody's fool.

The sudden jolting of the car brought Rita back to the job in hand. The waiting crowd surged forward like a wild herd, scrambling and shoving and yelling as they clambered aboard the tramcar. Rita's eyes narrowed and her arm came down like a guillotine, slicing the excess.A few determined passengers hung on to the rail, reluctant to let go. But Rita was just as resolute.

"AFF!" she snapped, "This caur is goin' naewhere till youse get aff. So, youse are wastin' yer time haudin' oan. It wull get youse and the rest o' us naewhere!"

Rita put her hand on her hip and stood grim-faced. Hesitantly and grumbling, the overspill let go of the pole and, with some curse words, went back to the pavement and jostled for position in the queue.

Only then did Rita bell the driver to carry on.

"Right, move up there," she yelled, "move up the caur."

"Fares, please...fares, please," she called as she squeezed onwards.... "Any more fares please...?"

A stoutish lady fumbled in her purse and retrieved two coins.

"Wan and a hauf tae Brigton Croass," she said, offering the money.

Rita took the coins and took another look at the woman's companion.

"Who's the hauf for?" she asked suspiciously.

The woman nodded to the figure slunk down at the window seat beside her.

"Him," she said.

"HIM?" Rita cried, "HIM..him there, slidin' doon the seat so that Ah canny see him in this light? The light might be dim, missus, but Ah am not. He looks like he's already had a hauf. Come on... nane o' yer snash."

The woman dug the man with her elbow and muttered as she delved back into her purse and reluctantly handed over the correct fare...which Rita, with a look of victory,rang up.

Rita left the woman, now rebuking her hiccupping companion with a razor-edged tongue and stabbing elbow, and moved on up the car.

"Any more fares please...fares please."

Rita had no time for any messing about...not after a hard day and now at the end of her shift, she had heard every sob story ever invented.

Wee Tilly McFadyen was there waiting as usual and the change over was done without fuss. Rita jumped on a twenty-six car going to Burnside and minutes later was checking in her cash at the Ruby Street depot. She wasted no time and caught a tram just leaving the depot for Scotstoun West. Ten minutes later she gave a cheery wave to her clippie colleagues and alighted in London Road, not far from Well Street.

As she neared home, the mouthwatering smell of fish and chips wafted down from Mario Valente's shop.

Mario, huge, tubby, forty-four and cheery, had a large printed notice in the front of his window. 'I have two sons serving with the British Army,' it said, and 'Long Live Bonnie Scotland'.Mario was proud of his adopted country and hated the Italian Fascist dictator, Mussolini, whose only claim to fame, as far as Mario was concerned, was that he had the Italian trains running on time.

Rita followed her nose and received a happy welcome from Mario, who threw his arms up in the air in a greeting.

"Ma wee-a Rita," he cried in his acquired Glasgow accent. "How is it a-gaun, eh? You just-a finished your-a work, eh, ma wee-a Rio Rita?"

Mario had learned his English from his Calton customers!

Rita leaned on the counter and rubbed her ankles.

"Ah think Ah left ma dogs at Brigton Cross," she sighed. Mario's face took on a sad expression.

"Aw, you loast your-a wee dug, eh? That's a sad, so it is!" Rita shook her head.

"Naw, naw," she smiled, "ma DOGS are ma feet...it's jist an expression." Mario commiserated.

"Ah know how it feels," he said.

"Ma – a feets get-a like that staunin' here in the shoap arra day."

"Ah'll steep them when Ah get hame," Rita said, sighing at the lovely thought.

Mario nodded.

"It's-a the only wey," he said knowingly. "You plank-a yer feets in a custard bath and that'll soon dae the trick. They'll-a feel like new...like wee, happy dugs, eh? Wee-a pups."

Rita laughed loudly.

"MUSTARD, Mario," she chuckled, "it's MUSTARD ye put them in. Custard is a dessert....a puddin'"

Mario laughed.

"Ah'm-a the bigga, daft puddin', eh?" Rita shook her head.

"Naw, naebody can ever say that, Mario. You're nae puddin'.Anywey," she went on, slapping her hands, "just as long as they're fit for Barraland the night! That's the main thing."

"You're-a goin' tae the juggin', eh?" Mario beamed. "That's a good. You don't-a let Jerry spoil yer pleasure.That's-a good," he repeated.

Rita smiled.

"Ah'm meetin' ma boyfriend," Rita said, "we're gettin' engaged a week oan Setturday."

Mario nodded his head and smiled.

"That's-a good," he said, "A nice-a boy, your Raspspittin."

"Rasputin', " Rita corrected, "He's called efter a monk."

Mario threw up his arms in glee.

"Mama Mia...a monk, you say? That's a wonderful. Mind ye Ah don't-a know any monks by that-a name. He is no' an Italiano monk...no' a saint that Ah have heard of...Nae Saint Rasputin tae ma knowledge."

"He's an angel as faur as Ah'm concerned," Rita said.She puckered her eyebrows.

"Ah just hope Ah hivnae put him in a spot," she said quietly. "Ah mean, Ah hope he can afford an engagement ring. An' Ah just hope, tae, that Ah hivnae pressured him intae this."

Mario dismissed the suggestion with a wave of the hand.

"Naw, naw," he said, "that's no-a possible. He would be-a nuts no' tae want you for his wife. You are ma favourite wee customer and if Ah was-a twenty years-a younger and no'-a married masel', Ah would be chasin' ye a' roon' the place."

"And Ah'd let ye catch me, Mario," Rita laughed.

Mario chuckled.

"He's no' in the army, then, Raspittin?" Rita shook her head.

"Naw, but he just might be called up at anytime. Maybe his eyes will keep him oot...maybe."

Mario grinned.

"There canny be much-a wrang wi' his eyes when he saw you and snatched ye up, eh!"

Rita laughed.

"Well, let's say that Ah'd rather he steyed at hame than go an' fight Jerries and YOUR countrymen."

Mario's jaw dropped and, hurt at Rita's statement, he sadly shook his head.

"It-a breaks ma heart," he said, "tae think that ma two-a beautiful countries should be-a fightin' wi' each other.It's the worst-a thing in the whole world."

He wrung his hands on his apron...despair clouding his face.

There was a pause and Rita wished that she had kept her mouth shut. It was easy to forget that this big, likeable man was a countryman of the enemy.

"I..er...didnae mean.." she began. Mario stopped her in her tracks. Clapping his hands loudly together he cried:

"Come oan, we are gettin' morbid. Whit you-a need is a good fish-a supper, eh? That cures everything!"

Mario turned and filled up a newspaper with the delicacy.

"Plenty salt and vinegar, eh?" he said, sprinkling the condiments on liberally. Then turning once more to the sizzling pan, he retrieved another piece of fish and slapped it on to the paper,

"A wee bit extra for ma wee extra special customer, eh!"

Rita took the package and flipped it from hand-to-hand as the heat from the steaming fish supper sent a roasting warmth through her chilled hands.

"Ye're a darlin', Mario," she said, turning towards the door. She blew Mario a kiss and he blushed.

"You're some man," Mario, "she called as she turned into the street.

Mario grinned. He liked Rita.Hadn't she knitted him a pair of socks one time?

"Don't-a forget the custard," he shouted.

Rita waved her hand, not looking back She walked on up London Road, past Mr Adams' newsagent shop and turned down Well Street, being careful not to bump into any of the baffle walls that sat on the pavement outside each closemouth. She often wondered what good they would do if a bomb ever did drop in the street? There had been more injuries in the district because of the walls than because of any enemy action. Still, they must know what they're doing, she reckoned.

The closemouth, too, had props fitted — solid timbers supporting the walls and roofs. Rita couldn't see these chunks of wood being any more effective than the baffle walls. But,she supposed,their presence might have given comfort to some of the more elderly neighbours.

Wullie was sitting relaxed and reading his Evening Times when Rita reached home.

Wullie sniffed the air and his face lit up:

"Ah...fish and chips," he uttered, smacking his lips.

"Aye,MA tea," Rita said, "But...for you Uncle Wullie, here...have a chip." She offered the vinegar-soaked paper and Wullie took a few of the golden delights and eagerly popped them into his mouth.

"Had a hard day, hen?" he inquired between chews.

"Wan o' the worst!" Rita sighed, placing the food on the table,flopping on to the chair and kicking off her shoes.

Annie entered the room carrying a milk jug and sugar bowl which she placed on the table.

"Ah see that you've been peyin' Mario's a visit!" she commented.

"Ah couldnae resist the smell," Rita said, licking her fingers.

"You'll no' be hungry then?" Annie said.

Rita shook her head.

"Naw, no' really," she said, "Ah just want tae soak ma feet an' get ready for Barraland."

Rita made to rise from the chair but Annie put up her hand.

"You just stey where ye are, hen," she said, "Ah'll get ye a basin of watter...and some mustard."

"Thanks, Mammy," Rita sighed and eased back on the chair.

Annie left the room and Rita closed her eyes. She thought of the busy day she had had. She smiled at the thought of the "cheeky wumman" trying to get away with half fare for her tipsy partner. Of Mario and his sadness at the conflict tearing at his loyalties.

"Auld McLatchie's deid," Wullie said, turning the page of his newspaper.

Rita sat bolt upright.

"EH?" she said, stunned at the suddenness of the news.

"Ina found him lyin' deid in bed. "

Rita let out a long sigh.

"Aw, whit a shame!" she said with genuine sorrow. "Poor lassie. That's her got naebody noo!"

Wullie nodded towards his room.

"She's lyin' doon in there the noo," he said, not taking his eyes from his paper.

"Where's her faither?" Rita asked, narrowing her brows.

"He's still in his bed," Wullie said. "Yer mammy and Ina are goin' tae Martha Street and the undertakers the morra tae make a' the arrangements."

"Aw, that's sad!" Rita sighed.

Annie entered carrying a basin and a kettle that was spouting steam. She put the basin down at Rita's feet and poured in the water.

"Test that," she said.

Gingerly, Rita put in her big toe and then, satisfied that she would not be scalded, slowly eased in the rest of her foot. Annie took a tin of dried English Mustard and sprinkled in a good measure, agitating the water with her hand. Rita slipped her other foot into the basin, smiled and sighed as the warm water did its soothing work. She leaned back on the chair and closed her eyes.

"Ye'll have heard the sad news aboot Mr McLatchie?" Annie said.

Rita nodded.

"Aye, whit a shame! Mind ye, he was a good age!"

"Ah'm surprised he lasted this long," Wullie said, looking up at last. "Where's he gettin' buried?" Rita asked.

"He should get buried at sea," Wullie said, "He's been lyin' in watter for the past forty years."

- Annie turned and glared at Wullie who caught her glance and hurriedly turned the pages of his newspaper.

"Don't you be so bloomin' cynical!" she snapped. "We'll get a' that fixed oot the morra when Ina is mair at hersel'. "

Rita wriggled her toes in the basin and finally, satisfied, dried her feet off with a towel Annie had thrown on to her lap.

"Ah'll just go away and get ready," Rita said and, with a final wipe of the towel, she tip-toed out of the room.

Annie watched her go. She was proud of 'her Rita'. She had turned out a fine looking girl and never gave any trouble.

Annie frowned.

"Ye know," she said to Wullie, "Ah worry aboot Rita goin' tae Barraland."

Wullie looked up.

"Whit are ye worried aboot?"

"Well, in case it gets bombed," Annie said, concern in her voice. "Ah mean, that's the kind o' place they aim for —- where lots of people are gethered...especially sojers."

Wullie put his paper aside.

"Ach, come off it," he cried, "ye don't think Goering lines up his pilots efter they have loaded up their aeroplanes wi' bloody big expensive bombs — they are nut cheap tae make, y'know — an' then says tae them....'Forget the docks and power stations, Mein Herrs, Ah want for youse tae plaster Barraland the night'."

Annie scowled:

"Don't be so stupid!" she said. "Whit Ah mean is that he might want tae demoralise us....spoil oor enjoyment."

Wullie shook his head.

"Naw, naw," he said, "you ur talkin' rubbish! Wan dance hall gettin' flattened isnae goin' tae chinge the course of the war. It would just be a waste o' bombs.Goering isnae daft! Ah mean can ye imagine his pilots returnin' frae a raid, comin' before him and clickin' their heels - 'Tell the Fuehrer that we've just flattened Barraland, Mein Herr. The morra we will go for the Dennistoun Palais, The Albert, The Locarno and the Plaza....and if we've any bombs left ower, we'll massacre the Masonic Hall, in Whitehill Street.'"

Wullie laughed at his own joke.

Annie's eyes narrowed.

"You can laugh if ye like," she snapped, "but that wee Hitler bloke's got eyes at the back of his heid."

Wullie grinned.

"Anybody that looks like Charlie Chaplin's got nae chance, hen...nae chance!"

Annie grimaced. She wasn't so sure. She sat down and sighed deeply.

"Ach," she said despairingly, "where will it a' end! Here we're sittin' here jist waitin' for that banshee wail."

"Auld McLatchie's deid," Wullie said,with an impish grin. Annie did not appreciate the sardonic comment.,

"Ah meant the sirens," she said flatly.

Wullie puckered his lip:

"Oh, Ah see!" he said."Well, if that's a' that ye've got tae worry ye, ye're a lucky wumman."

Annie sighed.

"Poor Ina!" she said aloud.

"Eh?" Wullie raised his eyebrows.

"Ina, "Annie said, more in thought, "she'll find it hard no' havin' a man aboot the hoose. We'll have her in at Rita's party, that'll maybe cheer her up a wee bit."

"Aye," Wullie said, frowning, "just keep her away frae me. She's got mair haun's than the Ark Royal."

Annie dismissed the sarcasm.

"She'll be very lonely, noo," she said. "It couldnae have been much fun sittin' in the hoose a' day wi' just that auld man for company! HE was nae company for her!"

Wullie shrugged.

"He was nae company for anybody 'cos he was never in the bloody hoose," he said. "He spent his time doon in that cludgie maist o' the time."

Annie opened her mouth to reply but was interrupted by Rita, who swept into the room and did a twirl.

"How dae Ah look?" Rita asked, spinning round once more.

Annie stood back and surveyed her daughter from head to toe. She smiled. Annie was proud of her Rita and wondered where she got her good looks from.

"Like Ginger Rogers!" she said, as Rita posed like a mannequin. Wullie gave a thumbs up.

"Stoatin'," he beamed, "just stoatin', hen!" Rita laughed.

"Ye were dead quick gettin' ready," Wullie went on. "Ye must be right keen meetin' that man o' yours!"

Rita nodded.

"Ah'm meetin' him in the hall," she said.

"Ah thought ye might," Wullie said with slight sarcasm. "Saves him peyin' ye in."

Rita's pencilled eyebrows furrowed.

"Are you suggestin' that ma Rasputin is mean?" she snapped. Wullie heaved his shoulders.

"Ah definitely am not suggestin' anythin' of the sort," he said. "Ah am makin' a definite statement. Ah am TELLIN' ye he's mean. Look at last Hogmanay. He arrived here efter the bells wi' his cairry oot-a Bells minia-ture. We a' toasted each other oot o' bloody thimbles."

"That is nut fair!" Annie hissed, coming to her future son-in-law's defence. "Rasputin was skint."

"That's right," Rita said, "he had been savin' up tae buy a microscope and had just bought it as a Christmas present for himsel'."

"Ye'd need a bloody microscope tae see his cairry-oot," Wullie said.

"Ah am not gonny argue wi' ye, Uncle Wullie," Rita said, a little hurt. "Rasputin wants tae get oan."

"Aye the boy wants tae better himsel'. He studies a loat," Annie said.

"He's a bookworm," she added with pride in her voice.

"He's just a worm if ye ask me," Wullie said. "Anybody that can turn up at a hoose on the greatest night of the year and present ye wi' a bottle of whisky ye take wi' an eyedrop is a traitor!"

Rita let out a wail and dabbed her mascara'd eye.

"Noo see whit ye've done!" Annie snarled, putting a comforting arm around her daughter.

Wullie shuffled his feet.

"Ach, Ah didnae mean anythin', hen," he said with sincere contrition.

Rita blew her nose.

"But ye must admit," Wullie went on, "that everytime ye ask him whit he's gonny be, he comes up wi' a different answer."

"That's because his brain is so active," Rita said, "There's that many things he wants tae dae."

Wullie shook his head.

Annie put her hands on her hips. "Are ye finished?" she snapped at Wullie.

Wullie shrugged his shoulders.

"A' Ah meant was ..."

Wullie did not get a chance to finish his sentence.

"Rita loves him an' that's he main thing," he said. "And, who knows, whit the future hauds for any of us!"

Rita smiled.

"He likes you, Uncle Wullie," she said.

Wullie laughed.

"Well, he canny be a' that daft," he said.

Annie nodded towards the door.

"Better get goin', hen, or you'll be late," she said to Rita, who was standing on one leg and, with knitted brows, surveying the calf of the other.

"Aw, mammy!" Rita wailed, "Ah forgot tae put ma legs oan!" Wullie looked up sharply.

"EH?"

Annie hurried out of the room and cried out "Ah'll put yer legs oan, hen. Just staun' there a minute."

Annie was back within a second. Wullie watched with interest as Annie, down on her knees, began to pencil in a stocking seam right up Rita'a tawny-stained legs.

"Couldnae go tae Barraland withoot ma legs,"Rita said, examining Annie's handiwork. Satisfied, she pecked her mother's cheek.

"The sooner stoackin's get mair plentiful the better!" she said. Wullie chuckled. "Aye, it would be daft gaun tae the jiggin withoot yer legs, right enough."

Rita went into her room and returned wearing her heavy coat and carrying her patent-leather handbag.

"Enjoy yersel', hen!" Annie said.

Rita sighed. "Ye know," she said softly, "Ah feel it's no' right me goin' oot tae enjoy masel' and Ina lyin' in there wi' her sorrows...it's no' right, is it?"

Wullie put an arm around her shoulder. "Life goes on, hen," he said quietly, "the world disnae stoap turnin'".

Annie nodded.

"Yer Uncle Wullie's right," she said, "and, besides, Ah'm sure that Ina widnae want ye no' tae go oot and enjoy yersel'...we've a' got tae just get oan wi' things the best we can these days." There was a pause. How wise her mother was, thought Rita. "Right," Rita said, perking up. "Ah'll away and Ah hope there's nae raids the night." Annie took Rita by the elbow and ushered her out. "Away ye go," she said, "and IF Jerry comes ower just make sure ye get tae a shelter. Ah still think he's got it in for Barraland." Wullie threw his arms up in the air. "Aw, we're no' gonny start THAT a' ower again", he cried . Rita laughed and gave a final wave. "Just make sure the McLatchie's door is shut, Rita," Annie called out. "Aye, a'right," Rita replied and Annie closed the door to the sound of Rita's high heels clicking down the concrete stairs. "A good lassie, that", Annie said, clearing the table. Wullie nodded assent. "She's soft hearted, so she is," he said. "Takes efter her faither," Annie said, her thoughts suddenly going to Big Sammy and the back row of the Arcadia Cinema.

"Ah said 'soft hearted', no' soft heided," Wullie said, cheekily. Annie glared at him and continued to clear the table.

Rita had made sure the McLatchie door was closed. She sighed and stepped out of the closemouth into the chill of the night. She shuddered as a gust of biting wind stung her face. Pulling her coat collar up as far as she could and making sure she dodged the baffle wall, she turned left and headed up the street towards Bain Square and across the Square into Gallowgate.

A queue of chatty, giggling dancers had already formed outside the ballroom. Rita looked down the line to see if there was anyone there she knew and could have, perhaps, eased in with them.

Rita saw nobody she knew and took her place at the end of the queue.

The queue moved quickly and, once inside the hall, there was the usual rush for the 'Ladies' Room'. Rita wasted no time and was soon in front of the mirror putting on a final touch of face powder. Then she pushed her way through the jostling crowd and made her way up to the ballroom proper.

The floor was already jam-packed with cheek-to-cheek couples, waltzing to 'I Wonder Who's Kissing Her Now' played by the mellow tones of Billy MacGregor and the Gaybirds Dance Band, the resident and popular orchestra.

The dance ended and the shuffling couples made their way back to their corners and tables. Rita stood at the back of the hall amongst the crowd, her eyes scanning round looking for a familiar face. The band struck up 'In The Mood' and the crowd swarmed on to the floor for the Quick-Step.

Rita leaned against a support and watched the dancers swish past, getting whiffs of all available scents being sold at Boots and Woolworths.

"Hi ya, Betty," a voice whispered in her ear.

Rita turned quickly. The big, cigar-chewing American soldier grinned, flashing a row of highly polished white teeth. He smiled broadly.

"Hi ya, Betty," he repeated.

"You talkin' tae me?" Rita's tone was flat.

The G.I. nodded and removed the eight-inch Havana from his mouth. "Sure," he said, "you ARE Betty Grable, aint ya?" His smile got broader.

Rita dismissed him with a wave of her hand. "On yer bike, pal," she rasped.

The big man was not going to break ranks by a mere wave of the hand. He pressed on.

"Ya mean you AINT Betty Grable?" he said, pouting his lip. "Aw, gee....but you sure do look like somebody Ah've seen in the movies."

Rita allowed herself a faint smile.It was a situaton that just a few years ago would never have arisen . There were few Americans, if any, frequenting the Barrowland Ballroom in decades past. This was really a war situation!

The tall soldier was not going to give up.

"Say, that Billy MacGregor's Band's got a great sound, eh?" he said, giving a thumbs up.

"We're no' a' pipes an' drums, y'know," Rita said dryly."We've even got electricity," she added with slight scorn.

The young soldier laughed and thrust out a huge hand.

"Ma name's Elmer Jubowski," he said, grinning from ear-to-ear.

Rita nodded and offered her hand.

"How dae ye do," she said, more in politeness than encouragement. "I say", the G.I. said, going into his tunic pocket and producing a wallet, "would you like to see a photo of ma range back home, in Texas?"

Rita shrugged.

"Ah am not interested in your fireplace," she said coldly. The soldier's jaw dropped.

"Eh?"he said, puzzled.

"Ah have never been interested in stoves or fireplaces or lums or anythin' like that," Rita said, "and Ah don't feel that the dancin' is a place for to discuss them."

The American shook his head.

"Naw, you're dead right there," he agreed. "Ah aint got anythin' goin' for me that way either. Ah guess you either like those things or you don't. Personally Ah don't."

"Ah mean," Rita went on, "Ah know ye're away frae hame an' that! But maist folk cairry photays of their families, their weans an' that aboot wi' them. NEVER their fireplaces."

The tall soldier decided not to pursue this particular dialogue.

"Aw, come on, be friends," he said. "After all...Ah've got Scotch blood in me. Ah am one of yer clansmen. "

"You've definitely got somethin' Scotch in ye," Rita replied. The trooper stuck out his chest.

"Ma ancestors are Scotch, y'know," he said.

Rita laughed:

"No' so much Scotch as vodka if ye ask me," she said."Ah have never heard of the Clan Jabowski...no' even MACJabowski. You'll be tellin' me they were Poles of the Clan Caber, eh?"

The G.I. grinned and felt he was breaking the ice and pressed on.

Flattery never fails, he reckoned. Dropping the name of Hollywood should impress this girl from the backwoods. It had never missed!

He gave a slight cough.

"Yeah," he said, "it's great to be back here where the old ancestors came from. Away from the hurly and burly of Hollywood."

"Ah thought ye said ye came frae Texas?" Rita chided.

The big man nodded.

"Yeah, but I'm...er... holed up in Hollywood right now. Ah'm...er..into pictures."

"Of fireplaces?" Rita quipped.

"Naw, naw...movies..An', y'know, with your good looks, Ah'm sure that Ah could get YOU into pictures, Baby."

"Look, son" Rita said, "Ah am nut interested. Ah don't WANT tae go tae Hollywood and Ah couldnae care less if Errol Flynn is yer next door neighbour and youse use the same lawnmower or even that Gene Autrey's hoarse supplies yer fertiliser. And the only pictures Ah want tae get intae is the Paramount, in Renfield Street, on a Setturday night...so there!"

The big Yank was hurt. The patter had worked in Manchester and London.

"Look, sister," he began, "Ah...."

"Don't 'sister' ME," Rita said, "Ah am nut a nun...no' even close."

Although, as faur as you're concerned, Ah might just as well be. So, if Ah was you Ah'd get oan ma hoarse and ride intae the sunset. And if ye ever get on ma caur ye'd better make sure that that torpedo you've got in yer gub is oot and back in yer inside poacket...beside the photay of yer grate."

They both stared at each other for a moment and then burst out laughing.

"You're some gal," the big fellow said. "And you're some guy!" Rita laughed.

The soldier slapped Rita on the back.

"Geez," he said, "for a minute there Ah thought Ah was back home in Brooklyn!"

"Oh, so it's Brooklyn, noo!" Rita exclaimed, "No' Texas, or Hollywood?"

The soldier guffawed.

"Brooklyn Heights...and we've got a lot of gals just like you there...you're international, baby!"

Rita laughed.

"Aye, and we've got a few just like you here as well," she said. They both laughed loudly and did not hear Rasputin's arrival.

"Sorry Ah'm late, Rita," he gasped, "Ah got loast in ma studies." Rasputin wiped the steam from his glasses .

Elmer nodded towards Rasputin:

"This the competition?" he said, smiling. Rita nodded. "Aye, and it's nae competition!" The soldier nodded. "Did Ah hear him callin' you Rita?" "That's ma name," Rita said. The G.I. shook Rasputin's hand warmly. "Ya got a great little lady there, pal," he said. Then, turning to Rita, went on. "Rita, eh? Ah told ya you had that movie look about ya...Rita Hayworth, eh!" He stuck the large cigar back between his clenched teeth and turning to Rita, gave a wink. "See ya in Hollywood, kid." Elmer Jubowski moved on and vanished in the crowd. Rita was silent and , with her handkerchief, dabbed the corner of her eye. Rasputin nodded after the American. "Was he annoyin' you?" he asked, showing a sudden, hidden boldness.. Rita shook her head. "Naw," she said softly, "he's just lonely." "Just as well," Rasputin said, clenching his fist. "Come on," Rita said at last, "let's dance." They took the floor and joined the jostling crowd. The band had struck up a sentimental number and the male singer was putting everything into, 'At Last My Love Has Come Along'.

Rita closed her eyes and floated on a dream cloud,

"This is lovely!" she purred.

Rasputin said nothing. He gave her an affectionate squeeze. "Ah've got somethin' tae tell ye," he said.

Rita stopped dancing immediately and took a step back.

"Whit is it?" she said, her brows knitting.

Rasputin took her arm and steered her off the floor, to the side of the hall and towards a dimly-lit corner.

"Let's staun' here," he said.

Rita bit her lip.

"Whit is it?... Whit's happened?" she asked anxiously.

Rasputin looked down at the floor. There was a long pause and Rita was getting more agitated.

"Well," Rasputin began, "Ah..er..got word this mornin'. Ah leave next Monday...just forty-eight hoors efter oor engagement party. Ah'll be a sojer!" He puffed out his chest.

A tear swelled in Rita's eye. She was stunned for the moment and, when it dawned on her that the moment she had been dreading had finally arrived, she threw her arms around his neck and burst into tears. "Aw, Rasp," she wailed, "it's no' fair, so it's no'!"

Rasp put a comforting arm around her shoulder.

"Try and look at it this wey, Rita. Noo that AH'M in, the war will be shoarter. Ah've got some good ideas. It'll be finished in nae time at a'!"

Rita looked at him and wailed all the louder.

She threw her arms around him and drew him closer.

"Oh, Rasp," she cried,

Rasputin tried to smile.

"Ah..er..knew it was comin'," he said..."And so did you."

Rita had put the fear at the back of her mind. She sighed.

"Ah know," she said quietly, "but Ah kept hopin' that they'd turn ye doon because of yer eyes. Ah'm really surprised that they took ye, Raspy!"

Rasp puffed out his chest.

"It's intellect they're efter, Rita," he said. "It's the brain cells that matter. They spotted ma superiority right away," he said proudly.

Rita dabbed her eyes.

"Whit regiment will ye be in?" she asked, trying to show interest.

"The Pioneer Corps," Rasp said with pride. Rita wailed!

Her loud howl was only drowned out by the sudden screaming of the air raid sirens. There was no panic and Raspy held her close.

"When this war's ower, hen," he whispered, "you and me will get a wee cottage somewhere and laugh at a' this."

Rita closed her eyes and sighed at the dreamy picture that filled her mind.

"It'll be wonderful,Rasp. You and me, the wee cottage. Me gettin' up in the moarnin' and puttin' on the porridge for you...tae put a wee heat in ye before ye go tae work."

Rita was in rapture!

"Ah don't like porridge!" Rasp said.

"A'right, then, corn flakes," Rita snapped, her bliss slipping.

"But the wey you make porridge," Rasp said quickly, sorry that he had offended her, "makes a' the difference. Ah would eat it by the bucketful," he said.

Rita was pleased.

"How will we live?" she asked, snuggling into Rasp's embrace. Rasp puckered his lips.

"Well, that depends," he said. "Ah am thinkin' seriously of goin' in for brain surgery."

Rita pulled away quickly.

"Are ye still hivin' they heidaches?" she said, a worried expression crossing her face.

Rasp shook his head.

"Naw, naw," he said, "nuthin' like that. Ah meant that Ah might become a brain surgeon...there's money in that gemme, y'know!"

Rita clapped her hands together. Wasn't that wonderful? she thought. Her man...a brain surgeon! HER man! What a status symbol! She saw it all. Meeting friends at the butcher's."A pun' o' links for ma man," says the woman in front of her in the queue,

Then turning to Rita, she says proudly:

"He's a coalman, y'know."

Rita will smile, order 'hauf-a-pun' o' coarned mutton' saying, "It's for MA man...he is a brain surgeon, y'know!"

She looked up into Rasp's eyes.

"That's marvellous, Raspy!" she exclaimed. "Ye'll never be oot o' work if ye become a brain surgeon. Ah mean everybody's got wan."

"Ah am definitely goin' tae be a heid bummer wan day!" he said with conviction.

"You have definitely got a fixation aboot heids, Rasp," Rita said, just a little worried.

Still, she was proud that Rasp wanted to get on in life. Although, a doctor's life can have its drawbacks, she thought.

"Ah suppose," he said, "Ah could just stey in the army efter the war. A general's pey's no' bad either!"

Rita shook her head.

"Don't build yer mind up on bein' a general,Raspy," she said. "Efter the war there'll no' be much work for generals. If it's a nice uniform ye want, join the caurs, like me....YOU could be the driver and Ah could be yer conductress."

Rasp shook his head.

"Naw," he said, "Ah want tae get oot there and gie you things that ye've never had....like pigs trotters in vinegar an' that. Ah want tae gie ye the finer things in life. Ah live for the day when Ah can drink champagne oot yer shoe!"

"No' oot ma shoe," Rita cried, "Ah dunk ma feet in mustard maist nights. No' only would yer breath be hoatter than it is this minute, but ye'd have skint lips as well!"

Rasputin was not listening. He had a faraway look in his eye.

"We've got tae look forward, Rita," he said dreamily. "We'll call oor wee cottage 'Tara' — like in 'Gone With The Wind'. On a Setturday we wull come intae toon tae shop and, wi' you proudly hingin' oan tae ma erm, Ah will stick oot ma chest as we promenade doon Argyle Street. Ah wull be like Rhett Butler and you, at ma side, wull be Scarlett!" he sighed a long sigh.

Rita's eyebrows quickly came together and a flash of anger crossed her face.

"SCARLETT?", she cried, "SCARLETT? Ah'll be bloomin' CRIMSON. Ah am not walkin' doon Argyle Street wi' you dressed up as a cowboy! Besides, crinoline froaks are definitely oot."

Rasp put his hand over her mouth.

"Shh!" he whispered, "or somebody will hear ye!"

Rita shrugged.

"Ah just want a normal marriage wi' weans an' that. Nae cowboys." Rasp put his finger to his lips.

"Ah was just speakin' metaphorically," he said.

"Ye wurnae speakin' English, that's for sure," Rita said.

She sighed and flopped back against the plaster wall There was a long silence as she screwed up her face and rubbed her head.

Outside the pencil beams of the anti-aircraft searchlights stabbed the night sky. The monotonous drone of the Luftwaffe's Heinkels was suddenly drowned out as the angry, heavy anti-aircraft batteries exploded with deafening regularity. The blackness of the night flashed vivid orange and green as the big guns thundered, spitting death into the heavens.

"Auld McLatchie's well oot o' it!" Rita said. "Who?" Rasp raised his eyebrows.

"Auld Mr McLatchie frae next door," Rita replied, "Ah'm sayin' he is well oot o' a' this. He's gone up there," she said, stabbing her thumb heavenwards.

"He's joined the Luftwaffe?" Rasp was puzzled. Rita shook her head,

"Naw, naw," she said with a despairing tone. "He is deid...has snuffed it."

Rasp sadly shook his head.

"Was that the auld man who wore a soft hat? Ah used tae meet in the stairheid landin".

Rita nodded.

"Aye, that's him," she said, "Poor auld sowel. Ah used tae tell him he'd catch his death o' cauld and that he should wear mair claeths than that when he went doon tae the toilet."

"Auld folk get set in their weys," Rasp said. Rita agreed.

"Aye, Ah know! His daughter Ina's got designs on ma Uncle Wullie."

Rasp's brows went up.

"Oh, is she a tattooist?" he looked, surprised.

Rita tutted and shook her head. "Naw, naw," she said impatiently, "no' they kind of designs. She FANCIES him...never gies him peace and it'll be worse noo that her faither has departed!"

Talking about her Uncle Wullie suddenly brought her mother into Rita's mind. Grabbing Rasp by the arm, an anxious look crossed her face. "Oh, Ah hope ma mammy is safe!" she exclaimed.

CHAPTER THREE

At the first high-pitched blast of the air-raid warning, Wullie had grabbed the two wally dugs from the mantleshelf. Annie had retrieved her coat from the back of the door and had wrapped a warm, woollen scarf tightly around her neck. Hurrying into Wullie's room, she shook Big Ina vigorously, rousing her from a deep sleep.

"Come on, Ina, it's an air raid!", she cried."We'd better get doon tae the shelter."

Ina clumsily swung her legs from the bed and on to the floor. She stood up, stretched and, half-asleep, rubbed her eyes. It then dawned on her what Annie had said.An air raid!

"Oh, ma da'!" she cried, her hand going to her mouth. "Ah canny leave ma da' just lyin' in there a' by hisel'," she wailed.

Wullie, clutching the wally dugs, turned at the door.

"Well,Ah'm no' bloody well cairryin' him doon intae the shelter," he cried. "It's packed enough doon there withoot me yellin' - 'move up doon there, gie this deid boady some room.' Think o' the panic it would cause!"

"Ma da's no' aggressive," Ina said, hurt.

"He's no' noo, right enough," Wullie said.

Annie took Ina by the arm and steered her towards the door.

"Yer faither will be a' right where he is, Ina," she soothed. "He's oot o' it."

Annie's eyes fell on the 'wally dugs' Wullie was carrying.

"Right, Wullie, leave they dugs where they were," she commanded. "You are not takin' them wi' ye doon tae the shelter for everybody tae see."

Wullie pulled the dogs closer to himself.

"You should be proud o' these dugs," he said with a hurt expression. "They belanged tae oor maw who bought them years ago at Paddy's Market for tae frighten the mice that were rampagin' in oor hoose at the time...remember?"

Annie nodded.

"Aye, well ye can just leave them here tae frighten the mice while we're doon in the shelter. Wullie followed Annie out of the door and made sure their door was locked before groping his way in the dim gaslit landing towards the top of the stairs.

He let out a startled cry as an arm was suddenly thrust through his.

"Come on, Wullie," Ina's voice cried, giving his arm a squeeze, "Ah'll feel a lot safer haudin' on tae you!"

Wullie sighed.

"And Ah would feel a lot safer steyin' up here wi' the Luftwaffe up there," he groaned.

The air-raid shelter was already filling up. Children, still in pyjamas and hastily wrapped in blankets, were carried by parents, some with just over-coats thrown on and others wearing siren suits, one-piece suits that resem-bled dungarees with a zipper from navel to neck. Speedy apparel made for emergencies!

Wullie and the two women managed to get together on the same bench. The long wooden seat ran the entire length of the brick shelter with a sim-ilar bench on the opposite wall. Some of the people had brought light, can-vas chairs with them.Others had quilted sleeping bags.

The shelter was soon packed although not all of the tenants had taken refuge. Many had merely turned over in their beds, blasé at the Luftwaffe's inconsiderate interruptions.

Others had taken a chance and fled to the deep dug-out shelters in Glasgow Green –ten minutes from Well Street if you hurried!

Settled on the benches, Annie suddenly thought about Rita. "Ah hope oor Rita's a'right!" she said anxiously.

Wullie nodded.

"Aye," he said, "and Ah hope that that wee bachle doon there disnae bring oot his mooth organ again! If Ah hear The White Cliffs of Dover wan mair time, Ah'll take him doon tae them an' personally chuck him ower."

Ina squeezed his arm.

"You hivnae a violent streak in yer boady, Wullie," she said with affection.

"You just forget aboot ma boady," Wullie snarled

A sudden blast sent a violent shudder throughout the shelter. Terrified women and children screamed as dust and grit showered down from the roof. Ina grasped Wullie's arm tightly.

Erchie McPherson's blackened face suddenly appeared at the entrance door.

"Everybody a'right in here?" he snapped. There was a chorus of "Ayes".

"Good," Erchie said. "That was McPhee's shoap that just got it...flat-tened, so it is." Erchie shook his head. "That's the poor man's shoap, his life, everything up in the air...a' in a flash!"

Erchie departed, shaking his head sadly. He would be a busy man this night, he reckoned.

Wullie clicked his teeth.

"Aye, an' that's his sex life up in the air as well," he said sardonically, "Nae tickles, nae pickles!"

Wullie chuckled.

Annie had suddenly become serious.McPhee's ruin was no laughing matter. Next Saturday was Rita's big day. Everything had depended on McPhee. All the food coupons she had saved with him...GONE!!

"Ah know whit's goin' through yer mind, Annie," Ina said softly. Annie sniffed.

"It's oor Rita Ah'm thinkin' aboot," she said. Wullie turned.

"Whit aboot oor Rita?" he said frowning.

"Well, if McPhee's has been flattened, it means that a' ma plans for Rita's engagement party have been flattened as well," Annie sniffed again.

Wullie leaned over and took Annie's hand in his.

"Don't you worry, Annie," he said quietly, "Ah'll think of somethin'."

Annie smiled. If anybody could help, Wullie could.

The three sat quietly for a moment, none of them knowing what to say. The mouth organ man, too, had remained muted and Wullie gave a quick, thankful, glance heavenwards.

It was Ina who finally broke the silence.

"Ma big fear," she said, "is that the Germans will invade us. Ye know whit they dae wi' us wimmen!"

Wullie looked up.

"In that case," he said, "you'll have nothin' tae worry aboot. Wan look at your coupon and it'll be..'Mein Gott...back to the boats, lads!'"

"Oh, ye're an awful teaser,Wullie," Ina giggled. "Ye know, Annie," she cried, turning to Annie who had now composed herself, "even when he's hingin' oot the windae an' Ah pass by, he throws wee taunts at me." Ina's guffaws echoed down the shelter.

"That's only because Ah've nae bricks near haun',"Wullie said frostily.

Ina slapped Wullie's back and roared with laughter.

"See whit Ah mean!" she said. "He's telt me himsel' that he loves tae tease me oot the windae."

Wullie shook his head.

"Naw, naw, Ah said Ah'd love tae TOSS ye oot the windae," he snarled.

Annie scowled at Wullie, then, turning to Ina, asked:

"Whit are ye daein' aboot yer faither's funeral, Ina?" She was ready for Ina bursting into tears. But she did not. Ina sighed.

"Well, "she said quietly, "it was always his wish that he be cremated and have his ashes scattered."

"A good idea, Ina," Annie agreed. "Where dae ye think he would like tae be scattered?"

"Well," Ina said, "he was dead keen on gardenin' and his request was that he be scattered in oor windae boax. Ye widnae credit it, but he had green fingers, y'know!"

"That's because he was always pickin' his nose," Wullie said dryly.

"WULLIE!" Annie bawled, angrily rebuking Wullie's insensitiveness. Wullie shrugged.

"It is no' hygienic...havin' yer faither in the windae boax!" he said curtly.

"You just cairry oot yer da's wishes, Ina," Annie said, "and YOU mind yer ain business," she snapped at Wullie.

Wullie did not like the idea of the window adjacent to his own having the remains of his next door neighbour planted on the sill.

"It is definitely no' right," he reiterated vehemently, "buryin' yer faither in the windae boax. Wan gust of wind and he'll be flyin' a' ower the bloody place. He will be pollutin' the air, gettin' up everybody's nose....just like he did when he was livin'. We'll a' be coughin' an' splutterin'...an epidemic of McLatchieitis..."

Annie was getting angrier.

"Just ignore him, Ina, he's an ignorant get at times," she said, glowering over at Wullie.

Ina sniffled once more, dabbed her nose at each side and looked at Wullie. She still felt that Wullie was just shy and had these tantrums as a defence mechanism.

"As a matter of fact, Wullie", she said softly, "Ah was wonderin' that noo ma faither has passed away if ye would do me a great favour?" Wullie drew in his eyebrows.

"Ah'm no' mairryin' ye," he said quickly.

"Naw, naw", Ina said, shaking her head, "it's nothin' like that. Ah was just wonderin' if you would collect ma da frae the undertakers, efter it's a' ower, and bring him hame here? Ah couldnae face daein' it masel'. He'll no' be heavy, Wullie, he'll be in an urn or somethin'.'"

Wullie looked at Ina's pleading eye and shifted uneasily. Before he could reply, Annie piped up.

"Of course he will, Ina....won't ye, Wullie?" Wullie could not escape Annie's scowl.

He nodded.

"Ah suppose so," he said reluctantly. Ina leaned over and pecked his cheek.

"Ah knew you would, Wullie," she said smiling.

Wullie's face flushed and Annie wondered if Ina was not the amateur tactician she pretended to be?

There was an embarrassing pause which was suddenly shattered by the wee man with the mouth organ who began to blast out 'Run Rabbit Run' with gusto.

Wullie immediately cupped his hands over his ears.

"That we nyaff should gie his mooth a rest!" he blurted.

"Ach, he's just tryin' tae cheer us up!" Annie said, tapping her feet in time to the music.

"So he is," Ina agreed, "he's just tryin' tae be nice." Wullie stared at her.

"You should gie yer mooth a rest as well," he said rising. "Ah'm away oot tae see whit's happening."

Wullie, hands cupped over his ears, shambled towards the door and was gone.

"Ah'm gled ma da's no' here tae see this!" Ina exclaimed. "For a start, he would never have made it tae the shelter!"

Annie nodded.

"True enough!" she said, "He sometimes couldnae even make it tae the toilet."

Ina nodded.

"The auld sowel never asked much oot o' life," she said. "His five Woodbines and an occasional pint doon at The Come Inn...when he could make it doon."

Annie sighed.

"Aye, well he's up there noo," she said nodding skywards. "Aye, God bless him," Ina sighed.

Annie nodded.

"Just think," she said, "Wullie's oot there lookin' up at thae German planes and your faither will be up there lookin' doon at them...funny world, int it?"

Ina nodded. She had never thought of her father up there looking down. Usually he was down there looking up!

"Aye, right enough!" she said.

Wullie stood in the backcourt looking up at the night sky. He could see nothing but could hear the thunder of the guns and, now and then, a flash would illuminate the heavens. He shivered in the cold and pulling his collar tightly round his neck, hurried back into the shelter.

"Is anybody oot there?" Annie asked.

"Ah met Andra McGinty who was sayin' that Auld McPhee is daein' his nut because they drapped a bomb on his shoap."

"Aye, well he would be, wouldn't he!" Annie sniped.

"Is his shoap in an AWFUL mess, Wullie?"

Wullie saw the worry in Annie's eyes.

"Devastated, hen," he said softly, adding, "Ah think a' his stock has been pulverised."

Annie fell back on the bench and stared into space. "Whit will Ah dae...Rita!!"

Wullie leaned over and patted her hand.

"Ah told ye that Ah would think of somethin'," he reassured her.

"Oh, Wullie, Ah hope so!" Annie sighed. Then, turning to Ina, she said: "Tomorrow mornin' we'll go doon and see the undertaker and go tae Martha Street as well tae register yer faither's death, Ina."

Ina squeezed Annie arm.

"Ye've been awful good tae me, Annie...like the sister Ah never had," she said.

Annie flustered.

"Aye, well...er.." she began, ". Ah..er..whit are neighbours for, anywey, eh?"

Any embarrassment was cut short by a sudden blasting fanfare from the mouth organ at the end of the shelter.

"And noo," a man's voice boomed, "we will have a chorus of the 'White Cliffs of Dover' followed by 'We Ur Gonny Hang out Our Waashing Oan the Siegfried Line'. All together now...."

Wullie shuddered.

"Somebody should bloody hang HIM oot on the Siegfried Line...any bloody line," he said, tightening his lips and slamming his hands over his ears.

Over the next few hours there were choruses of 'Mairzy Doats and Dozy Doats', 'Don't Fence Me In' and 'Keep the Home Fires Burning'.

The loud wail of the 'All-Clear' siren was a welcome release for Wullie. Wearily they spilled out of the shelters, stretching and yawning and carrying sleeping children and headed for home.

Annie made a cup of tea and fixed up a makeshift bed in the kitchen for Ina, who had looked in at her own house to make sure everything was all right.

Rasputin had seen Rita safely home and soon, lights switched off, all was quiet except for the deep snoring in Wullie's room.

Morning came with a cold snap. Already scores of volunteer workers were in the streets, clearing up and checking for casualties. McPhee's store was no more, along with a builders' yard and a derelict tenement. Luckily, no-one was hurt.

Annie had made a potful of porridge and had toasted bread on the grate. Rita, who was on the early shift, had already left for work and Ina had gone next door just to make sure that all was well.

"Ye never know, her auld man might've got up during the night tae go doon tae the cludgie," Wullie said sarcastically.

"You have some respect for that lassie's feelin's," Annie scolded.

"It's her feelin's Ah'm dodgin'," Wullie snapped.

Ina, dabbing her eyes, entered and sat down at the table.

"He's just lyin' there," she sobbed.

"Well, thank God for that," Wullie said. "It would've been worse if he had been staunin' up."

Annie scowled at him. "Aye, well, c'mon, Ina, we'll go intae Martha Street and then alang tae the undertaker, tae get things movin'."

Ina wailed and Annie put a comforting arm around her.

"Let it oot, hen," she said softly, "ye canny beat a good greet!" Ina wailed louder.

Annie turned on Wullie.

"Noo listen, it could be that Auld McPhee sent oot ma boax of messages before his shoap was bombed..it's just a chance. It might just turn up today. Anywey, Ah'll try and find oot. Ah only hope tae God that he has for Rita's sake. You keep yer eyes open just in case...a'right?

It was a command, not a request.

Wullie nodded. It was a forlorn hope, but, who could tell? "Aye, aye," Wullie replied with impatience.

Annie and Ina left Wullie reading his morning Daily Record and sipping tea. The wireless played 'Music While you Work', from a factory canteen 'somewhere in England'.

Henry Hall's Band played 'Smoke Gets In Your Eyes' and the war was a thousand miles away.

Wullie lit up his pipe and leaned back, listening to the music. It was too early in the day for 'Lord Haw Haw's' broadcast. Wullie was glad that the authorities, in their wisdom, had seen fit NOT to jam the pompous oaf's propaganda transmissions.

They were good for a laugh and were doing the exact opposite of what Nazi Minister of Propaganda, Josef Goebbels, had in mind. Only some gullible souls shook at the sound of Haw-Haw's dull monotone . Wullie listened in with scorn.

Workers Playtime ended and Sandy MacPherson came on playing the organ. Wullie turned down the sound and turned back to his newspaper. Harry Lauder had given an impromptu concert in John Brown's shipyard, in Clydebank. Last night's raid had done little damage according to an official statement. They hadn't mentioned McPhee's shop at all.Probably just because it was a wee shop, Wullie reckoned. If it had been Galbraith's, in London Road, that had been clobbered, it would have been all over the front page, he decided.

He read the paper from front to back and back again until he found his eyes getting heavy. Putting the journal aside, he sat back and closed his eyes and was drifting into sleep when he sat up with a start.

What if Auld McPhee HAD managed to send out Annie's box of goodies before that fateful bomb made a direct hit?

He could not take a chance of falling asleep in case the delivery man, getting no reply to the door, was apt to dispose of the messages in some other quarter...at extra cost, of course.

Wullie got up from his chair, stretched himself and ambled to the door leading to the outside landing. He opened the door and, leaving it slightly ajar, shuffled into the bedroom where he lay down on top of the patchwork quilt and closed his eyes.

As he found himself drifting into sleep, he sat up with a jerk,gave himself a shake and lay down again. But soon his eyes grew heavier and, once more, he floated towards slumber until he sank deeper and deeper into that sweet repose..

Annie and Ina left the Registry Office, in Martha Street, with the demise of Old Mr McLatchie now duly noted.

They crossed George Square, walked down Mitchell Street and into busy Argyle Street. The two girls did some window shopping although many of the windows were boarded up with only slats provided for passers-by to look through. Sandbags were everywhere, mufflers against bomb blast.

Annie and Ina walked on,across Union Street,past the Grant Arms Restaurant and under the Central Station Bridge, affectionately known as The Heilan'Man's Umbrella, and right, into Hope Street where they strolled up the entire length before turning into Sauchiehall Street...and Miss Cranston's Tearoom. They were lucky! A table was being vacated as they entered, to be met by a smart waitress, immaculately dressed in black frock and crisp, white apron.

The smiling girl showed them to the newly vacated seat and soon they were in deep conversation, munching freshly baked muffins and sipping sweet,hot tea from delicate,hand painted bone china teacups..

It was good to get away from everything, Annie thought, and this was the best way to take dear Ina's mind away from her pain. After tea, the girls walked down to Argyle Street once more and caught a tram going east. First stop was the undertaker's where arrangements were made for the funeral.

The undertaker, a small, roundish man with a black Earl Haig moustache, epitomized his profession.

"Would youse like for me to insert an intimation in the Evening Times for your friends to peruse?" he asked, almost in a whisper.

Ina smiled.

"Oh, that would be lovely!" she exclaimed.

The small man licked his pencil and made a note.

"Would youse be for wanting a verse of poetry on said intimation?" he asked, licking his pencil in anticipation.

"Aw, Ah think that would be nice!" Ina said.

The little man noted Ina's acquiescence with a smile.

"Would youse wish to compose your own verse or would youse like for me to furnish youse with 'one of the more standard, popular ones?" he said, pencil poised.

"Like for instance," he went on, "He never made it to ninety-seven, but he disnae care...he's now in Heaven!"

Ina looked perplexed and glanced at Annie, who pursed her lips and gazed at the ceiling.

Ina cradled her cheek in her hand and knitted her eyebrows and thought deeply.

"Naw, Ah don't fancy that!" she said. "He was an actor, ma da' and Ah think something mair appropriate would be desirable."

The wee man tapped his lips with his pencil and let his creative mind get to work.

"I know," he said, pleased with himself. "How about 'No more can he work for Twentieth Century Fox....He's gone off on a journey in a big, widden box'!"

Annie slapped her hand over her mouth to stifle the sound and gazed harder at the ceiling. Ina didn't know where to look.

"I can see from your expressions that youse are not inclined for to like that prose. Perhaps youse have something better in mind?" the wee man said.

"Ah think we'll just leave it," Ina said at last."If ye want tae be poetic, ye can say somethin' like 'He was a wee actor that worked wi' Max Factor'...somethin' plain like that but which informs of his profession."

The undertaker stuck his pencil behind his ear and said that they would just omit any verses in the Times' publication. They left him with his promise that he would see to things immediately and the deceased would be collected as soon as possible.

Next stop was Mary Fox's florist's shop, in London Road, where a suitable floral tribute was purchased — a wreath of white carnations.

"He just loved Christmas, so he did," Ina said, blowing her nose.

Curdy McVey shifted uneasily in the passenger seat as his colleague, Hector Tamson, speeded down Gallowgate. Curdy, small and rotund with a plump face and with the complexion of a well polished apple was apprehensive. This was his first day on the job...the beginning of his five-year apprenticeship. He thought that he would have been broken in quietly with just some of the mundane jobs to perform...tasks like sweeping floors, making the tea and running with bookies lines. But no! He was thrown in at the deep end. He looked over at Hector, tall and gaunt and with a sharp nose that could 'pick wulks oot', Curdy thought. Hector was cursing because he had run out of cigarettes. But Hector Tamson knew his business. He was a professional and the lady in the office told Curdy that he was lucky indeed to have been teamed up with him.

With a final curse, Hector stopped searching his pockets for a cigarette and braked quickly. He turned the gleaming black hearse into Well Street and drove slowly down, his head out of the window as he scanned the closemouths for number twenty-seven.

"Ah, this looks like it!" he said, coming to a stop. He studied his notebook and climbed out of the cab...followed by Curdy who suddenly felt his neck suddenly becoming moist under his collar.

"Aye, this is it!" Hector said finally, putting the notebook into his inside pocket.

"McLatchie's the name....Jake McLatchie..."

Curdy was standing rigidly to attention, waiting on Hector's orders.

"Right, noo look, Curdy," Hector said, "Ah am just nippin' doon tae that wee shoap tae see if they've any fags. You go up and make sure that somebody's in...a'right?"

Curdy nodded and touched his forelock.

"Right ye are, sir," he said with proper respect. Hector grimaced.

"Look, son," he said, "nae formalities. Ah've already telt ye..just call me Hector. If we are gonny be workin' the gether we are as well startin' off on the right fit, okay?"

Curdy touched his forelock.

"Right, sir...er..Hector," he stammered.

"Good!" Hector said. "Noo it's two up...tap flat. Just leave the coaffin there until we're sure there's somebody in, a'right?"

Curdy nodded.

"Right!" Hector said, "Away ye go...Ah'll no' be long."

Hector turned and hurried down the street towards Mary Welsh's corner shop.

Curdy tugged nervously at his collar and, pulling himself up to his full five-feet three inches, entered the closemouth. Gingerly, he climbed the stairs, going as slowly as he could and hoping his stalling would give Hector time to reappear. But his mate still had not turned up as Curdy arrived at the topflat.

There were three doors on the landing. The door on the right hand side had a brass nameplate proclaiming the current occupants were called Brown.

The middle and the left hand doors had no nameplates. McLatchie was the name Curdy was looking for and the door with the brass nameplate was immediately discounted.

Curdy rapped loudly on the middle door but received no reply. He noticed the left-hand door was slightly ajar. This had to be it, he reckoned. They were expecting him. Curdy knocked quietly on the door which opened wider at his touch. Warily, he poked his head inside.

"Anybody in?" he said, almost in a whisper. There was no answer. Becoming a little bolder, he stepped inside.

"Anybody here?" he called with a little more authority in his tone.

"Mr McLatchie...it's the undertaker...are ye in?" Only silence greeted him.

Cautiously, he tip-toed into the house, quietly tapping on doors and looking into the deserted rooms.

"Mr McLatchie...are ye in there?"

Finally he came to the bedroom door where Wullie was stretched out in deep and silent sleep..

Curdy felt his neck go clammy as he reluctantly edged towards the bed...all the time wishing that Hector would turn up.

He arrived at the top of the bed and, looking down at Wullie, he bit his lip.

"Geez!" he exclaimed, "he looks like he's just sleepin'!"

Curdy produced his measuring tape, the first tool of his trade, which had been presented to him by Hector, who proudly told him that it had been his grandmother's. He proceeded to take Wullie's dimensions, stopping now and then to mark his little, black notebook. He peered into Wullie's face, closer and closer until their noses almost touched.

It was at that point that Wullie suddenly woke up. His eyes stared in disbelief at the fat face just hovering two inches from his own.

Curdy's notebook went flying into the air and he went rigid, standing rooted to the floor, his hair bristling. He emitted no sound. His vocal chords were paralysed. His protruding wide eyes stared blankly ahead and only a slight quivering of his fingertips proved he was not in a comatose state.

Wullie leapt from the bed and surveyed the frozen apprentice.

"Hey, hey...whit's up wi' you, son?" he cried, "Ah'm no' THAT bad lookin'!"

Curdy began to stammer incoherently.

"Calm doon...calm doon," Wullie said soothingly, tapping Curdy on the cheek. "Ah've been lyin' here waitin' for ye."

Movement reluctantly came back to Curdy's incapacitated body. The blood began to pulse through and his voice croaked back into life.

"Ye...ye have?" he stuttered, his jaw dropping open.

Wullie steered Curdy to an arm-chair and eased him down into it.

"There, noo," he said, "take it easy, son. Sorry if Ah gave ye a fright! Did ye...er..bring the boax?"

"Er...aye," Curdy stammered.

Wullie was delighted and glad that he had left the outside door ajar. He might easily have missed this errand boy.

"Where is it?"he asked, his eyes sweeping the room. "Ah've..er...left it doon stairs,"Curdy said.

"DOON THE STAIRS?" Wullie bellowed. This boy was naive, he decided. He recalled how another young man had once left bedridden Granny McLeod's box down for a mere second or two, while he nipped round the back of the close to relieve himself. When he returned the box had been snaffled...gone!

He narrated the sad saga of Granny McLeod's stolen box to Curdy, who was astounded that anyone would pinch such a thing.

"Some folk wull pinch anything," Wullie said sadly."Mind ye, it wisnae your firm that was involved. It was Galbraith's."

Curdy shook his head.

"Ah didnae know Galbraiths had this service," he said.

"Of course they have," Wullie said. "Ye canny expect an auld wumman tae go doon three flights o' stairs and cairry her ain boax up. Ah mean, surely chivalry's no deid!"

Curdy shook his head in disbelief. Not only was he shocked that some people would stoop so low as to put an old lady through that terrible ordeal, he was surprised and humbled at her courage, and Wullie's, too, in lying and waiting for the delivery.

"Whit aboot the auld wumman?" he asked with genuine concern. Wullie shrugged.

"She just lay there in bed. It was a few days before they telt her that somebody had pinched her boax. The auld sowel was horrified." Wullie shook his head.

"If they waited a few days," Curdy said, "it's a wonder she wisnae mummified."

"Ah went ower tae see the auld sowel masel'," Wullie sighed, ignoring the remark. "It was pitiful so it was. She just lay there. Her face was like wax."

"It probably WAS wax!" Curdy exclaimed. "She was probably embalmed."

Wullie shook his head.

"Naw, naw," he said, "Ah widnae go as faur as that. She had a bit o' lipstick oan, right enough. Anywey, when the neighbours found oot whit had happened, they had a whip round and took up a wee hamper."

Curdy raised his eyebrows.

"Was she a midget?" he asked.

"Naw, naw. She was a wee wumman, right enough," Wullie said, wondering why Curdy asked such a question,

"Well, Ah think that was terrible!" Curdy said. "A hamper isnae dignified, so it's no'."

Wullie looked up.

"Whit does it matter?" he said.

"Oh, it matters, it definitely matters," Curdy was adamant."When that auld wumman's boax was stolen from right under her nose, they might at least have furnished her wi' another boax. If they had telt MA boss the circumstances, he would've been mair understandin'."

Wullie's face flushed angrily.

"UNDERSTANDIN'..? UNDERSTANDIN'?" he bawled. "YOUR BOSS...UNDERSTANDIN'? When was HE ever understandin'; That auld swine o' a boss of yours likes nothin' better than tae climb intae bed wi' his customers. It's blackmail...nae bed, nae boax."

Curdy stood still and silent as Wullie's words penetrated. Finally, shaking his head, he said.

"Naw, naw. Ma boss is a gentleman. He is not Dracula. You are definitely wrang aboot him!"

Wullie stood and drew himself up to his full height.

"Wrang, am Ah?" he snapped. " Wrang? Ah'll tell ye this, son. Ah would not trust ma granny wi' your boss. Noo, you get doon they stairs this minute and bring up that boax."

Curdy folded his arms and stood his ground.

"If ye ask me," he said, tightening his lips, "you don't look like ye're ready for a boax."

"It's no' for me," Wullie said. "It's for ma wee niece."

Curdy raised an eyebrow. He was sure his 'customer' was a man.

"Yer niece?" he queried.

Wullie nodded.

"Aye, ma niece, Rita," he said. "She'll be that pleased ye've arrived. It was her wan big worry... 'Oh, Ah hope they come up wi' ma boax'...that's a' she's been sayin' for days noo. Ye'll have made her day, so ye wull!"

Curdy gave an embarrassed cough.

"She'll no' be usin'it the noo, is that it? Lookin' tae the future, ye might say!"

Wullie shook his head.

"Naw, naw," he said, "A' her pals are comin' up next Setturday and when they see the boax has arrived ye can bet yer life they'll a' be gettin' intae it."

Curdy, exasperated, puffed his cheeks and let the air out slowly.

"It's no' that big, y'know!" he said at last.

"It'll be big enough," Wullie said, "Her maw's been savin' up for months for it....and her boyfriend will be delighted!"

"Er...where's yer niece the noo," Curdy hesitantly asked. "Is she in a bed in wan o' the other rooms?"

"Naw, she's at her work...she's a clippie on the caurs," Wullie said."But she'll dae cartwheels when she she gets in and sees her boax here!"

Curdy scratched his head. He had heard of forward planning but nothing like this.

"Ah thought the boax was for you," Curdy said.

"Naw, naw," Wullie shook his head. "Ah'm past it...although the big wumman next door has been chasin' me. She's tried tae pin me doon a few times but Ah've always managed tae wriggle oot of her clutches!"

"Is she a mad wumman?" Curdy looked worried.

"She could be," Wullie replied.

"Well, Ah'd get the polis if Ah was you," Curdy said. "Ye could be sleepin' in yer bed wan night when suddenly she could pounce. Ye could easily waken up deid!"

Wullie laughed.

"Surely no'!" he said.

"So, the boax is for yer niece, then, eh? How auld is she?" Wullie shrugged.

"Aboot twenty, Ah think"

"So young! It's a shame, so it is! Is she gonny kill hersel'?" Curdy sounded perplexed.

"No' that Ah know," Wullie said. "Unless it's wi' work."

Curdy was wishing that Hector would show up. He had not been trained to handle situations like this.

"Anywey," Wullie went on. "You're here and that's the main thing. Her maw can noo throw a party tae celebrate."

Curdy stared at Wullie in disbelief.

"It's a bit cauld, is it no'?" he said.

"Want me tae put the fire oan?" Wullie said, moving towards the small electric fire on the floor..

"Ah don't mean cauld, cauld," Curdy said

Wullie hesitated.

"Whit kinda cauld dae ye mean?" he asked.

Curdy scratched his cheek.

"Well, a' this cairry-on wi' yer niece....and her maw aboot tae throw a party tae celebrate. Ah personally think that whit's happenin' tae your niece is a tragedy."

Wullie's brows rose.

"Oh, ye've met Rasputin, have ye?"

"Whit's THAT?" Curdy asked narrowing his eyes.

"Ah've been wonderin' that masel'," Wullie said. "Rasputin is Rita's intended. It's because o' him that we need that boax you brought the day."

Curdy threw up his hands in frustration.

"Ah gie up," he said. "This is bizarre, so it is. Ah am here for to pick up a boady and a' the time it's oot there in the street goin' up and doon collectin' fares on a caur. That is not hygienic."

Wullie looked puzzled.

"Whit's a' this aboot a boady?" he asked.

"Ah have got a big boax doon the stairs...a coaffin tae be exact."

Wullie spluttered.

Curdy went on.

"Is your niece's name McLatchie?"

Wullie sighed with relief. His conversation with Curdy now beginning to make sense.

"It is not," he said. "Auld Mr McLatchie lies next door awaiting you. I have misinterpreted you as the lad frae McPhee's the grocer's. And while Ah am pleased that you have came tae the wrang hoose, it means that Annie, ma sister, is back in the same boat again!"

Before Curdy could open his mouth, there was a loud rapping at the door and Hector hurried in.

"Sorry Ah'm late," he gasped, " a big queue...everythin' a'right, Curdy?"

"Er..aye..."Curdy stammered. "He...er..says it's.no' him." Curdy jabbed his thumb towards Wullie.

The professional in Hector sized up the situation immediately. He always maintained that apprentices should never be left on their own...well, not until their fourth year at least.

"Aye, well..er.." Hector stammered, "I..er.. would definitely, but definitely take the gentleman's word for it, Curdy. If he staun's there and catagorically denies that he is not the gentlemen what we have called for, Ah would be inclined for to believe him!"

Curdy hung his head.

"Ah..er..came intae the wrang hoose," he said, making a pattern on the shiney linoleumed floor with his toe.

Hector turned to Wullie, who watched Curdy's embarrassment with some sympathy.

"Ah hope, sir," Hector began, "that you was not put to any inconvenience by my eager apprentice's 'fox par'...a boy Ah see that I will have to supervise in the future in case we should end up planting the wrang people."

He glared at Curdy who looked quickly away.

Hector went on.

"I mean by that, sir, people who are alive and kicking and not wishing for to partake of our professional services for the time being."

Wullie felt sorry for Curdy. He remembered his own young days when he made many a faux-pas making many red faces. Turning to Hector, he said:

"Your apprencice, good sir, is a lad who should be promoted to the highest ranks of your noble profession! He is a lad to be proud of, the soul of discretion and should undoubtedly be a sales representative in your fine organisation. This boy," he went on, pointing towards Curdy, "will have mair people queueing up ootside your premises, waitin' tae be measured, than you will see ootside The Fifty-Shullin' Tailors during a sale, and queuein' up for the same purpose."

Hector's sombre face broke into a huge smile.

"Your services are required next door," Wullie said, winking at Curdy who stood wearing a water-melon grin.

"Mr Jake McLatchie awaits you," Wullie continued, "A man who gave his whole life tae bein' on the boards and who is now as stiff as wan."

Hector scratched his chin.

"Aye, well...er...let's go, Curdy. We've got work tae dae." Hector hurried out. Curdy pumped Wullie's hand vigorously.

"Thanks a lot, pal," he said with genuine gratitude.

"Nae bother, son!" Wullie smiled, "Come on, Ah'll let youse in."

Wullie watched from his window as Curdy and Hector slid Mr McLatchie aboard. A group of children crowded round the hearse bawling for pennies and shouting 'Hard-Up...Hard-Up'.

"Hey, Mister, hurry up wi' the scramble, wull ye?" one ginger-haired boy yelled and screamed abuse when Hector took a swipe at him.

The hearse moved slowly off to the sound of expletives and wild gesticulations from the angry children, who had conveniently mixed up their wedding and funeral customs.

Wullie watched as the hearse turned into London Road and roared off at an acceptable speed. He turned back, went into the kitchen, switched on the wireless, flopped on to the chair and lit-up his pipe. He smiled to himself.

"Imagine thinkin' it was oor Rita!" he thought.

His mind turned to Annie and Rita and the coming celebrations. They would be very disappointed. He would have to make a move and take things into his own hands. Rita would not be let down, he would see to that!

He leaned back on the chair, puffed his pipe and watched the drifting smoke. How could he best tackle this situation, he wondered? He went into deep thought and then a slow smile crossed his face. Yes, he thought, yes!

Bud Flanagan and Chesney Allen's harmony filled the room.

"Underneath the Arches I dream my dreams away "

Wullie smiled and closed his eyes.

CHAPTER FOUR

Wullie, Annie and Ina sat quietly together in the Daldowie Crematorium chapel.

Hector and Curdy stood at the back, looking like two football players blocking vital body parts from a direct freekick. Ina dabbed her eyes as the minister gave a homily. He praised Auld McLatchie's contribution to the theatre. Of how he had risen from humble beginnings to the starry heights of the Metropole and the Queens, not to mention a rare personal appearance once at the Geggie, in Kirkpatrick Street, in Bridgeton, before making a lightning dash to the The Wee Royal, in Main Street, where one of his films, starring the great Rin-Tin-Tin was showing. Yes, the minister said, Jake had conquered Hollywood. He was a man who believed in taking his opportunities. Once, during high summer, he fell asleep on Malibu Beach and when he awoke he found that he had almost burned to a crisp and that he would be out of work for months. But, being the man he was, he just improvised and got work doing Al Jolson impressions. Yes, he had hit the big time and finally decided to leave Hollywood and settle down back home, two up, at twenty-seven Well Street, Calton, Glasgow....near The Barras. Telegrams were read out from the pulpit. And Ina wailed as the minister delivered the tributes. 'Good-Bye Old Timer from Al, Great-Grandson of Rin-Tin-Tin'.

Ina wailed in top 'C'.

Wullie looked round at Annie and, from the corner of his mouth, whispered:

"AL? Son of Rin-Tin-Tin? Ah take it AL is shoart for Aluminium!" Annie dug him in the ribs.

There were other messages. One from the great cartoon king, Walt Disney, who said that he would always remember Jake McLatchie with deep affection as the man who inspired him to create Goofy...and who had, indeed, modelled for the character.

As each communication was read out, Ina wailed all the louder. Annie gave her arm a comforting squeeze.

The minister ended his sermon with the only Shakespeare he knew.

"Parting is such sweet sorrow!" he said, as Jake McLatchie moved silently forward while a gramophone played 'There's No Business Like Showbusiness' and the coffin vanished and the drapes closed behind it.

It Was Auld Jake McLatchie's final curtain!

Annie invited Ina in for a cup of tea when they arrived home and Wullie's eyes widened when he saw the tin of John West salmon that she produced from deep in the depths of the sideboard.

"Ah was keepin' this for a special occasion," Annie said. "Ah've had it a long time!"

"Aw, ye shouldnae open it for me!" Ina exclaimed.

"Och well, this IS a very special occasion," Annie said, taking the tin-opener from the sideboard drawer.

Wullie nodded:

"True enough," he said, " it's no' often ye get a telegram frae RinTinTin's Great-Grandson!"

Annie glared at Wullie and poured out the tea.

The three of them sat sipping in silence. Ina had stopped dabbing her eyes but, now and again, gave a sniff that began its life somewhere d eep down in her nasal canyons.

It was Annie who finally broke the silence.

"Ah just wish ma Sammy was here," she said. "He'll be sorry he missed yer faither's funeral."

Ina sighed.

"Aye, well somebody's got tae go and fight the war," she said. "God help us!" Wullie said under his breath.

"Just where is your Sammy noo?" Ina asked, placing her cup on the saucer.

Annie shrugged.

"Who knows?" she said. "Ah think he's on some secret mission," she added, with pride in her voice.

"Oh! And whit makes ye think that?" Ina asked.

"It was just somethin' he said in his last letter," Annie replied, furrowing her brows. "Ah must say, Ah was really surprised when Ah got that letter frae him."

"Why was that?" Ina asked, taking up her cup, sipping her tea and peering over the rim.

"She didnae know he could write," Wullie sniped.

Annie ignored the remark.

She looked serious: -"Ah just got the impression that he was daein' somethin' dangerous," she said.

"Oh!" Ina exclaimed.

"He said that he was being drapped ower France," Annie whimpered. Ina gasped, bringing her hand up to her mouth.

"Oh, that is dangerous, Annie!" she cried.

Wullie wiped his mouth with the back of his hand.

"Especially when they're no' gien' him a parachute," he said dryly.

Annie glowered!

"Ma Sammy is that brave that he would gladly obey orders and jump withoot a parachute," she snapped.

"He's that daft, ye mean," Wullie said..

Ina began to feel embarrassed and got up from the table.

"Well...er...Ah think Ah'll just go in and tidy up the hoose and get things organised," she said. Squeezing Annie's arm, as she passed, she added:

"And thanks for everythin', Annie."

Annie blushed.

"Er..that's whit neighbours are for, Ina," she said in a matter-of fact tone, hiding her embarrassment. "If there's anythin' Ah can dae, just let me know."

Ina pecked Annie's cheek.

"Well," she said, "there's that wee thing Wullie could dae for me, if he would?" She glanced at Wullie.

Wullie screwed up his face. "Ah'm no' mairryin' ye," he repeated sourly.

"Naw, naw," Ina said quickly, "it's nothin' like that. Remember Ah asked ye if ye would collect ma faither's ashes and bring him hame?"

Ina dabbed her eyes once more. Wullie shifted in his seat.

"Aye," he said grudgingly, "for his implantation in the windae boax!"

"Aye, Wullie'll dae that for ye Ina," Annie said, glancing over at her brother.

Ina leaned over and pecked Wullie on the cheek.

"Aw, thanks, Wullie," she said as Wullie pulled away and vigorously rubbed the offended cheek.

Ina closed the door behind her.

"Well," Annie sighed, turning to Wullie, "that's that!"

Wullie leaned back and poked at his pipe with a dead match. Annie tidied the room and finally flopped down on the chair.

"Y'know Wullie," she said, biting her lip, "Ah'm gettin' really worried aboot gettin' the stuff for Rita's wee do on Setturday. Obviously Auld McPhee is not forthcoming!"

Wullie lighted his pipe, extinguished the match with a good shake and threw it into the fireplace with a flourish.

He slowly exhaled the smoke and leaned back. He had the look of a man with a secret...a smug, arrogant look, Annie thought.

Annie folded her arms and tightened her lips.

"A'right, Wullie," she said, "whit's the big secret?" Pointing his pipe towards Annie, Wullie said: "There's only wan man in the whole o' the Calton can get us oot of this dilemma!" "God disnae stey in the Calton," Annie said facetiously Wullie shook his head. "No' God," he said examining his pipe, "no' God." Wullie went irritatingly quiet. Annie began drumming her fingers on the table. "Well?" she snapped. "Who is this superman?" Wullie took a drag from his pipe and let the smoke ooze out slowly. "FINGERS McGEACHIE," he said at last. Wullie thought of Fingers McGeachie with deep reverence. He was a boy from the tenements who had made good.

Wullie lay in bed that night, planning his itinerary for the next day. Contacting Fingers McGeachie was top priority, he decided, but he would keep his promise to Ina and pick up auld Jake and bring him home to the box on the sill.

Fingers would come through, he was sure of that. The 'Big Man's' affluence had not gone to his head. He was still one of the boys. Fingers was in his late forties, tall and slim and with a Ronald Coleman moustache. He was called 'Two Fingers' at the beginning because of the depth of whisky he liked in his glass. That was the accepted story but some thought he got his name because of his gesture to authority. Wullie felt privileged to know him.

Wullie smiled. Tomorrow would be a busy day. He sank deeper into the soft pillow and was soon in deep sleep...only to be rudely awakened by the doleful wailing of the air raid sirens and Annie vigorously shaking the sleep out of him.

"Get away," Wullie said grumpily, pulling the bedclothes over his head, "Away ye go..."

"A'right," Annie snapped, "be it on yer ain heid!"

Annie left her brother settled snugly under the blankets and, muttering to herself, hurried down to the air-raid shelter across the road and up the pend.

Wullie was cosy, comfortable and relaxed. He dug his head deeper into the pillow.and breathed deeply. He would rather hear the drone of the German Heinkels than the sound of a certain 'wee nyaff's' mouth organ.

He closed his eyes...still smiling!

Wullie stepped into the crisp nip of an autumn morning. He took a deep breath, turned right and strode the fifty yards up to London Road, turning left and heading for Bridgeton Cross.

Hector stepped forward immediately Wullie entered the undertaker's reception.

"Hello rerr," he said, greeting him with a wide grin.

"Dae you dae everything here?" Wullie asked, taking Hector's out-stretched hand.

Hector nodded.

"It's the war," he said, "ye can see how it is! Even good apprentices are hard tae come by."

Hector laughed loudly.

Wullie joined in.

"Aye, right enough," he said, "but your boy's a'right!"

"Ah have surmised," Hector said, putting on his business accent, "that you have called to retrieve the deceased for his final planting, nae doot?"

Wullie nodded.

"That, Ah have," he said sombrely. "He is going intae the windae boax!"

Hector was silent for a moment.

"Ah see," he said finally, "but Ah must warn you that no matter how much watterin' youse give he will definitely not grow any."

"Ah appreciate your professional advice," Wullie said. They both put hands to mouths to hide their chuckles.

Hector vanished into the back shop, returning almost immediately and carrying an earthenware jar which he placed on top of the highly polished counter.

"Ah could've put him in an Indian Ginger Jaur," he said apologetically, "but he might've been a bigot for a' Ah know."

Wullie shrugged.

"Ah could not tell ye his affiliations," he said.

"Well," Hector said, sliding the jar towards Wullie, "sorry it is not in the accustomed metal urn but ye just canny get metal urns these days. They've all been melted doon for the war effort...just like a' the railin's an' that."

Wullie assured Hector that he understood and that he, himself, when the collectors came round had given up the tin mug he carried through the bloody trenches of the Great War.

"Ah am definitely congnizant of the situation," Wullie said. Hector slapped him on the back.

Wullie went on:

"Besides, Ah do not think that Auld McLatchie will mind being interred in his current container. He always liked gettin' a good jug in him ... noo it's the other wey aboot — he is in a good jug!"

Hector stifled a laugh.

Wullie took the jar, thanked Hector for his professional services and stepped out into the street...careful not to spill any of his old neighbour on to the pavement.

He walked back the way he had come, making only one slight diversion...through the hallowed portals of the Doghouse Pub, in Landressy Street.

He wondered why Dougal, usually a friendly little pooch, growled aggressivly, as he bent down to pat him.

Jimmy Smith the barman, raised his eyes when he heard the ungentlemanly behaviour of his little mongrel.

"Whit's up wi' him?" Wullie asked, placing the jar on top of the bar.

Jimmy shrugged.

"Beats me!" he said, "He's been in a good mood a' day. He had a rerr terr earlier wi' Mitzi...a wee King Charles Spaniel frae doon the road."

"Ach well, we a' have oor wee tantrums at times," Wullie said. "Gie's a pint, Jimmy."

Jimmy poured and, nodding towards the earthenware jar, said: "Whit's that, then?"

"Next door neighbour," Wullie said.

"It's for yer next door neighbour?" Jimmy asked, pushing Wullie's pint over the counter.

"It IS ma next door neighbour," Wullie said, taking a long gulp of the cold beer.

"In a jaur?" Jimmy's brows went up.

"Aye, he's deid," Wullie said, as though an explanation were necessary. "Ye canny get metal urns these days Ah am led to believe, so ye have tae dae wi' cley wans....no' that it makes much difference tae him."

Wullie took a swig from his glass and smacked his lips. He raised his tumbler once more:

"A toast," he said, "to Auld McLatchie...may he be up there enjoyin' himsel' wi' the real stars of the firmament!"

Dougal, sitting at his feet, growled fiercely and showed a perfect set of teeth.

Wullie looked down at the snarling mutt.

"Whit IS up wi' Wee Dougal?" Wullie said. "Ah always thought we were pals!"

Jimmy leaned over the bar.

"He seems tae be keepin' a wary eye on yer jaur, there," he said. "Who did ye say was in there?"

"Auld Jake McLatchie," Wullie said.Jimmy burst out laughing.

That's it!" he exclaimed. "Nae wonder Dougal's takin' umbrage. Auld McLatchie used tae come in here for his afternoon pint....and he did NOT like dugs, that's for sure! It's no' the first time he gave Wee Dougal a good kick on the erse —- and the dug's never forgotten by the looks o' it."

Wullie looked down and Dougal bared his teeth, showing more gum this time.

Wullie shook his head in amazement.

"Ye mean Dougal can recognise Auld Jake even in this powdered state?"

"Dugs are very perceptive," Jimmy said, knowingly. "Dougal forgets NOTHIN'!"

Jimmy threw Dougal a piece of pie crust, which was quickly gobbled up. But if he thought the wee dog was going to be bribed or pacified, he was barking up the wrong tree!

Dougal continued to keep his eye on the earthenware container.

"Ah did hear wance, right enough,"Wullie said, "that the old boy hated dugs efter he had a slight altercation wi' Rin-Tin-Tin."

"Well, he didnae like Dougal, Ah can tell ye that!" Jimmy said. "He wance said that if he ever met Dougal oot in the street and away frae his safe environment in here, he would have nae hesitation in droonin' him. That is no' a nice thing to say to a wee dug, Wullie, so it's no'...no' nice'."

Wullie agreed.

"Ye're dead right there Jimmy," he said, "especially dugs that understaun' English."

Jimmy took Wullie's pint and topped it up on the house. Wullie was an an old and valued customer!

"Aye," Jimmy went on, wiping the bar with a damp towel, "there's something wrang wi' people that don't like dugs! Dougal used tae snarl the minute Auld McLatchie walked in the door. Auld Jake would gie him a kick and tell him tae take a powder."

Wullie bent down and lifted Dougal on to the bar beside him.

"There, there, ma wee pal," he said, petting the dog, "you get the last laugh. Auld McLatchie maybe kept tellin' YOU tae take a powder, but noo he IS a bloody powder...it is definitely providence!"

Dougal barked, stuck out his tongue and panted...but never taking his eyes away from the jar on the bar.

Jimmy continued to wipe the bar counter. "Whit brings ye in here the day,

Wullie?" he said, looking up. Wullie looked around to make sure no ears were listening. He leaned over the bar. "Ah'm lookin' for Fingers McGeachie," he whispered. "It is very important that Ah contact him!" Jimmy leaned forward. "Fingers is..er..keepin' a low profile the noo...understaun'?

Wullie did not understand but nodded anyway. He tapped the side of his nose with his forefinger. "Mum's the word," he said, "But Ah really must get a haud o' him, Jimmy....and soon!" Jimmy Smith saw a plea in Wullie's eye. He leaned over. "Well," he said quietly, "between you and me, he'll be in here the morra night....aboot six o'clock." Wullie sighed with relief. "Thank God for that," he said, pushing over his pint glass "Fill it up again, Jimmy...and wan for yersel'." Jimmy replenished the glasses. "Here's tae us," Wullie beamed, raising his pint. "Tae us," Jimmy concurred. Jimmy took a sip and put his pint down to one side. He gathered up some empty glasses from the bar and put them into the small sink behind the counter, turning on the cold tap and rinsing them through.

Dougal, still sitting on the bar next to Wullie, had not taken his eyes off the McLatchie container.He growled and bared his teeth like a tiger stalking his prey. Suddenly, unable to contain himself, he moved. As quick as lightning he leapt forward snarling, tail wagging like a car's wipers, he was a blurred flash...pouncing ferociously on to his quarry. With a clatter the earthenware jar crashed into the sink and smashed into a thousand pieces. The cold tap was still gushing, full on and Wullie's mouth fell open as he peered down into the wally basin and saw Old Jake McLatchie vanish, in a swirling motion,down the plughole.

"Oh my God!" Wullie cried in dismay, slapping the side of his face with the palm of his hand. "Never mind Auld McLatchie threatening tae droon Dougal...Dougal has just drooned Auld McLatchie!"

Dougal stood in the sink, his paw digging and scraping at the plughole and yelping as one whose victim had just escaped. Then, giving up, he stood erect with tongue out and tail wagging at a great speed. He stared up at Wullie and barked loudly.

"Whit's he want?" Wullie said.

"He wants ye tae clap him," Jimmy said, gathering up the shattered pieces from the sink.

Wullie shrugged.

"Well," he said, "He is the victor. Ah suppose he deserves a wee clap."

Wullie stood up and began to applaud Dougal and soon the entire bar had joined in. The clapping was thunderous.

When the applause and whistling had died down, Wullie leaned on the bar and cupped his chin in his hands.

"Aw, whit am Ah gonny dae?" he groaned. "Annie'll kill me....no' tae mention wailin' Ina. Ah'm done for, Jimmy!"

Jimmy lifted the dog from the sink and, rebuking it, placed Dougal on the floor.

"Ye're a bad dug!" he said sternly.

The dog ignored the remark and, with a final, defiant bark dashed out of the door and, it is assumed, went on another hunt.

"Here," Jimmy said, pushing a glass of whisky towards the commiserating Wullie. "It's on the house."

Wullie downed the liquor in one gulp. He smacked his lips.

"Thanks, Jimmy....but whit am Ah gonny dae? Ah canny go hame empty handed!"

Jimmy nodded.

"It's awkward, right enough," he said.

"Ah mean," Wullie moaned, "if Ah had drapped him oan the pavement or the flair, Ah could easily have retrieved him....swept him up again.But, my God, he'll be haufwey tae Rothesay by noo!"

All was lost! Wullie could picture the scene as he walked in the door without an urn.

"Where is ma da'?" Ina would wail, dabbing her eyes. "A wee dug shoved him doon a sink," he would say.

Ina would utter a shrill scream and Annie's wrath would be pitiless.

Wullie cradled his head in his hands.

Jimmy came round from the serving side of the bar and put a comforting arm around Wullie's shoulder.

"There's...er..wan wey ye could...er..get oot o' this terrible situation," he said quietly.

Wullie perked up.

"Tell me, Jimmy..tell me...Ah'll dae ANYTHIN'"

"Well," Jimmy went on, "naebody's...er..seen Auld McLatchie in his present form, Ah mean..er..wan jug of ashes looks pretty much like any other jug of ashes....if ye get ma meanin'?"

Jimmy winked.

A grin began at the corner of Wullie's mouth and quickly spread into water-melon proportions.

"BRILLIANT!" he cried. "You ur a genius, Jimmy," he extolled.

Jimmy smiled and polished his nails on his lapel. He hurried round to his proper place behind the bar and pushed a chunky pint glass, with handle, over to Wullie.

"Talkin' aboot sweepin' up, Wullie," he said, "oor lum was swept this moarnin', so there's nae ashes in the grate. But the sweep left a bag o' soot roon the back. Ye can help yersel' tae some of that. It's roon' the back there."

Jimmy nodded towards the back door.

Wullie did not hesitate.Grabbing the glass he hurried through and found the bag of soot stacked in a corner. With one deft movement he had the glass filled almost to the brim. When he returned to the bar Jimmy was waiting with a piece of greaseproof paper which he covered the top of the glass with, securing it with a rubber band.

Wullie held up the soot filled glass and a worried expression crossed his face.

"A pint tumbler?" he grimaced.

"Well, there's a war on!" Jimmy exclaimed.

True enough, Wullie thought! You must compromise and utilize in times of deep crisis, he decided. He suddenly felt better.

Holding up the glass, he smiled.

"He's got a good tan, eh?

"Aye," Jimmy grinned, "it..er..'soots him." The two men howled.

"Well," Wullie said finally, "Ah'll have tae go, Jimmy. Ye're a pal and ye'll undoubtedly get yer reward in Heaven."

Jimmy laughed as Wullie walked gingerly towards the door. Wullie turned.

"Ah'll be in tae see ...er..oor friend the morra night.Ye can maybe tell him that Ah would wish to have converse with him, eh?"

Jimmy raised a thumb and Wullie walked through the swing doors. He walked jauntily down the street towards the tram stop. A short queue had already formed and Wullie, glass in hand, took his turn.

A small gent, with a Royal Stewart tartan woollen muffler around his neck and a bunnet, with frayed skip, stood, hands thrust deep into his pockets, beside him in the queue. A cigarette, broken in two, dangled from his lips and, with perfect synchronization, he swayed with the slight breeze. The drunk kept eyeing the pint jar clutched firmly in Wullie's hand and was about to say something when the tram trundled up. Most of the queue stood back,waiting on the car travelling their own particular route.

Wullie was delighted that he had not long to wait for the car....and more pleased when he saw Rita hanging out, arm outstretched.

"Right," Rita hollered, "two inside!"

Wullie and the wee man with the tartan scarf scrambled on board. Rita nodded.

"It's yersel',Uncle Wullie," she said in greeting before immediately turning on the inebriated gent.

"Right you, get that fag oot," she demanded. "Nae smokin' doonstairs."

The drunk protested vehemently.

"Smokin'? Ah canny even bloody light it, hen. And, anywey," he went on,"that's no' fair, whit aboot him, eh," he said, pointing to Wullie. "he's cairryin' a portable ashtray aboot wi him."

Rita stared at the glass in Wullie's hand.

"It is not a portable ashtray, " Wullie said, glaring at the drunk man.

"It's no' a pint o' Guinness, is it?" Rita snapped. "There's nae drinkin' oan the caur either...upstairs OR doonstairs."

"It's no' an alcoholic beverage either," Wullie growled.

"Mmm!" Rita murmured suspiciously before turning and climbing the stairs.

"Fare's please," she called, "Any more fares please...?"

The drunk bent forward until his eyes almost touched the glass in Wullie's hand.

Not satisfied, he stood up, swayed slightly and looked Wullie in the eye.

"Whit is that?" he said, nodding at the glass.

"THAT?" Wullie replied, "is ma next door neighbour."

The drunk took another close look, staggered back and tipped his skip.

"How do!" he said politely. And, turning to Wullie,asked: "Are ye takin' him oot for a wee walk?"

Wullie nodded.

"Aye," he said, "he's no' been hisel' recently."

"He looks like he's no' been anybody," the drunk remarked.

The two men stood in silence swaying to the car's motion as it rattled along.

"Is he a wee dwarf?" the drunk suddenly asked. Wullie shook his head.

"Naw, it's his brother that's the dwarf," he said. "Ye'll often see me at weekends taking HIM oot for a walk. Ah just need a hauf-pint tumbler for him!"

Rita stomped down the stairs.

"Right, you two, fares please..."

The drunk dug into his pocket and paid up. Wullie hesitated but, reluctantly, produced the fare when he saw Rita's determined look and her outstretched hand.

"Hey!" the drunk suddenly cried out, "this is ma stoap."

Rita belled the driver and the tram screeched to a stop. The wee man got off, staggered to the pavement and swayed back and forwards for a moment.

Looking round, he tipped his bunnet and called out to Wullie as the car moved off slowly:

"Ah'll look out for ye, pal, and if Ah happen tae see ye cairryin' a couple of whisky glesses Ah will just assume that you're takin' the weans oot for a walk."

Wullie grinned as the car gathered speed and the drunk, head shaking, staggered off down the street.

"Whit was he on aboot?" Rita asked.

"Ach, he's had wan ower the eight," Wullie said.

Rita belled the driver to let someone off at the next stop.

"Well," she said on returning to Wullie's side, "are ye gonny tell me?"

"Tell ye whit?" Wullie asked.

"Whit's in the tumbler," Rita said nodding towards the glass. "It's no' Guinness, is it? 'Cos Ah will not have alcoholic drink on MA caur. It is against the rules for a start."

Wullie held up the glass:

"Does that look like Guinness tae you?" he said, irritated by all the fuss.

Rita shrugged.

"Ye canny tell these days,"she said."Ye get powdered everythin'...powdered milk, powdered eggs...why no' powdered beer?"

Wullie shuffled his feet.

"If ye must know," he said quietly, "Ah'll tell ye...but Ah'm swearin' ye tae secrecy."

Rita licked her finger and crossed her heart.

"Ah am the soul of discretion," she said, suddenly intrigued.

"Well," Wullie said,almost in a whisper,"it's Auld Mr McLatchie." Rita stuck her tongue in her cheek.

"Oh, aye," she said, "Ah knew that a' the time!" Wullie's brows rose sharply.

"Ye did?"

"Of course Ah did," Rita said. "How could Ah mistake him. Know whit that means, don't ye?"

Wullie shrugged.

"Naw, whit does it mean?" he asked, puzzled.

"It means," Rita said, "that it's gonny cost you another tuppence fare....naebody, Mr McLatchie or no', gets a free hurl on MA caur."

Rita held out her hand.

"Ah am not kiddin' ye, Rita," Wullie said seriously."Ah'll tell ye whit happened..."

Wullie whispered the whole story and Rita's jaw fell open. When he had finished she burst out laughing. No one could make up a story like that, she reckoned.

"Promise ye'll no' tell?" Wullie pleaded.

"Ah promise," Rita said, "but just for YOUR sake. Ah feel rotten for Ina. The less said aboot a' this, the better! You'd just break the poor lassie's heart!"

Wullie thanked her profusely.

Wullie put his arm around Rita's waist and gave her a loving squeeze.

"No' be long till yer engagement party noo,hen!" he said. Rita nodded.

"Aye, and no' a sausage roll between us," she said dolefully. Wullie sighed.

"Aye, if Auld McPhee hadnae had that terrible misfortune....! Ah, well," he said, giving her another affectionate squeeze, "somethin'll turn up...just you wait and see!"

Rita gave a nervous laugh.

"Just as long as Raspy turns up," she said, adding, "he's that shy!"

Wullie's eyebrows shot up.

"SHY?" he cried. "He's got mair gall than Hitler. Ah'll bet he sees himsel' as a general before his square-bashin' is up. Five'll get ye ten that he's already been stockin' up on Brasso."

Rita dug her uncle in the ribs.

"Just you wait and see," she said. "When ma Rasputin puts that uniform on and gets a gun in his haun's, not wan German will be safe!"

Wullie shook his head.

"Wi' a gun in his haun's and they eyes o' his, NAEBODY'LL be safe," he cried.

Rita's lips tightened. She did not like references made about Rasputin's prowess or his weak eyesight. She belled the driver.

"Right," she snapped, "this is your stoap. Tell ma mammy that Ah'll be a bit late the night."

The tram squealed to a halt and Wullie stepped off.

"Tell ma mammy we're havin' a special Workers' Playtime Concert at the depot," Rita hollered.

Wullie turned.

"Aye, a'right," he called. "If Vera Lynn's on the bill get her autograph."

"Ah didnae know you were a fan of Vera Lynn's," Rita shouted as the car moved off and gathered speed.

"Ah'm no' particularly," Wullie replied, "but we could maybe swap her autograph for a dozen sausage rolls."

He laughed loudly and sauntered down London Road, carrying his precious cargo.

Wullie's sensitive nose detected the pungent smell of disinfectant as he turned into the closemouth. Climbing the stairs, the antiseptic odour got stronger and, after rounding the bend at the first storey, he saw the reason.

Annie, down on all fours, was finishing cleaning the last step. Hearing Wullie's footsteps, she turned.

"Wi' a' the runnin' aboot," she said, wiping her forehead with the back of her hand, "Ah nearly forgot it was ma turn o' the stairs."

"Ina's in oor hoose," She said, rising. "Everything go a'right at the undertaker's?"

Wullie flushed.

"Er...aye," he stammered. "Ah've got him here."

He held up the pint tumbler and, noticing Annie's jaw drop, he hurried on up the stairs and into the house before she could comment.

Wullie tip-toed into the room and quietly placed the glass on top of the kitchen table.

"Is that ma da'?"

Wullie spun round as Ina came in from the adjoining bedroom. He nodded.

"It is. The auld man is at peace. "

Annie entered and emptied the dirty water from her pail down the sink. Wiping her hands on her apron, she turned, looked at the glass on the table and glared at Wullie.

She looked at Ina who was trembling and staring at the pint of soot sitting in the middle of the table. Ina suddenly let out a wail and turned away.

"Ah canny look," she sobbed."tae think he was such a big man...and look whit he's come tae!"

Annie hurried over and put her arm around Ina's heaving shoulders.

"There, there," she said, comforting the distraught girl.

Ina dabbed her eyes and turned with great reluctance towards the table. She stood as though mesmerised gazing at the glass container. Then her brows knitted and she let out a piercing shriek. Pointing a trembling finger at the glass, she blurted.

"THAT...THAT is NOT ma faither!"

Wullie was taken aback by Ina's sudden outburst.

"Ye..ye mean Ah've been walkin' aboot wi' a stranger a' mornin'?" he cried.

Ina's hand was shaking uncontrollably.

"Ma da'," she cried, "was not a black man!"

"He is noo," Wullie shrugged.

Ina turned to Annie .

"Annie," she said pleadingly, "would you look at that...that PUB MEASURE and honestly say that that is ma dear auld faither inside it?"

Annie felt a little embarrassed and a good bit angry at Wullie turning up with such a receptacle. She glowered at Wullie, who looked quickly away.

Annie looked perplexed. "It's hard tae say,Ina,"she replied.

Ina looked over at Wullie, who was shuffling his feet. "Incineration chinges ye," he volunteered.

"How come ma faither is in a pint tumbler?" Ina asked, her eyes narrowing.

Annie folded her arms and gave Wullie a scathing look. She too wanted to know the answer to that one.

Wullie pulled himself up.

"Well," he said authoritively, "there is a war on and it is hard for tae get metal urns...them all being melted doon tae make guns and ammunition — like railin's and things. A' Ah can say tae you, Ina, in all honesty is that that is yer faither. He was the only wan on the shelf, unclaimed. There is nae mistake. They even showed me his saft hat."

Ina sighed. She believed Wullie's story. Hadn't they come round the back-court just a few weeks ago and removed all the iron railings to be put to the furnace and re-cycled?

"Och, it's sad!" she said.

Wullie agreed.

"So it is," he said, "tae think ye work hard a' yer life and end up as a cairry-oot!"

The insensitive remark sent Ina into another attack of frenzied wailing with Annie, once more, becoming the pacifier.

"Come on", Annie said, "let us sprinkle yer da' on the windae boax as was his last request."

Annie steered Ina towards the table, picked up the glass with all due reverence and put it into her shaking hands.

Ina gave a weak smile.

"Wi...will ye come wi' me, Annie...please?" she said quietly. Annie nodded.

"Of course Ah will, Ina," she said, giving her arm a squeeze. "And you, tae, Wullie?" Ina pleaded.

"Er...Aye, sure,"Wullie said.

Ina took hold of the pint glass and , with Wullie and Annie, in solemn procession, walked slowly through the doors, on to the landing and into the McLatchie house where the window was open and the window box was in full view.

Ina approached the box and stood over it with bowed head and glass poised.

"Would you say a wee prayer ower him, Wullie?" she said, a plea in her eye.

Wullie hesitated for a moment and only a sharp jab on his ankle from Annie's toe made him move.

"Er...aye, sure," he said. "It's been a while since Ah've been in personal contact wi' the Almighty, but Ah will dae ma best."

Clearing his throat, he began:

"You loved him when he was a star, Though he was rude and curt,

But we know that you will love him still, Though he's just a pile o' durt."

Ina howled as she solemnly sprinkled the contents of the glass on to the window box, dabbed her eyes and turned away. Annie glowered at Wullie, her fist clenched in anger.Then, putting an arm around Ina's shoulder, she guided her towards the door.

"Come on," Annie said, "we'll go intae ma hoose and have a wee cuppa tea."

Wullie sighed with relief. He was glad the episode was closed. Auld McLatchie had gone to his rest. He was probably enjoying sailing down the Clyde, flapping against the Rothesay pebbles, Wullie thought. Who would want to spend their time stuck in a window box anyway? No, he did McLatchie a favour, he reckoned.

Ina, too, was glad it was all over. Wullie had been good and faithful, she thought. She made sure that she sat next to him at the table and the handkerchief was gone now, stored away in her bag. She took a deep breath. Life had to go on.

Annie switched on the radio saying "Might as well liven the place up a bit."

The toe-tapping music of 'In The Mood' filled the room and Ina smiled broadly. Clapping her hands in time to the beat, she exclaimed:

"Oh, 'In The Mood'...ma favourite!"

"It could be your signature tune," Wullie said, lighting up his pipe.

"Ah'd better get Rita's tea on," Annie said, filling the kettle. That reminded Wullie.

"Oh," he said, "Rita says she will be late the night. They've got a Worker's Playtime doon at the depot."

Annie shook her head.

"Ah wish some people would let me intae their plans. Ah didnae know that!"

"Ah think Ah'll have forty winks," Wullie said. "Ta-Ta the noo." Wullie vanished, yawning widely. Annie replenished the teacups and sat down facing Ina. "Er..Ah often wondered why Wullie never married," Ina said hesitantly. Annie shrugged. "Nane o' the young lassies in the street would look at him. In fact nane o' the auld wimmen would look at him." Annie laughed. "When ma maw died, he came tae live wi' Sammy and me." Ina smiled and took a deep breath. "Well," she said, "there's time enough. Wan o' these days some good wumman will come alang and get her hooks intae him." "Dae ye think so?" Annie said with a slight smile.

Ina gave a knowing look: "Did Ah ever tell ye that Ah was the runnerup in the Claythorn Street Angling Club's Championships?" Annie's eyebrows went up. "Oh, ye were, were ye?" she smiled. "Ah was," Ina said with a mischievous smile, "and very seldom did wan get away." From Wullie's room came the deep, heavy sound of snoring. Ina and Annie's eyes met....and they burst out laughing.

CHAPTER FIVE

It was a quiet and peaceful night!

The Luftwaffe had directed its activities further south and into England.

Only the occasional blast of an air-raid warden's whistle disturbed the night as somebody's blackout blind had moved a fraction to allow a narrow shaft of light to escape into the darkness.

Ina McLatchie had returned to her own house and had slept soundly.

Annie had found it hard to sleep. Her mind raced with the events in hand. She worried about Rita's engagement party and wondered how her Sammy was doing and where he was?

Wullie had no problem in finding sleep. Fingers McGeachie would fix things, he was sure of that...well, almost! He just hoped that Fingers would manage to arrive at the pub without being picked up en-route. Wullie quickly discarded that thought. The Big Man was too smart and, besides, it was not definite that the police had anything on Fingers...although THAT seemed unlikely. No, everything would be all right, he had convinced himself and, closing his eyes, had drifted into peaceful slumber.

Annie had made tea and toast for breakfast.

Sandy MacPherson was playing the theatre organ on the morning wireless when Wullie staggered in, yawning and stretching. He nodded a sleepy greeting to Annie and flopped down at the table.

Wullie reached over for his morning paper and was surprised to see a packet of ten Woodbines lying on top.

"Whit's this?" he asked, picking up the cigarettes.

"Ina haunded them in for ye," Annie said, spreading the margarine on his toast.

"Oh, aye?" Wullie said with suspicion.

"The lassie is just trying tae be nice. It's her wey of thanking ye for doing her that wee service yesterday," Annie said, pouring the tea.

"Aye, well that's the only service Ah'll be gien' her," Wullie said, biting into his toast.

After breakfast Wullie ambled down the street towards Stevenston Street and spent some time with the 'Coarner Boys' who gathered daily at the foot of Well Street. He popped into Mary Welsh's shop and bought a couple of 'Lucky Potatoes'. As usual, he did not find a penny coin inside the delicacy but enjoyed the cinnamon chew.

Wullie's chat with the lads at the corner was shattered by a commanding voice blaring out from a public address system mounted on a coal cart. Two brown and white Clydesdale horses pulled the cart plodding along, heads bobbing and looking quite unconcerned.

From two loudspeakers mounted on top of the cart a tinny voice urged people not to waste food and, on the side, was painted the stark message: 'One Ton of kitchen waste per week will provide food for forty pigs', and, 'By saving food scraps you are saving shipping space for planes, tanks and guns...YOU can beat the U-Boat!'

Wullie raised a thumb to the carter:

"That's the stuff!" he shouted, "although Ah could be daein' wi' forty sausage rolls."

The cart carried on down the street proclaiming its tinny message and Wullie said cheerio to the gossiping corner boys. He had time to kill and it would be a few hours before his encounter with Fingers McGeachie.

With hands deep in his pockets, he strolled up Well Street, crossed London Road and noticing that Peter Rossi's ice-cream shop was quiet, entered and ordered himself a McCallum ice...with raspberry. He sat down at a table and picked up a copy of The Bulletin that had been discarded on an adjacent seat.

Wullie grimaced, turned the page on his newspaper, gave it a shake and snarled:

"Aye, and whit dae you want?"

Ina slid into the seat opposite.

"Ah saw ye comin' in," she said, "and Ah just thought Ah'd treat ye."

"Ye would treat me by goin' away and lettin' me read ma paper in peace," Wullie said without looking up.

"Ah just wanted tae thank ye for whit ye did for me yesterday," Ina said quietly.

Wullie felt uneasy. Guilt swept over him and he hoped that Ina did not notice the flush that had suddenly sprouted on his face. He shifted in his seat. To tell Ina what really happened would only break her heart, he decided. Better that he said nothing!

"Ye don't have tae treat me," he mumbled. "Ye gave me the double Woodbine, that's plenty. Ah don't want any mair treats."

Ina smiled.

"Let me buy ye the McCallum," she said when the young girl arrived with Wullie's ice. She ordered one for herself and insisted on paying.

Wullie muttered an incoherent 'thanks' and the pair sat eating in silence.

"Ye'll be gettin' organised for Rita's engagement party?" Ina said finally.

Wullie nodded.

"It's the biggest thing in Annie's calendar," he said

"Rita's red-letter day as well," Ina said. "and Rasputin's such a nice boy!"

"Well, depends on how ye look at it," Wullie said. "Whit dae ye mean?" Ina asked.

Wullie shrugged.

"Well, personally," he said, "Ah am not entirely convinced that Rasputin is a' there."

Ina tut-tutted.

"Oh, that's a terrible thing tae say," she scolded. "It's no' sayin' much for Rita, either. SHE is no' the type to choose somebody who is..er...wanting."

"Well," Wullie went on, "again, and it's just ma ain personal opinion, Ah think he is wanting a good kick in the erse tae bring him doon tae the real world. Anywey, long as Rita's happy, Ah suppose.!"

"That's the main thing," Ina said.

"Aye, well, Ah just hope there's gonny BE a party," Wullie said, adding "Auld McPhee's shoap is pulverised and Annie's messages wi' it....well, ye can see the problem."

"Ah've got some tins stashed away for a rainy day," Ina said, "and Annie's mair than welcome tae them."

"Whit kinda rainy day are you expectin'?" Wullie asked suspiciously.

"Well, ye never know," Ina smiled, "they might just be waitin' there for an engagement party."

Wullie did not like the tenor of this conversation.

He rubbed a finger under his collar, thanked Ina for her 'treat' and made a hasty retreat.

Ina smiled as she watched him dash across the road and back down Well Street.She heard the rumble of a tram and, quickly buttoning up her coat, she hurried to the stop and hopped aboard the car, heading for the city centre. Ina had a busy day ahead! Wullie did not look back. He joined the 'coarner boys' and was soon in deep and serious coversation...about the war and its turns.

Wullie and the corner boys applauded as a Glasgow Corporation truck passed slowly by with messages splashed across its side panels:

"We want your old Wellington Boots...hot water bottles .. galoshes ... sponges ... bath mats ... tyres ... gloves. Have you a rubber tree in your garden? No....but you can produce as much rubber in your own home. Bring your rubber here...HELP TO SINK THE U-BOAT!"

Wullie gave another thumbs-up sign as the truck snaked its way down Stevenston Street.

"God, they U-Boats hiv nae chance," he said, "between stuffin' a' they tons of waste food doon their hatches and then ,when they surface, kicking hell oot o' them wi' oor wellies !!!."

Wullie turned. Annie smiled as she pulled her loaded washing basket which was mounted on a set of old pram wheels. Annie was going to the public wash-house. Annie was off to the 'Steamie'..

The Doghouse pub was in full swing when Wullie entered. Jimmy, the barman, caught his eye the minute he walked through the door and nodded towards the far corner. Wullie acknowledged the signal with a nod and a wink and indicated to Jimmy to send up a pint. He pushed his way through the crowd and finally found himself standing before the Big Man himself.

Fingers McGeachie was alone and sipping a large gin and tonic. His brilliantined hair shone like polished ebony and the fawn, gaberdine coat hung loosely, showing the expensive dark serge suit underneath. His crisp, white shirt dazzled and the deep maroon, silk tie was fastened with a gold pin with a white pearl setting. Wullie was awed! Fingers didn't get that lot with a Provident Cheque, he thought.

Fingers looked up and smiled broadly when he saw Wullie. The gold-capped front tooth flashed like a twenty-two carat wink as it caught the light.

He stood up immediately and greeted his old friend with outstretched hand:

"Wullie...ma auld china!" he exclaimed. "Sit doon, son, sit doon."

The two men shook hands and Wullie sat opposite Fingers, still overawed by his presence.

Jimmy arrived with Wullie's pint.

"Gie's a large gin, Jimmy and, let's see, noo," Fingers tapped his head with his forefinger, "a Bells...a large Bells, that's your drink, Wullie...Bells,eh?"

Wullie nodded. Imagine Fingers remembering that, he thought!

"Ah never forget whit a pal's favourite tipple is," Fingers said, as though reading Wullie's mind.

"That's awfu' good o' ye, Fingers," Wullie said.

"That's nothin', son ... nothin'."

Fingers leaned back on his chair and cupped his hands steeple fashion.

His fingers glistened with gold and diamond rings.

"Noo," he said, "Ah understand that you have been wantin' an encounter wi' me, Wullie?"

Wullie nodded.

"Aye, well...er...Ah've been wantin' a meetin' wi' ye right enough, Fingers," he said, a little nervously.

"You've got a wee problem, eh son?" Fingers said, sipping the last of the gin in his glass.

"Spit it oot, Wullie," he said, "naebody lingers when they come tae see Fingers."

He laughed loudly.

Jimmy arrived and placed the drinks on the table, giving Wullie an encouraging wink before returning to the busy bar.

Fingers pulled out a twenty packet of Du Maurier, lighted up with a gold-ribbed cigarette lighter, leaned back and nodded to Wullie. Permission had been given for Wullie to continue.

Wullie cleared his throat.

"Well..er.." Wullie began, "ye remember ma wee niece, Rita?"

Fingers blew out a stream of blue smoke.

"Indeed, Ah do," he said. "An ugly wean wi' a nose like a saxophone!"

Wullie vigorously shook his head.

"Naw, naw," he said, "that was her pal, Maisie Dolan. Oor wee Rita was the ugly wean wi' teeth like a pianna. Her an' Maisie used tae gie back-court concerts, so they did!"

Fingers nodded.

"Ah remember noo," he said, "wan playin' her nose and the other playin' her mooth."

Wullie's back was getting up.

"Look, Fingers," he snapped, "Ah am not here for to discuss the physical characteristics of the weans in the street."

Fingers threw up his hands.

"I diverse," he said apologetically.

"Aye, well Ah've nae time tae sit and listen tae yer poetry the noo, Fingers," Wullie said.

Fingers' jaw dropped open. "Eh?"

"Ma meetin' wi' ye this night is a matter of life and death," Wullie said, an urgency in his tone.

"Wullie," Fingers said, "If Ah can help somebody as Ah pass along, ma living will not be in vain."

Fingers took a sip of his gin, a drag of his cigarette and a slow glance at his well manicured fingernails.

Wullie looked on. He could only admire this man, brought up in the slums and who now looked like he stepped out of a Bearsden bungalow.

Wullie could not contain himself.

"Ye know, Fingers," he said, "lookin' at ye noo ye widnae think that ye were the same wee boy who used tae run aboot the street wi' a patch on his erse!"

Fingers smiled.

"We a' did in they days, Wullie," he said.

"Aye, but the rest o' the weans wore troosers, Fingers," Wullie said seriously.

Jimmy arrived with another round.

"This is in anticipation," he said.

"Good on ye, Jimmy," Fingers said, pulling out a wad of banknotes and peeling a couple off.

"Here ye are, Jimmy," he said. "Wan for yersel' and keep the chinge."

"Aw, thanks, Fingers," Jimmy said smiling.

"Aye, they were poor times, Wullie," Fingers went on, reminiscing. "Ah decided tae pull masel' up and get oot o' it. Ah wanted tae escape ma environment!"

Wullie's brows went up.

"Ah thought ye steyed in a tenement?" he said, surprise in his voice.

"Aye, Ah did...that's whit Ah mean," Fingers said. "but Ah had tae escape tae better masel'...and tae dae that ye need money."

Wullie's admiration for the man soared.

"How did ye dae it, Fingers?"

Fingers gave a long sigh.

"Ah decided tae forge ahead."

"How did ye dae that," Wullie asked, moving his chair closer.

"Ah forged the head o' the king on five pound notes and made a packet," Fingers said proudly.

Wullie's mouth fell open. Their eyes met and they burst out laughing.

"Aw, ye're some man, Fingers!" Wullie cried. Fingers enjoyed the compliment.

"Ye've got tae crash oot, Wullie," he went on. "Get oot there and intae the world and look tae new horizons. Look at me noo! Ah used tae live in a wee tiny single-end in Green Street. Look at me noo, Wullie....Ah used the heid. Ah got oot o' it."

Fingers leaned back and his chest puffed all of two inches.

"Where are ye steyin' noo, Fingers?" Wullie asked, sipping his drink.

"Ah'm in a big room and kitchen in Green Street," Fingers said, quickly adding, "up a wally close."

Wullie shook his head in admiration.

"That is definite progress, Fingers, so it is," he said.

Fingers thrust his arm forward and let his fingers ripple under Wullie's nose. The gold and diamond rings twinkled and danced in the electric light and Wullie threw up his hands and covered his eyes in mock blinding discomfort.

Fingers smiled proudly. "Whit dae ye see there, Wullie?" he asked.

"Yer haun'," Wullie replied, still dazzled by the illuminated handful.

"The RINGS, Wullie, the RINGS" Fingers said, with a note of impatience. "Pure gold, they are! That wan," he said, pointing to a large diamond cluster, " was gied to me by Rabbi Seamus O'Reilly for services rendered." Fingers gave a knowing smile. "Ah..er..did a wee turn for him at his wean's Barmitzvah."

"Whit kinda turn?" Wullie asked, showing interest.

"Ma Charlie Chaplin act," Fingers said, pride in his voice. Wullie shook his head and clicked his lips in admiration.

"Can ye put yer haun's on anythin', Fingers?" he said.

"Ah steer clear of dugs' crap," Fingers said.

Wullie leaned back on his chair and surveyed the man before him.

What a man he was! Fingers knew everybody...anybody that counted, Wullie reckoned. He had never heard of Rabbi Seamus O'Reilly but he knew that Fingers McGeachie had no particular religious affiliations. In fact he remembered how the Bernard Street Orange Band, in Bridgeton, had its big drum stolen and Fingers had talked the Kent Street Hibernian Flute Band into lending them theirs...after it being properly blessed by Father Hourigan, of St. Alphonsus' Catholic Church.

"That Rabbi Seamus O'Reilly," Wullie found himself saying, "that's a bit unusual, is it no'...havin' a name like that, Ah mean?"

Fingers shrugged.

"Ah presume he fled frae the faith," he said, "and when Ah mentioned it tae Cardinal Goldberg he had to agree."

Fingers certainly moved in high circles, Wullie thought. It suddenly occurred to him that Fingers was here alone. The man with the golden handshake was ALWAYS accompanied by a retinue of pugnosed attendants. Could be that all of them had been drafted and were on other fields of conflict, Wullie thought.

"Where..er..are yer..er..friends, Fingers?" Wullie asked, hoping that Fingers would not think him too inquisitive.

Fingers leaned back and threw his arms in the air and gave a cry of disgust.

"They're a' in uniform," he said.

"Servin' His Majesty?" Wullie said.

"Yep," Fingers said, "servin' His Majesty."

"Nae doubt, in some foreign field," Wullie sighed.

"In Barlinnie," Fingers said, referring to Glasgow's notorious prison.

Wullie commiserated and remarked that the Big Man himself was fortunate not to have accompanied his cronies to the 'Bar-L'.

Fingers shook his head.

"Naw, naw," he said, "they were daft! "They said they were Conscientious Objectors and refused tae go intae the army and fight for their country. They deserved a' they got!"

"The polis didnae believe them that their consciences widnae allow them tae fight?" Wullie asked.

Fingers nodded.

"Especially when they found a pair of socks oan Clatty Shug," he said.

"Whit's that got tae dae wi' them bein' Pacifists?" Wullie asked, puzzled.

"The soacks were loaded wi' lead," Fingers said, shaking his head in obvious contempt. "Ah have never been wan for violence," he went on, "and Ah always warned them that Ah would have nane o' it...so, it bloody serves them right!"

The Big Man immediately went up another two notches in Wullie's estimation. He was so full of respect that he found himself calling Jimmy over and ordering their glasses be replenished. He had done this before he could stop himself.

Jimmy was back at the table almost before Wullie had drained off the dregs in his glass. As Wullie fumbled for his loose change, Fingers insisted in paying and Wullie did not object.

"Have wan for yersel', Jimmy," Fingers said and dismissed him with two pound notes and a wave of the hand. Jimmy mumbled his grateful thanks and hurried off.

Fingers leaned forward and cupped his hands.

"Right, then, Wullie," he said, "You still have not embellished me wi' your urgent problem!"

Wullie cleared his throat.

"You:.er...heard that Auld McPhee's got flattened?" he said.

Fingers nodded.

"The Luftwaffe have made a lot of jealous men very happy!" he grinned.

Wullie grimaced.

"Aye, well it's no' made oor Annie very happy!" he exclaimed. "She had saved up her food coupons wi' McPhee so that she could gie Rita an engagement party that befits yer only daughter. When McPhee's shoap went up in the air, so did Annie's grub. Noo she's a' worried she's gonny let the lassie doon!"

Fingers was sympathetic. He remembered his own mother's joy the day she got engaged to his father. In fact, the delight had rubbed off on the entire family. He, his two brothers and three sisters had wept with gladdened hearts when they heard that, at last, their dad had proposed to their mum. He thought of Annie, too. Good, kindly Annie. He would have married her himself at one time and the only thing that stopped him was that she didn't like him. It just was not to be! He thought back and wondered if he would have been a better man with Annie at his side? He decided not! He had married Jessie Ogilvie from up the pend. Jessie had promised him excitement. She was a bookie's runner and, just five weeks after they wed, she ran off with a bookie. You can't bet on women, he had decided and had never married again. Annie had done the right thing in marrying Big Sammy. He was dependable and laughed a lot when he had his teeth in.

"Yer mind's away!" Wullie said.

"Just thinkin', Wullie, just thinkin', Fingers sighed. "Noo," he said, straightening up, "If that's yer only problem, have nae fear. Rub-adub-dub, Fingers will get the grub!"

Wullie smiled broadly.

"Ah jist knew ye widnae let us down, Fingers," he said, relief in his voice. "Ah knew we could depend on YOU. Ah telt Annie that. 'Annie', Ah said, 'we can depend on Fingers McGeachie', that's whit Ah said so help me God!"

Fingers smiled.

Wullie continued.

"We don't need anythin' exotic," he went on. "some ham or sausage rolls or somethin'...know whit Ah mean?"

Fingers held up his hand.

"Say nae mair,Wullie," he commanded. "How many will be participatin' at this feast?"

Wullie shrugged.

"Ah don't rightly know," he said. "There'll be Rita's pals frae the depot and neighbours and freen's an' that, y'know?"

Fingers nodded.

Examining his fingernails, he said:

"Ah have reason tae believe that Ah will be acquiring a full, deid pig shortly....very good for pork chops an' that, if ye know whit Ah mean?" Fingers gave Wullie a knowing wink.

Wullie's eyes lit up.

"Aw, that would be great!" he exclaimed. "Ah am very partial tae chops an' that, so Ah am!"

Fingers was pleased at Wullie's obvious delight and response.

"Have ye got a spit?" he asked.

Wullie shook his head.

"Naw, but Ah've got a bad cough," he said.

Fingers smiled. "Naw, naw," he said, "Ah mean a SPIT....tae roast the pig on — know whit Ah mean?" Wullie drew his eyebrows together. "Eh?"

Fingers sighed. "A spit...where ye stick the pig on and rotate it...ye hivnae got wan?" Wullie shook his head. "Definitely no'," he said. "We have only got a range, nothin' fancy. This is because Annie disnae usually come hame wi' a deid pig and we have never considered purchasin' wan of them things. Oor eating habits are modest....usually somethin' wi' totties." "Corned beef?" Fingers suggested. "Ah am a bit," Wullie said, cleaning out his right ear with his little finger. "Naw, Ah meant would ye like a bit o' corned beef if Ah could get it?" Fingers said. Wullie nodded. "Oh, aye, Fingers, ANYTHIN' just as long as it's eligible. Fingers grinned. "Edible, Wullie, Edible," he corrected, "and whit aboot some aipples, eh?" Wullie threw up his hands. "Aw, this is too much, Fingers...too much! "

Fingers puffed out his chest. Wullie's accolade suited him beautifully.

Wullie was shaking his head as he reminisced:

"It's been years since Ah saw an aipple," he said, almost licking his lips. "The last time we had them was wan Friday night before the war. Annie came in wi' a bagful and stuck them in a pot wi' sugar. Ah stood ower that pot for ages...jist watchin' them bubblin' away, and sniffin' that lovely aroma. Ah took wan big sniff and swayed, did Ah sway or did Ah sway!!"

"Stewed?" Fingers asked.

"Naw, Ah was quite sober," Wullie said.

"Naw, Ah meant was the aipples stewed?" Fingers retorted, adding, "ach, never mind!"

"We used tae get candy aipples as well," Wullie sighed, remembering.

"Aye, well Ah canny get ye candy aipples for the party," Fingers said, "but whit aboot they other things?"

"Whit other things?" Wullie asked, coming back to the present.

Fingers shrugged.

"Well," he began, "there are usually other items that pertain to weddin's and engagements an' that. Rings for instance. Ah just happen tae be daein' a very good line on rings...weddin' rings, engagement rings, masonic rings and even gas rings. "

Wullie grimaced.

"Ah would think that Rita's boyfriend would be attendin' tae that sort o' thing, Fingers...know whit Ah mean?"

Fingers nodded.

"Aye, sure Wullie, Ah know whit ye mean," he said. "But surely you will want tae gie yer wee niece an engagement present—something ... some wee memento of the great occasion, eh?"

Wullie had not thought about that. He thought that making arrangements for the food was quite enough to expect of him. But, considering what Fingers had said, he had to agree that some little gift would be appropriate and, probably, expected. He was glad now that Fingers had brought up the question.

Wullie nodded.

"You are right, Fingers," he said, "Ah hadnae thought aboot that. Whit had ye in mind? Maybe a wee tea-towel, eh? A vase?"

Fingers screwed up his eyes and shook his head.

"Ah was thinkin' mair in the line of a Bed-settee suite," he said..

Wullie gulped. "Ah am not A.E. Pickard," he said, referring to the well-known Glasgow millionaire. "Ah could maybe stretch tae a Morris Chair....although even THAT is beyond ma poacket. Whit aboot a wee stool?"

Fingers decided to let the subject drop. Wullie was obviously in dire straits.

"Point taken, Wullie," he said. "Point taken. Here, let's have another drink."

Wullie smiled happily as Fingers held up his glistening hand. Jimmy nodded as the glint caught his ever watchful eye.

"Well," Fingers said, "tell me, Wullie, whit's this boy who Rita is gettin' engaged tae, dae for a livin?"

Wullie puckered his lip and shrugged.

"Ah'm no' sure," he said, "but Rita says he's a genius. He's the wee, specky type wi' his nose always in a book...know whit Ah mean? Like Horace Broon in the Sunday Post."

Fingers nodded.

"Maybe he IS a genius," he said. "Ah mean ye don't have tae come frae Bearsden or Newton Mearns tae be a genius," he went on, referring to the city's more affluent areas.

Wullie nodded in agreement.

"Ye can get geniuses brought up in the slums," Fingers said in all seriousness. "There's a very thin line between being a genius and being an idiot."

Wullie looked up.

"Well, Ah think Rita's intended might just be an idiot," he said, "but a nice idiot," he added quickly.

"Aye, well Ah remember Horace McGroarty," Fingers went on, "who lived up the next close tae me.Everybody said he was daft...everybody. Then, just as war started, Horace stunned everybody by claiming to have invented a pill that would allow men tae stey underwater for hoors withoot comin' up for air....a complete revelation, it was!"

Wullie leaned forward, his interest aroused.

"And had he?" he asked, a slight excitement in his voice.

"Well," Fingers continued, "naturally, the War Department were very, very interested. They could see endless possibilities wi' Horace's wonder pill. We could have regiments marching undetected underneath the English Channel...right intae France.Nae wonder the brass-hats were excited!"

Wullie shuffled in his chair.

"Ah never read anything aboot it in the paper," he said sceptically.

"Well, ye widnae, would ye?" Fingers said. "Anywey, the big-wigs frae the army a' gethered doon at the Clyde, near the Govan Ferry, and Horace popped wan o' his pills intae his mooth tae gie them a demonstration. He was out tae show them that, although he was not a native of Bearsden or Newton Mearns and that he was just a specky wee fella frae the Calton, he was nae idiot."

Wullie cocked his head with pride.

"Good for him!" he said, his heart swelling.

Fingers continued.

"Well," he told his captive audience, "as Ah say, he popped the pill intae his mooth and stepped intae the freezin' watter. He turned and waved tae a' the onlookers and waded oot until his heid disappeared under the flowing river. Well, the generals and a' them high heid yins jumped intae a motor boat and dashed across the river tae the other side and waited for Horace tae clamber ashore. It was a great day for everybody!"

Wullie shifted nervously in his seat and moved closer.

"Did they gie him a big cheer when he stepped ashore?" he asked excitedly.

Fingers shook his head.

"Naw, we never saw him again," he said sadly. "He WAS an idiot, right enough!"

Wullie slumped back on his seat, deflated.

The anti-climax was too much for him.

"Whit a shame," he mumbled, shaking his head, "Whit a bloomin' shame!"

Fingers agreed.

"Ah merely repeat this story," he said, "so that you can keep a wary eye on this bloke, this genius, who is about to join your family circle."

What a wise man, Fingers is, Wullie thought. He nodded. "A good idea," he said with a sigh.

Wullie did not see Rasputin enter and sweep his eyes around the crowded pub. Spotting Wullie and Fingers in the corner, he pushed his way through the happy gathering.

"Excuse me, Wullie," he said, "Ah thought Rita might be here. She's no' hame yet."

Wullie looked up, surprised to see Rasputin inside a public house.

"Oh, it's yersel'!" Wullie exclaimed. "And whit makes ye think Rita would be in here?"

Rasputin shrugged. "Ah know she sometimes goes for a wee sherry wi' her colleagues when she finishes work," he said.

"Well, she's no' here and she's no' been here,"Wullie said, turning away.

Rasputin looked worried.He removed his glasses and cleaned them with his handkerchief before slumping down on a vacant chair at Wullie's table.

"Ye don't mind if Ah sit doon, dae ye?" he asked apologetically.

Wullie shook his head.

"Not at all!" he said. "It's no' often we see you in a pub. This," he said turning to Fingers, "is Fingers McGeachie, a very old pal o' mine and wan who is about to fix things for your engagement do on Setturday."

Fingers leaned over and offered Rasputin his extended and expensive hand.

"Don' squeeze too hard, son," he said, "the diamonds jab."

"This is Rita's boyfriend, Rasputin Plunkett," Wullie said.

Fingers smiled, his gold tooth glinted and he gripped Rasputin's hand firmly.

"Would you care to partake of some refreshment, Rasputin?" he asked.

Rasputin nodded.

"Thank you very much," he said, "Ah'll have a shandy."

Fingers signalled Jimmy, who hurried over, and ordered a half-pint shandy and two large gin and tonics.

"An unusual name, eh, son?" Fingers smiled. "It should be vodka you should really be drinkin'."

"His maw liked monks," Wullie interrupted.

As usual, Jimmy was quickly back at their table with the order.

"Wan for yersel', Jimmy," Fingers said, handing over a note. Jimmy mumbled his thanks and cleared the empties from the table.

"Tae the happy couple," Fingers said, raising his glass.

They clinked glasses. "Cheers," Wullie and Rasputin said in unison.

Fingers smacked his lips. "So," he said, patting his lips with a pale-blue silk handkerchief, "when's the big day then?" Rasputin took a diary from his inside pocket, flicked through the pages and, licking his finger, ran it down the column of the page he stopped at. "Well," he said finally, " Ah reckon that Ah should be walkin' Rita doon the aisle four years come January the twenty-fourth."

Wullie gulped on his drink. "FOUR YEARS?" he spluttered.

Rasputin nodded. "We'll need tae wait until the war's ower....which will be a lot quicker noo that Ah'm joinin' the fray." Fingers raised his eyebrows. "You've got plans, eh?" Rasputin nodded. "The minute Ah get intae uniform," he said, "Ah intend havin' a powwow wi' the top brass...tae outline ma plans." Wullie and Fingers' eyes met. Wullie shrugged and Fingers stroked his chin. "Can Ah ask ye what yer war plans are, Rasp?" he said, leaning forward.

Rasputin shook his head.

"Sorry," he said, "Ah'm afraid it's top secret...but it involves elephants."

Wullie nodded.

"Ah thought it might," he said. Fingers smiled.

"Ah like yer style, Rasp," he said. Rasputin smiled broadly.

"Thanks, Fingers," he said. "Ah frequents Burtons, The FiftyShullin' Tailors."

Fingers leaned back on his chair, slapped his thigh and guffawed. "Naw,

naw," he roared, "Ah meant yer confidence. You're a man efter ma ain heart!"

Wullie put a thumb up.

"Ye've hit the button there, Fingers," he said, "Rasputin was thinkin' aboot that as well....hearts, that is."

Rasputin agreed and nodded.

"Ah was thinkin' seriously aboot goin' in for heart surgery...or maybe brain surgery," he said, eyes puckered.

"Very commendable!" Fingers said.

Wullie agreed.

"He should go intae erse surgery," he said, "he's the only bloke Ah know who can talk through his."

Rasputin ignored the remark.

"Wullie here tells me that you and Wee Rita, of pianna-teeth fame, are havin' problems wi' yer intended engagement party!"

"Ah'm leavin' everythin' tae Annie," Rasputin shrugged. Fingers said.

"Fingers is gonny help us," Wullie said quickly.

Fingers puffed out his chest.

"There will be nae problem, son," he said. "Ah can assure you that your party wull go with a swing. In other words, Have nae fear, Fingers is here!"

Rasputin smiled and, leaning over, grasped Fingers' hand.

"It's very good of ye. Ye'll make Annie and Rita very happy people and there's an auld saying... 'You'll get yer reward in Heaven....but you wull not need tae wait that long, Fingers because when Ah'm the Lord Provost, Ah wull personally see that the City recognises ye."

Fingers laughed loudly.

"Just as long as the polis don't recognise me," he roared.

Wullie and Rasputin joined in the laughter. But the hilarity was short lived. The air-raid siren suddenly wailed its banshee warning and the chatter in the pub stopped abruptly. Glasses froze before touching lips as drinkers listened intently for the drone of the Luftwaffe's Heinkels.

Jimmy's commanding voice broke the silence.

"Right, noo....everybody doon tae the cellar," he yelled, lifting up the trap door behind the bar. "Come on noo everybody doon the stairs"

Still clutching their spilling glasses, the drinkers hurried towards the bar where Jimmy stood, ushering them down into the safety of the bowels of the building.

Rasputin began to rise from his chair but was stopped by Fingers' firm hand on his shoulder, pushing him back into his seat with a curt command.

"Just keep yer seat and finish yer drink!"

Wullie had not moved and the three men sat silently sipping their drinks and ignoring the departing customers around them who were vanishing down a hole behind the bar.

Rasputin and Wullie admired Fingers' coolness. But, Wullie decided, any man who lives with danger all the time can easily become immune.

Fingers was always one step ahead of somebody...or any hostile situation.

The three men were now the sole occupants of the upstairs bar. Jimmy, the barman, knew better than to insist that Fingers McGeachie should scurry for cover just because a few dozen German raiders were going to rain down destruction on their heads. Fingers ran from nobody!

Outside, the searchlights stabbed upwards with long, straight yellow beams and the ack-ack guns blazed and spat tongues of fire out into the night sky.

The ubiquitous air-raid wardens' whistles were blowing wildly everywhere, followed by angry shouts from the men with tin hats. Fingers ignored the outside clamour, rose and strolled over to the bar and poured out three large gins. He rang up the till, placed two notes inside and returned to the table.

"Cheers," he said, placing the glasses on the table.

Wullie and Rasputin responded and raised their glasses.

"Er..whit business are ye in?" Rasputin asked Fingers, looking over the rim of his glass.

Fingers carefully placed his glass down on the table.

"Well," he began, "YOU might think, Rasp, that Ah am not doin' ma bit for the war effort...but you would be wrong!"

Rasputin opened his mouth to protest but was silenced by a gesture from Fingers.

"Ah have just been placed an order," Fingers went on, "a contract by our illustrious Home Guard for to provide them with a quantity of a certain item which is hard to come by...but of which I have special connections."

Rasputin clicked his teeth. He was impressed.

"Could Ah...er..inquire as to whit these special items are?" he asked.

Fingers leaned back and puffed his chest out.

"Ah should not really imbibe you with this knowledge," he said, "but seein' you are a friend, if not a relative, of ma dear pal, Wullie, Ah think Ah could trust you with this information."

Wullie puffed out HIS chest.

Fingers sipped his drink, placed his glass down and leaned forward. In almost a whisper, he said, "Ah have been ordered to supply for the Home Guard's mobile patrols….a quantity of bicycle pumps….Ah can't reveal the quantity for obvious reasons."

Fingers sat back, pleased with himself. Wullie never knew that the Home Guard HAD mobile patrols and said so.

Fingers was adamant.

"Aw, aye," he said, "they keep vigil at the beaches in case Jerry invades us."

"Whit good could they dae if an entire German army landed on the shore at the mooth o' the Clyde?" Rasputin scoffed.

"Well," Fingers said, "as soon as the Jerries stepped on the beach, oot would come the boys with their bicycle pumps."

Rasputin laughed.

"Whit good would THAT dae?" he cried.

"The boys would blaw the Germans up," Fingers said, winking at Wullie. Wullie laughed loudly.

"Aw, very funny!" Rasputin said, feeling embarrassed. Fingers leaned over and tapped him lightly on the cheek.

"Just a joke, son," he said grinning, "just a joke!"

"Ye had me goin', there," Rasputin said.

"Well," Fingers said, "as a matter of fact, Ah really have been asked tae supply the Home Guard wi' bike pumps."

"How come they ask you?" Rasputin asked flatly. Fingers splayed his arms. "Ma boy," he said, "the lads are finding it difficult to acquire their needs through official channels….but they know they can rely on Fingers." Fingers clapped his hands together. Wullie stood up. "Aye, well Ah'd better be gettin' up the road or Annie will be sendin' oot a search party," he said, stretching his arms. "Aye, me tae," Rasputin said, rising. "Ah'll just get away hame. Wull you tell Rita Ah was in lookin' for her?" he asked Wullie. Wullie nodded. "Ye'll no' forget aboot whit we were discussin', Fingers?" Wullie asked his old friend. "Nae probs," Fingers said with assurance. Happy, raucous singing exploded from the cellar as the drinkers, now settled down, chorused "You Made Me Love You". "Here," Wullie said, "maybe we should wait till the all-clear before we go oot intae the street." "If it's for us, we'll get it," Rasputin said philosophically. "Dead right there, son," Fingers agreed. Rasputin and Wullie turned towards the door. "And don't forget," Fingers called, "If there is ever anythin' ye need, Fingers will do the deed." Rasputin nodded. "Ah'll remember that," he grinned.

Wullie had walked on as Rasputin stepped out into the street. He had taken just a few steps when Fingers called him back.

"Tell me," Fingers said, "how many elephants dae ye think ye'll need?"

Rasputin grinned broadly and Fingers turned back into the pub, a twinkle in his eye.

Rasputin saw the dark figure of Wullie vanish down the other side of the street and he ran across the road to catch up with him.

Coming from the depths of the pub and above the dreary drone of the bombers echoed the tuneful tonsils of the Doghouse revellers singing 'Deep in the Heart of Texas'.

Rita sat at the table, licked the tip of her pencil, and jotted down the names of some girlfriends on the pad before her. She leaned back and closed her eyes, her mind going back to the Workers' Playtime concert, at the depot. Frank and Doris Droy, from The Queens Theatre, were there. Their Glasgow humour rocked the canteen roof. Sarah Bell was there, too, in the guise of her creator, Sammy Murray.

"Aw, it was a great show, Mammy!" she said. "Ah only wish Bing Crosby could have been there!"

Annie laughed.

"Bing Crosby?" she said, carrying on with her knitting.

"Oh, aye," Rita said dreamily, "just tae hear him singin' 'When the Blue of the Night'." She sighed deeply.

"We've got enough blues these nights," Annie commented without looking up.

Rita nodded.

"Aye, ye're right!" she said, and, licking her pencil once more, went back to the task in hand.

"Ah'll get this list o' folk Ah'm wantin' tae come up on Setturday night finished yet!" Rita said.

Annie looked up at her daughter and sighed. Rita's engagement party in the context of world events was unimportant. But for HER it was THE red-letter day of the year. She did not want to let her only child down and knew the thoughts of every excited young girl preparing her 'Bottom Drawer'.

She smiled as she recalled her visit to the 'Barras' where Sammy purchased a very special gift, not a ring.

She had to smile at his boyish naivety! There was no engagement party because there was no money. You just did not ask parents, who were surviving on 'The Parish' for a hand out for celebrations! But they DID whoop-it-up with a pie and peas and a botttle of Tizer down at Peter's Cafe, in London Road.

Annie and Rita turned round as the door opened and Wullie, looking pleased with himself, entered.

He hung his coat behind the door and flopped down on his favourite chair by the fireside.

"Well?" Annie said

"Hello Uncle Wullie," Rita mumbled and continued with her chore. Wullie lit up his pipe and leaned back, a smug expression on his face. "Well?" Annie repeated with impatience. "Ah just left your intended there," he said to Rita. "He was lookin' for ye."

"He's loast withoot me," Rita quipped. "He's loast, period!" Wullie said. Rita ignored the remark, licked her pencil and once more bent over her jotter. "WELL?" Annie said for the third time, louder and commanding. Wullie took a long draw at his pipe and let the smoke out slowly. He had centre stage and was enjoying it. "Did ye see Fingers?" Annie demanded. Wullie nodded. "Ah did," he said. "WELL?" Annie cried. "He says you've no' tae worry. He'll take care of everythin'. In fact he's got his eye oan a pig." Rita looked up. "A PIG?" she said sceptically. "Aye, a deid deid pig. ..for makin' pork chops and ribs and that, know whit Ah mean?" he said, pleased with his success.

Annie tapped the side of her cheek with her finger."How are we gonny cook a pig?" she murmered.

"Just get a bloody saw and get stuck intae it,"Wullie snapped, adding,"Ye can make great brawn wi' the pig's heid wi' some ingins an' that!"

Rita laughed.

"Right enough," she said, "we should just be pleased that Fingers McGeachie is goin' tae a' this trouble for us. The preparing of the food is up tae us. In fact you could say that Fingers has saved oor BACON!" Rita chuckled and Wullie slapped his thigh and chortled loudly.Annie smiled:

"Aye, Ah suppose ye're right, hen," she said. "We should be grateful right enough!"

"Aye," Rita added between giggles, "there's another thing that we should be grateful for."

Wullie wiped his eyes.

"Oh! And whit's that?" he said.

"That we're no' Jewish," Rita replied with a gleeful chuckle.

"Whit's THAT got tae dae wi' it?" Annie asked, frowning.

"Well, they don't eat ham or pork," Rita said. "Tae them, pigs is unclean." Annie shrugged.

"Ah'll just gie it a good wash in the auld zinc bath," she said. "There wull be nae dirty pigs in MA hoose!"

Wullie and Rita's eyes met and they burst out laughing. Annie, in her naivety, frowned and wondered what the merriment was all about.

Annie turned away , put the kettle on the gas ring and proceeded to set the table.

"Right, there we are," she said, placing four cups and saucers on the table. Wullie raised his eyebrows.

"FOUR cups? Is Rasputin comin' up...he didnae tell me!" he said, annoyed.

"Rasputin's no' comin up the night,"Rita said without looking up. "He knows Ah'll be washin' ma hair."

"Ah..er...thought Ah'd ask Ina in for a wee cup o' tea," Annie said quietly. "She must be feelin' lonely the noo."

Rita agreed.

"Aye, right enough," she said, "she's got naebody noo. You should take her oot some night Uncle Wullie—– gie her a wee break." Wullie spluttered on his pipe and went into a fit of coughing. "Gie ME a break, hen," he said at last. "Ah am not inclined for to take Ina, or any other female oot....except, if the occasion should ever arise, Betty Grable."

Annie put her hands on her hips, leaned backwards and laughed scornfully.

"Betty Grable? She widnae look twice at ye. In fact she widnae even look wance at ye! In fact ye should be lucky that Ina even looks at you at all!"

"She's got a nice face, so she has!" Rita said.

"It's her LEGS that's her fortune," Wullie said, puckering his lip and throwing a kiss in the air.

Annie's eyes narrowed.

"And when, may Ah ask, did YOU start lookin' at Ina's legs?" she said dryly.

"Ah'm talkin' aboot Betty Grable's legs," Wullie sniped back, adding, "Ye canny even see Ina's legs!"

"That is NOT funny," Annie snapped angrily. "That lassie has been a prisoner in there for years. She has been lookin' efter her auld faither wi' a daughter's devotion and she deserves a break!"

Wullie sniffed loudly. He felt guilty. Scratching his jaw, he looked away.

"Ah..er..didnae mean anythin'," he stammered.

"Aye, well you just mind yer lip," Annie growled. "Ah've asked her in for a wee cup of tea and that's that!"

Wullie was silent. He puffed harder on his pipe, got up from his chair and switched on the wireless.

Rita smiled. Nobody ever got the better of Annie and she was proud of her mother sticking up for Ina. She looked over at Wullie, now back in his chair, fumbling with his Evening Citzen and avoiding all eye contact.

Rita turned over a page in her jotter, licked her pencil and continued with her list.

Annie finished setting the table and let her eyes sweep around the room. The vase with the artificial roses in it was out of allignment on top of the sideboard and she corrected it. Annie had a keen eye and liked things to be just right. From the wireless the soft strains of an anonymous orchestra played 'Tea For Two'. Annie smiled!

Ina McLatchie had stepped from the car at the Argyle Cinema, in Argyle Street, crossed the road and entered Marks and Spencers, where she went from counter to counter searching for a blouse. She smiled with pleasure when she picked up exactly what she was looking for....and overjoyed to see that the white-silk blouse had been reduced by five-and-sixpence. She was more than delighted to note, too, that the garment was just the right size for her ample proportions. Leaving the store, she turned right and went into Woolworths, making straight for the make-up counter. Guided by the pleasant salesgirl's expertise, she left with a suitable lipstick, box of face-powder, seam-lining and leg tanning liquid. She had left her bottle-green skirt freshly ironed and hanging on the rope pulley in her kitchen. All she needed now was to have her hair done and that appointment was already made.

Ina stood at the tram stop outside Woolworths and waited for a red car going east. A number nine, going to Auchenshuggle, was first to come along and, boarding it, Ina went upstairs and sat in the privacy of the empty compartment above the driver's platform. She was happy with her day's shopping and she was looking forward to tea in Annie's house. She smiled at the thought. Yes, it was a nice thought!

Ina alighted in London Road, just a few yards from the premises of La Maison de Petit Nellie, coiffeuse to the elite. She hoped she was not late for her appointment and, clutching her purchases, hurried in, the doorbell greeting her with a quick burst of the opening notes of La Marseillaise.

Wee Nellie, top coiffeuse, was already waiting, tongs in hand. Her blonde, frizzy hair made Ina think of a film star...Harpo Marx. White, porcelain teeth flashed a welcome.Wee Nellie, it was said, had studied her profession under the great Antoine, of Paris. But others reckoned she had studied her profession under the Central Bridge.

"Good efternoon, Modome," Nellie said, ushering Ina to a seat.

"How do you do, Madame Wee Nellie," Ina replied, removing her coat.

"Just Nellie," the hairdresser said, "we have no formalities here at La Maison de Petit Nellie."

She sat Ina down, stood back and surveyed her cranium from every angle. "Mmm!" she said, putting her finger to her cheek.

Ina shifted uncomfortably. Her hair wasn't THAT bad, she thought. She had washed it in Derbac soap just the other night!

"Did Modome have anything speshul in mind?" Wee Nellie asked. Ina thought for a moment.

"Mmm!" she murmered, "it's awfu' hard tae make yer mind up, int it? Ah mean ye've got tae get a style that complements yer face..How aboot croppin' it?"

"We don't crop faces, Modome," Nellie said.

"Naw, naw...ma HAIR Ah meant. Whit aboot cuttin' it shoart?" Nellie shook her head.

"Non, non, mada..er..Modome,"she said. "vous's face is too baw...el fato!"

Ina had to agree. Sitting looking at herself in the mirror, she saw the advertisment for Creamola Custard staring back—a large beaming moon. "Whit aboot the Shirley Temple look?" Ina said. "Ah've still got a young face." Nellie shook her head. "But modome's face is BIG...mair like a Mormon Temple look!" Ina felt deflated. Nellie saw the despair in her customer's eyes. "Is modome going out somewhere speshul tonight?" she asked "Well, no' really special," Ina said. "Just intae ma next door neighbour's hoose for a wee cuppa tea," Nellie threw up her arms. "And vouz is going to all zis trouble?" she said incredulously. Ina flushed. "Well, it's her brother, y'see. Ah..er..." She did not get a chance to finish the sentence. "Ah...voila!" Nellie exclaimed.. "Ah see! You like him, this brother, eh? You like...amour, eh? Ina shook her head. "Oh naw...he's a Christian," she said "Non...non...," Nellie said. "I mean AMOUR...LOVE...no' a MOOR...a Turk." Ina wondered why Madame Nellie had the impression that Wullie was a Turk. "He's Glesca born an' bred," she found herself saying.

Nellie continued to study Ina's head from all angles. Finally she made up her mind.

"I theenk madome should have zee Marcel Wave, non?" she concluded. "It would enhance el faceo." The porcelain smile flashed brightly and Ina was convinced.

Wee Nellie got to work and Ina closed her eyes.

"Does modome live alone?" Nellie inquired, between dives into Ina's hair.

Ina nodded but was immediately rebuked by Nellie for nearly causing a calamity.

"There was just me and ma da' for years," Ina said, "but noo there's just me." A lump came to her throat.

"Where is he noo?" Nellie asked, "in some faraway land where the grass is greener?"

"Naw, he's in the windae boax," Ina said.

"Well," Nellie shrugged, "ask a stupid question !"

Nellie fussed around Ina's head, stopping only now and again to spit on the hot tongs.

"You will have great success with this man tonight, Ah can assure you," Nellie beamed, putting the finishing touches to Ina's crowning glory. "Ah can smell it!"

"Eh?" Ina cried, over the noise of the blow drier.

"Can vous not smell it?" Nellie shouted.

"Aye, Ah can,"Ina yelled.

"That's success vous is smelling," Nellie hollered.

"Oh!" Ina said, "Ah thought it was yer oaxters."

Wee Nellie laughed.

"Oh, zee joke!" she chuckled.

"Well," Ina said, "it'll be nae joke the night if Ah don't make an impression on Wullie McSorley...efter peyin' oot whit Ah'm peyin' oot this day."

Nellie patted her shoulder.

"Don't vous worry," she said. "When Madame Wee Nellie is finished with vous he will be stunned."

"He always is," Ina said sadly.

"Stunned?" Nellie asked, puzzled.

"Oh, Ah thought ye said 'stoned'," Ina laughed. Nellie threw up her arms and laughed loudly.

"There is only one way to treat a man like that," she said knowingly. "Vous must give him ze cold shoulder, non? Ze bums rush. Deflate his ego...be not nice to him when he talks to vous."

Ina perked up.

"Dae ye think it'll work?" she asked, excited by the thought.

"But of course it weell work," Nellie answered in her best Parisienne patois.

Ina's heart was suddenly burning...just as her hair was. The last tong sizzled in her dome and Nellie quickly pulled it away. Madame Wee Nellie was right, Ina decided. Who could know how to handle a man more than a Frenchwoman? She looked at Nellie with admiration.The girl with the porcelain smile knew her business. She wielded her tongs with the deftness of a surgeon handling a scalpel.

Ina was glad that she had decided to go all out and have her hair done! The Marcel Wave would probably cost her about one-and sixpence...but she didn't care. It would be money well spent!

Madame Wee Nellie began to sing in French as she worked on Ina's head....a song Ina found familiar. She found herself humming along with the diminutive hairdresser. Their singing got louder and louder until they were chorusing in full gusto. Ina had caught the flavour of France from the wooden seats in the Arcadia Cinema stalls, at matinee time. As they sang she had visions of the great French actor, Maurice Chevalier, of the Beaujolais vineyards, of the squeaky honking of the Paris taxicabs, of the wafting aroma of coffee from the sidewalk cafes...dreams from a dream-world.. Ah, yes...Paris in Spring! They finished the song in unison and laughed loudly.

"Aw, memories, memories!" Ina cried. "Whit was that song called, again, Madame Wee Nellie? Ah know it but Ah just canny place it!" Wee Nellie threw up her arms.

"But it ees "Vous Canny Shuff Yer Granny Affa Bus," non? A great Glesca song, mon ami!"

"Oh!" Ina exclaimed, feeling inwardly embarrassed. "Well, anywey, it sounded good in French, so it did!"

With a flourish, Nellie finished her masterpiece. She stood back and, turning Ina's head every way, she examined her handiwork. Nellie was pleased. Voila!" she said, her white, glossy teeth flashing.

Ina stared at herself in the mirror and was delighted at what she saw! Nellie stood back:

"It is good, non?" she said, "Vous looks like Rita Hayworth....a fat Rita Hayworth, but still !"

"You're a genius, Madame Wee Nellie!" Ina said
Nellie smiled.

"Good,!" she said, "Noo vous know what vous must do with thees Vullie....be rude, insult him...tell him he has a face like a peeg....pull no punches. Get stuck in there. Let him theenk effery man in Glesca is chasin' vous."

"Dae ye really think Ah should?" Ina asked. looking a little worried.

"But of course, mon ami," Nellie said. "Jist tell the nyaff where tae get aff!"

Ina raised her eyebrows at the sudden loss of Nellie's accent.

"Ye sounded right Glesca there," Ina said.

Nellie smiled.

"Aye. ..well...er. ..," Nellie stuttered. "Ah. ..er. Ah'm goin' oot wi' a bloke frae Govan and his patter is rubbin' aff on me," she grinned.

Their eyes met and both went into fits of laughter.

"Oh, ye're a fraud, Madame Wee Nellie!" Ina chuckled, gathering up her belongings,she paid the bill, leaving a threepenny tip and a took one last pleasing look at herself in the mirror and turned and waved at the door.

"Don't forget tae gie him the auld wan-two," Nellie cried.

Ina laughed. She felt like a million Francs!

CHAPTER SIX

Annie placed a plateful of soda scones on the table. She had baked them herself and had kept them well hidden from Wullie, who had an insatiable appetite for soda scones. The minute Annie put the scones down, Wullie sat bolt upright and sniffed like a dog discovering a forgotten bone that had been hidden.

"You just keep yer eyes oaff them!" Annie snapped. "Ye'll get yer share when Ina gets here and no' before."

Rita entered from the room pulling on her woollen gloves.

"Ah've chinged ma mind," she said, "Ah'm goin' oot tae meet Raspy....youse don't mind dae youse?"

"Not at all," Wullie said.

"It'll be a' the mair for youse tae eat," she said, looking at Wullie with a twinkle in her eye. She knew how her uncle had a passion for soda scones.

"You just go and enjoy yersel', hen," Annie said. Rita waved and closed the door behind her.

"She's as well makin' the maist o' Raspy while she's got him," Annie said. "He'll soon be goin' away...just like ma Sammy," she added, coughing slightly to camouflage the lump she felt coming in her throat.

Rita had gone only a few minutes when there was a frantic urgent rapping on the door. Startled, Wullie took the pipe from his mouth and looked over at Annie whose hand had gone up to her mouth.

"Who the hell could that be?" he said, hurrying to the door. Annie heard a garbled conversation and looked anxiously at her brother who came dashing back in spluttering: "It's an agitated wumman for you." Annie wiped her hands on her apron and went quickly to the door. She returned seconds later with Ina, who looked resplendent in her attractive new out-fit and Madame Wee Nellie's hair fashioning masterpiece.

"Whit dae ye mean 'A WUMMAN'?" Annie rapped, "it's Ina...INA...did ye no' recognise her?"

Wullie gawked. She looks like a fat Rita Hayworth, he thought.

Annie was thrilled.

"Aw, ye look lovely, Ina!" she exclaimed.

But Ina was not seeking flattery. She WAS agitated and excited.

"Come. . .come quickly. . .intae ma hoose. . .hurry, there's somethin' Ah must show ye!"

Ina hurried ahead, shaking and fidgety, all the time turning round to see that Annie was following.

Annie and Wullie were close on her tail as they crossed the stair landing and hurried into the McLatchie house. Ina made straight for the window box.

"Look," she said, her voice quivering.

Wullie, Annie and Ina gathered round and stared into the box. A small green shoot had appeared. Annie gasped and Wullie scratched his chin.

"Dae ye think it's ma da'?" Ina asked, a tremble in her voice. Wullie shook his head.

"Looks mair like a geranium tae me," he said dryly.

"It's definitely no' yer faither," Annie said, shaking her head. Wullie nod-. ded.

"If it was yer faither," he said, "Ah would imagine he would come back as something mair pertaining tae whit he was in THIS world. Ah mean, if he was being re-incarnated as a flooer —-it widnae be as a geranium ....if ye know whit Ah mean."

Ina nodded.

"Ah suppose ye're right," she said. "If his new nature was tae pertain tae his previous existence in this world, he would probably have come back as a rose or somethin'. Is that whit ye mean, Wullie?"

Wullie shook his head.

"Ah was thinkin' mair as a dandelion — or, as we say in the Glesca vernacular,. a 'Pee-the-Bed."

Annie glowered at Wullie and gave him a sharp kick on the ankle. "THAT is not nice!" she said angrily.

Wullie scowled.

"Well, it's the truth," he said, rubbing his foot.

"It just means, Ina," Annie said, "that life goes on."

Ina sobbed quietly as Annie led her out on to the landing and into her own house.

Wullie flopped on to his chair and lit up his pipe. Annie indicated to Ina where she was to sit and proceeded to pour out the tea.

"Soda scones?" Ina said in surprise.

"Ah baked them masel'," Annie said proudly.

Annie sat down, slapping Wullie's wrist as he tried to take TWO soda scones.

"Don't be greedy," she snapped.

Wullie sipped his tea and was silent. Now and then he peered over the rim of his cup at the transformed Ina. He had to admit that she was look-ing quite attractive. Ina caught his glance and he looked quickly away.

"Ye're really lookin' nice, Ina," Annie said, "That new hairstyle does won-ders for you,...doesn't it Wullie?"

Wullie shrugged and nodded.

He grudged giving Ina any flattery. She might misconstrue it as a signal to come with smoking guns.

"It's a wonder you noticed, Wullie," Ina said, patting her hair at the back. "Especially wi' they cock-eyes of yours." Ina took a dainty sip from her teacup.

Wullie spluttered. "EH?" he gasped.

Annie, too, raised an eyebrow. She smiled as she detected a mischievous twinkle in Ina's eye.

Annie rose, went over to the sideboard and rummaged in the top drawer. She stood back, put a finger to the corner of her mouth and murmured thoughtfully:

"Ah was sure there was a packet of Capstan in there! Ah'll..er..just nip doon tae Mary Welsh's and see if any came in!"

Annie took her coat from behind the door and hurried out saying: "Ah'll no' be long."

"Aye," Wullie called after her, " and nane o' this three Woodbine or Capstan and three Pasha. It's blackmail, so it is, havin' tae take three o' they Turkish smellies just tae get a few good Scottish fags."

Ina and Wullie were now alone and facing each other across the table. Wullie slurped his tea and snatched another soda scone. "Ah just love soday scones," he said, taking a large bite.

"Soday scones, soday heid," Ina said. "It figures."

Wullie gulped.

"You're gettin' helluva cheeky!" he said, narrowing his eyes. "Ah think they curlin' tongs have been too hoat and have melted yer brain!"

"Look who's talkin' aboot brains," Ina said, putting down her cup. "The brainless wonder of Well Street. Ma faither was right aboot you. He said ye were a waster and that you would end up a nothin'."

Wullie threw up his arms.

"Listen tae her!" he cried, "That's a good wan, that is! Ah would end up a nuthin'? THAT comin' frae an auld git who has ended up as a bloody geranium."

Ina looked across at him. Madame Wee Nellie was right. Wullie was irri-tated and puzzled by Ina's nonchalance. She would keep it going, but hoped that her coolness would not backfire on her.

"And Ah'll tell ye another thing," Wullie grumbled, "Ah have never in ma life gied you cause tae think that Ah was any wey interested in you romantically."

"Huh!" Ina cried, "Don't flatter yersel'. Ah widnae have you if ye went doon on yer knees and pleaded wi' me tae walk doon the aisle."

"ME? GO DOON ON MA KNEES?" Wullie bawled. "Let me tell you, hen. Ah have never gone doon on ma knees in ma life...for ANYBODY!"

"Is that so? Ah've seen you comin' up the stairs many a time oan yer knees," Ina said dryly.

Wullie fumed. He drummed his fingers on the table top and puffed rapidly on his pipe until the smoke filled the room like a fog.

"Take the last soda scone, Wullie," Ina said. "Ye look like you could dae wi' it. Ye're that skinny, you remind me of an act Ah saw wance on ma faither's bill at the Metropole....Wullie, The Human Pipe Cleaner!"

Wullie exploded.

"Ya cheeky midden," he hollered, jumping up. "That new hairdo has gone tae your heid."

"Aye, well," Ina said, "Ah'm just hopin' it might go tae somebody else's heid in Barraland...a rich American's, maybe!"

Wullie doubled up in mock laughter. "A rich Yank!....YOU!" he scoffed.

Ina was hurt. The hard veneer cracked and she saw that Nellie's advice was having the opposite effect to what was expected. She felt a tear ooze from the corner of her eye and she turned quickly away so that Wullie would not notice. Ina rose from her chair. "Ah'll have tae go," she said, hurrying towards the door. "Whit aboot the last soday scone?" Wullie asked, nodding towards the delicacy.

Ina turned.

"Dae ye want jam on it, Wullie?" she said quietly

Ina hurried out leaving Wullie with his jaw drooping. Patting her eyes with her handkerchief, she almost knocked Annie down in her haste to get into her own house.

Annie's eyes narrowed when she saw how distressed Ina was. Her matchmaking attempts had backfired.

Her jaw firmly set, she marched into the house, slamming the door behind her.

Wullie was sitting on his chair munching into the soda scone. He looked up and faced an angry Annie. But before his sister could utter a word the air-raid sirens screamed. The rebuke would have to wait until another time.

Wullie McSorley had been saved...by the Luftwaffe!

Fingers McGeachie had it on good authority that Broon, the butcher, in Hunter Street, would be having a delivery of pigs from the Gallowgate Meat Market this very day. His informants were usually reliable and the Big Man was already at his stance keeping watch from a nearby closemouth.

He had 'borrowed' a pram from a backcourt in Green Street...after making sure that it was empty. Fingers had had tussles with the law many times, but never for kidnapping babies. He leaned against the wall of the close, lit up a cigar and waited. Gone was the gaberdine coat with the velvet lapels and he was garbed instead in a brown corduroy jacket, blue flannels and a checked cap.

His disguise would not fool any of the local lawmen, especially Erchie McPherson, but his normal attire seemed out of place for such a mission as this. He kept his eyes open for any of the beat policemen who might come his way and would undoubtedly wonder why the sophisticated Fingers McGeachie was pushing a battered old pram. No sign of a blue tin hat around and Fingers reckoned that whistles had been stashed away and it was 'Rest' time for the law behind the closed doors of the Come Inn pub.

He was annoyed at having to do this job himself! Normally he would have delegated it to one of his minions but, unfortunately, they were all doing post office work ...sewing mailbags in Barlinnie.

As a rule, Fingers would never have entertained such a petty, trivial job as this.

But Wullie McSorley was an an old and valued friend. He remembered Rita, too, ever since the days she skiffed up and down the close wearing her mother's high-heels with her doll in her arms. Or the days when he had to squeeze past Rita and her playmates who had set up shop at the foot of the stairs and where the 'cakes' were made of clay, patted into all shapes and sizes, and where the 'money' to purchase them, was broken glass from discarded bottles. Where a good piece of green glass could buy the shop.

He remembered, too, how Wullie had hidden him in a kist under the bed when Big Rab, the beat man, was searching for him, after he had stolen a pair of herring from the slab of Fyffe's fish shop, with its open window onto the street, putting temptation in the way of nimble fingers.He had given the fish to Auld Beenie Boal who showered blessings on him.

He took a long drag at his cigar and had just checked the time on his gold pocket watch when the delivery van turned the corner and pulled up outside the shop. Fingers immediately threw the cigar to the ground and crushed it with his heel. The driver jumped down from his cab and opened up the back roller door on his van. Fingers' eyes widened. The carcasses of at least a dozen pigs, heads attached, lay piled in a stack. The driver lifted the top carcass and threw it over his shoulder and entered the shop.

Fingers waited and timed the man from the time he entered the shop until he emerged again for another load. Half-a-minute. After the delivery man had taken four carcasses into the shop Fingers made his move. Like lightning he was over at the van and a pig was snatched and thrown into the pram. With a quick flick, the blanket was pulled over the carcass with only its head showing. A dummy teat was rammed into its mouth and Fingers strolled nonchalantly away and vanished round the corner.

The thought that by taking the pig he might be depriving others had occurred to him. But, he reckoned, the market would make up the loss and he knew himself that a lot of pilfering went on and that no-one would suffer. All was fair in love and war, was his motto and this escapade covered both!

Fingers felt quite pleased with himself and felt in his pocket for a fresh cigar. Finding none, he crossed the street to a tobacconist's shop, parked the pram outside and entered, hoping the shopkeeper had such a luxury in his premises.

The drunk with the tartan muffler, who had encountered Wullie in the tram queue, turned the corner and, with great difficulty, was attempting to light his broken cigarette. In his consistent state of sublime bliss, he bounced along the wall towards the tobacconist's shop with the intention of purchasing another box of matches, to replace the entire box he had just wasted.

He threw his broken cigarette away and peered into the pram where the flesh coloured face, with the dummy teat, stared up at him.

He looked again at the pug nosed face and tickled it under the chin.

"Coochy-coochy-coo," he slurred. "Coochy, twoochy....Geez, ye're an ugly wean!...Ah've never seen an uglier wean in ma entire life!...whit happened tae yer nose, eh?..hiv ye been batterin' it aff a wa'? You should sue yer maw for bringin' ye intae this world, so ye should , hen! Whit are they feedin' ye on, that's whit Ah would like tae know....so that Ah can steer clear o' it....whit a kisser! It's a shame, so it is!"

Fingers emerged from the shop lighting up a King Edwards cigar, which, fortunately, the shopkeeper just managed to purchase from a lorry with a broken back door. He looked into the pram, making sure his charge was all right.

The drunk staggered against the shop window, turned and eyed up Fingers, who was about to push off with the pram.

"Hey, jist a minute, pal," the muffler said, grasping Fingers' sleeve.

"Eh?" Fingers muttered.

"Is that your ugly wean in there," the drunk said, nodding towards the pram.

"And whit if it is?" Fingers retorted. "Whit's it got tae dae wi' you, eh?"

The drunk pulled himself up to his full five-feet height.

"You are feedin' that wean too much ham," he said. "Weans of that age should not have ham stuffed intae them....look at the poor wee sowel, eh..look...whit a coupon!"

Fingers shrugged. "Aye, well...er...he..er...he's no' hisel' the day."

"He's no' ANYBODY the day," the drunk said.

"Aye, well you just get oot the road," Fingers said, pushing on, "the wean needs some air."

"He needs a shave as well," the drunk said.

Fingers hurried off, not wanting to draw notice to his encounter with the man with the tartan muffler.

The drunk stood swaying and watched the retreating Fingers vanishing down the street pushing the pram.

"Ye should take yer wean oot in a whisky gless like everybody else," he called. Then, turning, he fumbled in his pocket, found a penny piece and shuffled into the shop.

"A boax o' pigs," he gabbled. "Ah've ran oot o' pigs tae light ma fag."

The shopkeeper nodded knowingly.

"Sorry," he said, "Ah've ran oot o' pigs. Ah could gie ye a boax o' Swans."

"That'll dae," the drunk said and, with his purchase, staggered out into the street and began the marathon task of lighting up his dangling ciga-rette.

Fingers hurried on, all the time his eyes sweeping around for any sign of the law...and Erchie McPherson in particular. Erchie was no friend of Fingers...not since he heard how Big Rab was outfoxed in the case of the stolen herring. It brought shame on the force and Erchie didn't like that.

It would not have mattered to Erchie that Fingers' theft was a Robin Hood gesture and that Auld Beenie Boal was hungry and finding it hard to make ends meet. Erchie went by the letter of the law and his dearest wish was to join the regular police force. But he was turned down because he was two inches under the minimum regulation height.

Erchie had made up his mind that he would show them that what he lacked in quantity, he made up in quality. Yes, Erchie would show them!

Fingers quickened his pace, all the time keeping his eyes peeled for Erchie or any of his colleagues. All was quiet and Fingers gave a sigh as he turned into Annie's closemouth.

He parked the pram at the foot of the stairs, intending to return it to its rightful place later on, wrapped the pig up in the blanket and hurried on up the stairs.

Annie hastened in response to the quickfire rapping on the door. Fingers stood with a broad smile on his face.

"Fingers!" Annie muttered in surprise. "Come away in...through there." She indicated the kitchen.

Fingers marched through followed by Annie, who was wondering about the baby bundle in her visitor's arms.

"Whose is the wean?" Annie asked.

"It's yours, hen," Fingers grinned, thrusting the bundle into Annie's arms.

Annie flustered and, pulling the blanket aside, gasped as the pig, still with teat in its mouth, stared up at her. She almost let the bundle drop but suddenly burst out laughing and gave Fingers an affectionate shove with her elbow.

"Ya big galoot, ye!" she cried, "gien me a fright like that." Fingers laughed.

"Aye, well, that's just for starters, Annie. That'll gie ye enough chops to feed an army, eh?"

"No' half!" Annie said, giving the bundle a squeeze.

"Ah would've got a coo but the pram wisnae big enough," Fingers grinned.

They both laughed loudly

"Ah've still the trimmins tae get ye yet," Fingers went on, "totties and sausage rolls an' that. Ah'll bring them up immediately Ah have acquired them!"

Annie shook her head, relief showing in her face

"Ach, you're a good man, Fingers McGeachie!" she said with sincerity. "Come on...have a wee cuppa tea."

Fingers shook his head.

"Naw, thanks, Annie. Ah canny wait," he said, impatience in his voice. "Ah have very important business tae attend to for the Home Guard....and Ah must return the pram Ah've got doonstairs tae its rightful owner."

Fingers headed for the door, turned and added:

"Ah will be up wi' the rest of the stuff before the party."

Annie hurried forward and pecked him on the cheek. Fingers shuffled his feet and his face flushed.

"You'll get yer reward in Heaven, Fingers!" Annie said cheerily.

Fingers laughed.

"Of course Ah will," he said, "Ah'm doin' a deal wi' Cardinal Goldberg."

Fingers closed the door behind him and Annie could still hear his laughter all the way down to the closemouth. She let the blanket fall from the pig and held it at arms length.

"You're just the very dab!" she said, propping it on a dining chair at the table.

"Noo," she said, "you sit there while Ah make a pot of tea." Annie filled the kettle, put it on the ring and went into the bedroon where she had hidden a packet of Rich Tea Biscuits...kept for special occasions.

There was a knock on the door and Ina popped her head round.

"Anybody in?"

"Come in, Ina," Annie called from the bedroom. "Ah'll be wi' ye in just a minute and don't let that wee pig bother ye!"

Ina came into the kitchen and sat down at the table.

Annie entered and moved the carcass into Wullie's room.

The two women sat sipping tea and Annie told how Fingers McGeachie was going to supply all that was needed for Rita's engagement party and explained about the pig.

"Ah only wish we could make it a double celebration, Ina," she said, looking affectionately at her neighbour.

"Whit dae ye mean?" Ina asked.

"Well, you know," Annie began, "you and..er..Wullie." Ina shook her head.

"Your Wullie's a confirmed bachelor," she said. "You've been too good tae him, Annie. Ye've got him spoilt!"

Annie had to agree.

"Aye, ye're right!" she said, "Maybe wan o' these days he'll come tae his senses."

Ina nodded.

"Aye, and maybe pigs'll fly," she said.

Their eyes met and they roared with laughter.

Wullie had quietly entered the house but, on hearing Ina's voice, crept into the bedroom. Annie and Ina were still chuckling when a sudden shriek made them jump. Wullie, ashen-faced, staggered into the room clutching his heart. He fell into his chair.

"Oh my God!" he gasped, "Ah got the bloody fright o' ma life there! Who put that pig on ma bed?"

"Ina thought it was you," Annie said with a wry smile. Ina nodded.

"That's right," she said, "it was they ears and the baldy heid that did it." Wullie's eyebrows narrowed.

"Is that a fact?" he snapped, "Well, you've a cheek tae talk aboot anybody's appearance. You, the original model for barrage balloons."

Ina ignored the remark.

"Ah was just goin' doon tae the shoaps for a present for Rita," she said, turning to Annie, "but Ah don't know where tae go first."

"Schmidt's have a sale on the noo," Wullie volunteered.

"Oh! Where's their shoap?" Ina showed interest.

"Nuremberg," Wullie said snidely.

Annie was quick.

"WULLIE!" she scolded, giving him a look that would have sunk The Tirpitz, the ominous Nazi battleship.

Ina rose. Inside, she WAS hurt by Wullie's acid tongue.

"Ah'll..er...go noo," she said quietly. "See youse at the party the morra night." Annie nodded. "Aye, a'right, Ina....see ye," she said softly. Ina gave a faint smile and, not looking at Wullie, closed the door quietly behind her.

There was an uneasy silence as Annie cleared the dishes from the table. Trying to hide her anger, she noisily began to rinse them in the sink. But she could contain herself no longer. Turning on Wullie, she snapped.

"You're awfu' hard on that lassie!"

"LASSIE?" Wullie cried, "Geez, if she's a lassie Ah'm still at school!"

"Aye, well you could dae wi' some education on how tae treat people," Annie retorted. "Ina is a fine wumman and Ah canny even see whit she sees in YOU!"

Wullie sat up straight.

"Is that a fact!" he cried. "Ah tell ye this...AH would be a catch, so Ah would!"

Annie threw back her head and roared.

"A CATCH?" she hollered, "A CATCH? Wullie, you would be the wan that's thrown back."

"Naw, Naw," Wullie said, "Whit YOU mean is that Ah was the wan that GOT AWAY." He leaned back pleased with himself.

Wullie was happy with his smart replies and was now confident enough to press on.

"And another thing," he said, "get that pig oot o' ma bed. A pig lyin' in yer bed is bad enough, but a pig lyin' in yer bed wi' a dummy-tit in its mooth is somethin' not tae be tolerated!"

"Naebody's askin' ye tae sleep wi' the pig," Annie said angrily.

"Aye, well...er...Ah'm...er..just as gled it wisnae a hoarse Fingers brung up....a bit of the old cheval."

Annie turned away and, followed by Wullie, went into the bedroom. Looking down at the pig, she said

"It's an ugly lookin' thing, int it?" Wullie nodded.

"Better lookin' than some folk Ah know, mind ye!" he said. Annie ran her hand over the pig's face.

"Dae ye think it's cured? "she said.

Wullie shook his head.

"Naw, it's definitely deid," he said with a straight face. Annie dug him in the ribs with her elbow.

"Ye know fine whit Ah mean," she said. "Ah meant they cure ham an' that an Ah was... "Ah know whit ye mean," Wullie said. "Ah think we'll just have tae carve it up the best we can....should be nae problems."

"Fingers says he'll be bringin' up mair stuff. Oh, Ah just hope everythin' goes a'right!" Annie said, a flash of worry crossing her face.

"Just as long as the grub's good and we're no' bringin' it up," Wullie said with a twinkle.

Annie lifted the carcass from the bed and cradled it like a baby.

"Ah'll put this away in the wardrobe," she said. "Keep it clear o' the moth-balls," Wullie cried.

The door opened and Rita breezed in and flopped down on the chair by the fireside.

"Whit a day this has been!" she sighed. "Ah think everybody in Glesca was travellin' between Auchenshuggle and Dalmuir West."

Rita kicked off her shoes and wiggled her toes.

"Never mind," her mother said coming into the room. "It's better than being in the Land Army!"

The Land Army had never appealed to Rita. She was a city girl who loved the rattle and clatter of the streets. Who loved shouting and having a conversation with Mrs McWhachle, who was leaning out of her third-storey tenement window. She loved the shop at the corner, the 'wulks shop', in

Gallowgate. The gruff, coarse voice of the coalman announcing his arrival in the street with his horse and cart stacked with hundredweight bags.

Or the whistle of the man selling buttermilk and the nearness of Barrowland and the Dennistoun Palais, the Paramount Cinema, in Renfield Street. Or 'The Polly', in Argyle Street, Lewis' polytechnic to give it its proper name, where you could buy anything in the world...just so long as you had the coupons.

Rita had considered going into factory work. They were manufacturing barrage balloons in the city's Kelvin Hall and, at the Morris's furniture works, in Wilton Street, they were turning out armaments. Rolls Royce had taken over a large site at Hillington, on the south side and were hard into war production. There was plenty of work —but folk had to get to their work in the factories and the workshops. And Rita was getting them to their benches on time, fresh and ready to work hard. And THAT was important work, too, she reckoned. They need clippies —- even for just a cheery word in the mornings. She was doing her bit for the war effort as best she could.

"Rita would be nae good in the Land Army!" Wullie said. "No' wi' HER hay fever. She would spend the whole bloody war sneezin'!"

Annie laughed. Wullie was right! Rita was a hard worker who was in the correct job and who never missed a day. Yes, Rita was doing her bit all right!

"Whit's the latest aboot the caterin'?" Rita asked with some concern.

"Fingers brought up a wee pig," Annie said, lifting Rita's shoes and putting them under the sideboard in case anybody should come in unexpectedly.

"A wee pig?" Rita said, screwing up her face. "No' that Wee Bowly Campbell, Ah hope....Ah don't trust that wee yin!"

"Naw, naw," Annie said, shaking her head. "A wee pig...a pig pig...for eatin'. It'll go doon well wi' the guests, hen, so it wull."

"Oh, Ah must see it!" Rita said, jumping up. "Where is it?" Annie nodded towards Wullie's bedroom. "In there," she said, "hingin' up in the wardrobe." Rita hurried into the room followed by Annie and Wullie. Opening the wardrobe door, Wullie stood back. "Voila!" he said. Rita stared at the pig, still with the dummy in its mouth. "Aw, would ye look at it!" she exclaimed. "The wee sowel!" "That wee sowel has saved oor bacon, if ye don't mind the pun," Annie said. "There's mair than a pun o' bacon there," Wullie said with a grin.

Wullie's remark went un-noticed. Rita was suddenly thinking of the coming party...and her father. "Oh" she said wistfully, "Ah just wish ma da' could've been here for the party." Annie sighed. "Aye, it's funny, Ah hivnae heard frae him for ages. He's probably on a mission."

"Probably MISSIN', ye mean," Wullie said sarcastically. "You shut yer face," Annie snapped. "It's worryin', ye know, no' knowin'." Annie wrung her hands. Rita put a comforting arm around her mother's shoulders.

"Don't you worry mammy," she said softly, "ye know ma da'....he always bounces back."

Wullie nodded. "Usually frae wan wa' in the close tae the other," he said dryly. Annie ignored the facetious remark. Turning to Rita, she asked: "Are ye goin' tae Barraland the night, hen?" Rita shook her head.

"Naw, no' the night, mammy. Raspy's steyin' in tae dae some swattin up. He's right intae a Swahili dictionary the noo." Wullie looked up.

"Is he learnin' it?" he asked, trying not to show his admiration. "Naw, writin' it," Rita said without looking up. Wullie's mouth fell open. Rita was now sitting and massaging her aching feet.

"That's better!" she said, relief in her voice. She stretched her legs out fully and wriggled her toes

Her toes now fully exercised, Rita got up and ambled into her room where she flopped down on top of the horsehair mattress.She lay gazing at the ceiling and a feeling of wellbeing swept over her. She wondered what kind of engagement ring Rasputin would surprise her with? For Rasputin was always full of surprises! He would not let her down, she was sure of that. She shivered with delight. It would be something nice to show off to the girls down at the tram depot! Rita saw herself standing in the canteen, arm outstretched and turning her left hand this way and that and dazzling her colleagues with the blinding emblem of her new status.

Rasputin had hinted that he had something very special in mind for her engagement finger — "romantic and symbolic of their uniting," he had said. Rita had pleaded with Rasputin to tell her what he had meant but he had refused to add to his intriguing hint. And now Rita wondered. Not only was Rasputin tight lipped, he was often tight, period. Still, Rita decided, her man was a genius and a poet and geniuses and poets are allowed their little idiosyncrasies. Rita sighed once more and closed her eyes.

She slipped into a dream world. There was the church, packed to the door and Rasputin was there, at the altar with the best man. Raspy looked resplendent in his general's uniform. The gold and silver medals pinned on his chest glinted in the shining shaft of blinding sunlight that stabbed through the stained-glass window.

The best man looked dignified in black frock-coat and silver silk cravat. His gleaming white, bushy hair encircled his head and caught the sunlight, turning it into a shimmering halo. She had never met this man but Rasputin had often shown her photographs of him and she recognised him immediately. Rasputin always talked highly of him. So, she was not surprised that her bridegroom had asked him to be his chief attendant at their wedding. It was, indeed, Albert Einstein.

The scene suddenly changed to outside the church where a magnificent Guard of Honour, men from Rasputin's regiment, The Calton Blues and Greens, made up from men of the San Toi and Billy Boys gangs, stood stiffly to attention. These men have been known to be stiff often.

The Sergeant Major, who looked remarkably like Erchie McPherson, stood grasping a silver cord attached to the neck of the regimenal mascot....a noble pig with a golden dummy tit in its mouth.

Then she saw herself arriving and stepping daintily from a number nine Auchenshuggle car. Her flowing dress caught the wind and had to be held down by her ladies-in-waiting, all beautifully dressed out in their green clippies' uniforms. Rita's exquisite wedding dress had been designed and made by Old Mrs Cominsky, from up the Paddy Close, in Well Street, known throughout the Calton for her expertise in making patchwork quilts. As she serenely entered the church, she was rival for the stained glass window.

On entering, Wullie stepped forward with arm crooked and offered her a pint of Guinness he was holding. The music suddenly struck up and everybody stood. The wee man from the air-raid shelter had tuned his mouth organ well. As Wullie escorted Rita down the aisle the dulcet tones of Bing Crosby, who was standing in the pulpit, flooded the church with 'I'm Dreaming Of a White Wedding'.

The preacher,who wore a Royal Stewart tartan muffler,swayed and stepped forward as Rita and Rasputin took their places.

Looking at the bride as straight as he could, the preacher said. "Wan and a hauf tae Brigton Croass."

Then suddenly the preacher with the muffler vanished and his place was taken by Erchie McPherson, who wore a blue mitre with the word 'Polis' emblazoned in gold printed vertically on it.

Erchie took a pencil stub from behind his ear, licked it and opened a small black book. Pencil poised he looked at Rita.

"Dae you take Rasputin for ye're lawful wedded husband — and don't you forget that Ah know a' aboot the law...so nae funny business." Rita found herself stammering.

"Ah..er...Ah...."

"Come on OPEN UP OPEN UP " Erchie snarled, repeatedly banging the book with the pencil "OPEN UP, OPEN UP "

Rita awoke with a start and sat bolt upright.

The landing door was being battered by an authorative pencil and Erchie McPherson's demented voice was bawling:

"OPEN UP...open up this minute!"

Annie and Wullie were already at the door as Rita hurried through, wondering what all the commotion was?

Erchie stood, his face contorted and, not waiting for an invitation, swept past Annie into the house. He made straight for the kitchen.

"Ah am here in ma official capacity!" he snapped.

"Oh, aye?" Annie retorted, with arms defiantly folded and with a steely glare.

Erchie's eyes narrowed as he scanned the room. "Take yer hat aff!" Wullie growled.

"And why should Ah?" Erchie snarled.

"'Cos it's obvious ye've got a bee in yer bonnet," Wullie replied coldly. "And, besides, there's a lady present...two ladies!"

Erchie shuffled his feet and removed his helmet.

"Right! Whit's a' this aboot?" Annie demanded.

Erchie cleared his throat.

"Ah have reason tae believe," he began in his best authoritative tone, "that you have got a pig in here."

Wullie suddenly felt his face flush and ran a finger under his collar.

"Oh aye!" Annie said coolly, "and whit would Ah be daein' wi' a pig in here,eh?"

Wullie stepped forward and glowered into Erchie's eyes.

"We've no' had so much as a rasher in this hoose for a month," he said boldly.

Erchie ignored Wullie's declaration and began to move about the room, opening cupboard doors and peering under chairs. He finally stood up and, replacing the tin hat on his head, growled.

"A man - as yet unidentified - was seen tae enter this close pushin' a pram wi' a deid pig wrapped up in a blanket in it!"

Rita put her hands on her hips and stood before him, looking straight into his eyes.

"An how dae ye know it was a pig?" she said defiantly. "It could've been a wean."

Erchie pulled himself up to his full height.

"If it was a wean," he said, "it had cleft feet....four of them!"

"And so, you think that we're harbourin' a four-legged wean in here, is that it?" Wullie thundered.

"Listen," Erchie said, "Ah have searched every hoose up this stairheid except this wan. Ah deliberately left this tae the last owin' tae the fact that Ah could not bring masel' tae think that lovely Annie here would be the recipient of stolen goods....especially deid pigs."

"Ah suppose Ah should be flattered," Annie said dryly.

"You should be ANGRY, Mammy!" Rita piped up. "He's got a cheek in him! Comes up here for wee fly cuppas and thinkin' that o' ye."

Wullie nodded.

"A' HE ever wants tae dae is feel yer bum, Annie!"

Erchie gave a slight cough.

"Ah..er..am just daein' ma duty," he stammered. "Ah wull have tae search this hoose."

Wullie's knees suddenly buckled. He glanced over at Annie, who was keeping a cool head and showing no signs of anxiety — although Wullie knew that inwardly she was alarmed at the prospect of Erchie's glee should he discover their hidden secret. "Search away," Annie said with nonchalance. "And if ye see a pig in here, ye must be lookin' in the mirror."

Wullie chortled at Annie's facetious remark.

Erchie marched into Rita's room, followed by Annie, Wullie and Rita. They watched quietly as he searched, leaving no cushion unturned....even turning up the corner of the linoleum.

"Geez!" Wullie sneered, "if it can hide under there, there canny be a pick oan it. It widnae be worth pinchin'."

Rita cleared her throat.

"Er..Uncle Wullie," she said, "did ye see ma fags anywhere?" Wullie's eyebrows shot up.

"Eh? Yer fags?"

Rita nodded.

"Aye, ma fags. The last Ah saw them was in your haun's when you were puttin' yer jaicket away...IN THE WARDROBE."

"Ah never had yer fags," Wullie said, puzzled.

"Ye had so!" Annie said, catching Rita's drift.

Wullie shrugged...and cried out as Annie gave him a kick on the ankle.

"Gie the lassie her fags," Annie snapped.

"Ah'm tellin' ye, Ah hivnae got " Wullie caught Annie's glare and suddenly he understood.

"Oh, THEY FAGS?" he cried, "The wans in ma jaicket poacket....?"

Rita sighed with relief.

"That's right, the wans in the wardrobe.."

"Ah put them in ma poacket withoot thinkin'. Ah'll get them, hen," Wullie said, hurrying from the room.

Rita looked over at Annie, who raised her eyes to the ceiling in gratitude. Wullie dashed into his bedroom, threw open the wardrobe door and grabbed the hanging pig, still with the dummy in its mouth. Grasping the carcass tightly to his chest, he frantically looked around for a less conspic-uous hiding place. There was none. It was too thick to shove under the bed and, besides, that would be the first place the eagle-eyed Erchie would look. Wullie panicked as he heard the entourage head his way. In blind ter-ror, he rushed to the window, threw it open and chucked the pig out, into the street,quickly slamming the window shut, leaning against it and wiping his brow with his handkerchief.

Erchie entered, followed by Annie and Rita. He made straight for the wardrobe and peered inside. Satisfied his prey was not there, he looked under the bed. Rita and Annie's eyes met and a knowing smile passed between them. They looked over at Wullie, who had a mischevious grin on his face.Erchie finally gave up the hunt and stood up, looking embarrassed.

Shuffling his feet, he turned to Annie:

"Ah'm sorry tae have bothered ye, Annie," he said. "Ah should've known better. Ah'll...er...conduct ma investigation elsewhere....but that pig was definitely seen comin' up this close, so it was. Ah'll get tae the bottom of this!"

Wullie murmured.

"Aye, you're good at gettin' tae bottoms."

Annie said nothing. She turned on her heel and threw the outside door wide open ignoring Erchie as he mumbled leaving and slammed it shut as he stepped on to the landing.

Wullie, Rita and Annie sighed with relief as they heard Erchie's size-tens clattering down the stairs. They exchanged glances and burst out laughing.

"Where is it, then?" Annie asked, her eyes scanning the room.

"Aye, whit did ye dae wi' it?" Rita said, puzzled.

Wullie gestured with his thumb.

"Oot there....Ah chucked it oot the windae!"

All three rushed to the window , threw it open and jostled for room as they looked down into the street.

There was no sign of the pig!

"Maybe Erchie saw it when he left the close?" Annie cried.

"Naw...naw...look," Rita said, "there's Erchie goin' up the street...and he's no' cairrying a pig."

Annie came in from the window and sighed a deep sigh.

"Aye, well, that's it," she said quietly. " the ba's oan the slates noo!"

Biddy O'Flaherty lived at number ten Stevenston Street,near the corner of Kent Street,where the famous Glasgow barrows, the street market, began and mushroomed out from and just one hundred yards from St Alphonsus' Chapel house. Round the corner, in London Road, the impressive red-brick building of the chapel itself stood.

Naturally, Biddy, from County Cork, in Southern Ireland, was a daily communicant at the church and a search party would have been sent out if her presence was missing just once from the ten o'clock morning mass. She was now thirty-years-old, small and plump and rosy-cheeked and the proud mother of Marietta,now fourteen months-old.

Work was hard to come by at home and Biddy and her husband, Barney, had decided to come to Glasgow, where Barney hoped to join the navy.

Having failed the navy medical because of flat-feet Barney now worked as a train guard for the L.N.E.R.,at the Bridgeton Cross station. The London and North Eastern Railway was a secure job and well paid. Things were good and only the food rationing got them down.

Biddy laid down a mug of tea and slice of toast and marmalade for her husband's breakfast that morning.

"No ham?" Barney asked, sliding into his chair.

"Now, Barney, you know there's a war on!" Biddy said, "and, besides, it's Friday...and we don't eat meat on Friday!"

Barney grimaced.

"We hardly eat meat at all these days," he said. "A workin' man should be goin' out in the mornin' with a full belly, so he should."

"Aye, well your belly's full enough comin' in at night," Biddy replied in her soft Irish lilt.

Barney laughed.

"Ah, me wee darlin', you're quite a wumman, so ye are. Ah'm not really complainin' y'know."

Biddy kissed him lightly on the cheek.

"Ah know ye're not, Barney. And, believe me, if I could give you a plate o' ham and eggs every mornin' in life, I would pile it on so that ye would have to go out the door sideways."

Barney gave Biddy a playful slap on the posterior.

Biddy sent Barney off to work that day with an extra two slices of brown bread and marmalade.

But her good husband's words had registered in her heart. Barney was right, a workin' man needed his food. Barney loved his bacon and eggs and had sometimes considered going back home where he knew his family were eating them in abundance. Like the Prodigal Son, he knew he would be made most welcome. But work was work and he was settled now.

Biddy thought about her breakfast time conversation as she pushed her pram down Kent Street and into London Road. After mass, she would go down to the Lady Altar, light a candle and have a chat with The Virgin Mary to whom she had great devotion. Ask and you shall receive,was her belief and 'Our Lady is never outdone in generosity' was her sincere conviction.

Father Hourigan said the mass that morning and,in his deep, gruff voice preached about how the Blessed Virgin intercedes for all who ask her. To Biddy, it was a confirmation of her intentions...like a personal message that had been directed straight to her.

After mass, she made her way down the righthand aisle, lit a candle and knelt before a statue of The Virgin and Child.

"Dear Blessed Mother," Biddy said, hands tightly clasped, "I know you are a busy wumman with a lot of important t'ings on your plate and maybe my wee petition to you seems trivial and unimportant. But it's important to me, my wee lamb, and YOU did say to come down anytime and give you our worries....not to mention the good Father Hourigan this very mornin' who said the very same t'ing you might have heard. It's my Barney, y'see, dear Mary.

"He's a good, hard-workin' man who looks after me and the wee one the best he can. And I would like to give him a wee bit extra in the mornin's before he goes out to work in the railway....a wee bit ham would make him, and me, very happy. So, Sweet Mother, d'ye t'ink you could see your way to doin' somet'in' about t'at? Maybe raise the rations a wee bit...know whit Ah mean? If you'll just turn your merciful eye to me and grant me this little favour, Ah promise to make a nine-Friday novena for your own, personal intentions. I t'ank you wit' great expectations and sincere belief."

Biddy finished her prayers, collected Marietta, in her pram at the side of the pew, and dropped a penny in the 'St Vincent De Paul Box' on the way out.

Turning left, Biddy headed along London Road, stopped in at Mrs Mills' newsagent shop, where she bought a copy of The Bulletin and turned down Well Street, towards Stevenston Street.

She had gone just halfway down the street, wondering what to make Barney for his supper when he got home from work, when there was a thud as a pig came suddenly down from the sky and landed at her feet.

Biddy stopped and looked at the pig with the dummy-tit lying on the ground. And then she looked up at the sky and crashed down on her knees.

"Oh, Mother of Mercy," she cried. "You didn't waste any time. I only put a PENNY in the box and I only asked ye for a wee bit extra ham....and you've went and gone the whole hog —if you'll pardon the pun. I know you're never outdone in your generosity...! Wait till Ah tell Barney...aw, thanks dear Mother, and thank yer big son as well...!"

Biddy placed the pig at the opposite end of the pram from Marietta, who was sleeping soundly. Then, looking skywards, she did a quick genuflection and hurried down the street, stopping at Mary Welsh's. Parking the pram in the street outside the shop, she hurried in. Trembling and clutching her chest, she blurted out the story of her miracle to the young, wide-eyed girl behind the counter.

The girl, seeing how elated and excited Biddy was, brought round an old chair and eased the shaking woman into it

Biddy had her hands clasped tightly and was chanting to herself.

"It's a miracle!" she gasped, "A miracle! I'd just been to chapel and asked Our Blessed Lady for a wee bit extra bacon for my Barney. And Glory Be to God, she heard me. She never said anythin', mind ye. But, as I was walkin' down this street here, down came a pig from Heaven. And, kind mother that she is, it wasn't even an old pig but a nice fresh baby pig wit'the blessed dummy-tit still in its mouth. Can ye believe, t'at, eh? A lovely wee, Heavenly pig!"

Biddy went into raptures.

"You just sit there and Ah'll bring ye a wee cuppa tea, hen," the young girl said and vanished into the back shop.

Biddy decided that it would be bad manners to delay her gratitude to her heavenly benefactor and, producing her rosary beads from her pocket,fell down on her knees and began to recite her devotions.

Outside, the drunk in the tartan muffler staggered down towards the shop where he intended purchasing another box of matches —- to replace the box he had used up trying to light up his broken cigarette. Seeing the pram, he stopped and stared in. His jaw fell as he noted Marietta sleeping at one end and the pig in the other.

"Coochy-coochy-coo," he slurred. "Geez, it's you again....and ye've got a wee sister,eh? Gawd, ye'd think yer maw would've gave up efter lookin' at your coupon. Yer wee sister's got a nice face, mind ye! But Ah'll bet ye her erse is better lookin' than your kisser. It's no' fair, sure it's no'!"

The drunk looked into the shop and saw Biddy on her knees and oblivious to the world. Taking a deep breath, he swayed and staggered in.

"Hey missus," he said, "is that your wee ugly wean oot there wi' a dummy-tit in its gub?"

Biddy was halfway through the second Glorious Mystery but anger swept over her. Making a hurried sign of the cross, she jumped to her feet and clobbered the man with her message bag.

"THAT," she said, "is a Celestal Being, an angel from Heaven....so you have more decorum."

The drunk stared at her through glazed eyes.

"Well," he said, "that angel wean has nae sense o' direction if ye ask me. It must keep flyin' face-first intae wa's. And if a' the weans in Heaven look like that, whit must their maws look like, eh? Ah'm gled Ah'm no' goin' there, Ah can tell ye that."

The girl arrived from the back shop carrying a cup of tea which she handed to Biddy, who thanked her profusely.

"Whit dae you want?" she asked the drunk. He shook his head.

"Nothin'," he said, "Ah WAS gonny ask ye for a boax of matches...but Ah wisnae gonny beg ye for anythin'....like she was. Ye can stick yer matches up yer nose!".

The drunk hiccupped, staggered out, crossed the road and, on half tilt, entered the swing doors of the 'Come Inn' pub, muttering:

"If that wean was Jewish it would be excommunicated!"

Marietta woke up and began to cry. Biddy gulped down her tea, thanked the girl once more and hurried out into the street. A man, passing by, heard the baby's cries and was looking into the pram as Biddy arrived at his side.

The man's eyes widened when he saw the pig lying staring up at him. The passer-by was Erchie McPherson.

"Whit's this here, then?" he said, his eyes narrowing.

Biddy had lifted Marietta out of the pram and was comforting her, patting her on the back.

"THAT?" she said proudly, "is a wee present that was given to me, personally."

"Oh, aye," Erchie said dryly, "And who gave it tae ye?"

"The Blessed Virgin Mary," Biddy said, looking skywards.

Erchie tongue went to his cheek and he scratched his chin.

"The Blessed Virgin Mary?" he said.

Biddy nodded.

"Our Blessed Mother herself," she smiled.

"She jist came doon tae earth, walked up tae ye an' said, 'want a pig'?" Erchie said gruffly.

Biddy placed the pacified Marietta back in her pram. Shaking her head, she said, "No, no. I went to chapel and prayed for a wee extra bit of bacon for me man's breakfast. And, as I was on me way home, comin' down this street, this pig came flying down from the sky and landed at me feet."

"Oh, aye!" Erchie said. "Nae note wi' it?"

Biddy frowned and scowled at the obvious athiest that stood before her.

"There was no note," she said curtly, "nor was one needed. The Holy Mother does not go around giving out notes."

"She jist goes around givin' oot pigs, is that it?" Erchie said dryly.

"God forgive you your blasphemy!" Biddy said and started to push the pram away, only to be stopped by Erchie's restraining arm.

"No' so fast," he commanded. "Ah am not finished wi' you yet."

"Well I'm finished wit' you," Biddy said and attempted once more to move on.

Erchie lifted the pig out of the pram and propped it under his arm. Then, taking Biddy's arm, he said.

"Well, Oor Lady must shoap at Broon's, in Hunter Street, 'cos that's where this heavenly pig was last seen. Come on you, you can explain yer celestial encounter tae the sergeant."

Biddy protested vehemently but could not free herself from Erchie's iron grip. With Biddy pushing the pram and the pig safely tucked under his arm, he headed up Well Street, towards the police box in Bain Square, where he would call in and request a van be sent out to transport himself and his prisoners to the police office in Tobago Street.

The police waggon arrived within minutes, coming only a short distance.

Erchie and colleagues lifted the pram and the angry, kicking Biddy up the few steps into the back and they roared off.

Sitting in the back of the van as they headed for the police station, Erchie, stroking his chin, said.

"Know somethin'? If Mary DID gie you this pig, she must have a great sense of humour."

"She DID give me it, from out the sky it came, and I don't know what that's got to do with her sense of humour," Biddy snapped back.

"Well," Erchie said, "if it's a Mary that gave ye the pig, it's another Mary that's takin' it aff ye."

"Oh, and how is that?" Biddy said scowling. "Cos this is a Black Maria we're in, hen!" Erchie burst out laughing.

Rita, at the window, saw Erchie,with the pig under his arm go up the street,escorting a woman, who was pushing a pram.

"Well, noo we know whit happened tae the pig!" she said, turning to Wullie. "There it is...in custody and it looks like Erchie has arrested a wumman wi' a pram!"

"Let me see," Annie said, hurrying over. "They're away noo," Rita said.

"Aw, that poor wumman," Annie said worriedly. "She's an innocent victim."

"Ach, they'll no' haud her for long," Wullie said. "Wance they've had a talk wi' her, they'll drive her hame!"

"Are ye sure?" Annie asked, concern in her voice.

"Of coorse Ah'm sure," Wullie said. "She'll be oot in two shakes o' a lamb's tail....or a pig's tail!"

He laughed at his weak joke.

Annie did not join in his jollity. She felt sorry for the lady who had been carted off. She was worried, too, because her banquet was gone as well. She had planned to begin preparing the porker for its final destination. Now she felt that she was back to where she started...and only twenty-four hours to go.

"A' they folk comin' up the morra night...tae nothin'!" she groaned.

Wullie put a comforting arm around her shoulder.

"Don't you worry, hen," he said softly. "Fingers will not let us doon, you'll see."

Annie forced a smile.

"He DID say he would be back," she said.

"And he WILL be, he WILL be," Wullie said with confidence. "Mind you, Ah'm right surprised that Erchie McPherson even came to oor door at a'...knowin' the wey he feels aboot you, Annie. Ah mean, even if he HAD discovered the pig, Ah wonder if he would have taken any action....know whit Ah mean?"

Rita puckered her lip.

"Naw, it widnae have made any difference tae Erchie," she said. "Wi' HIM, duty comes first. He goes by the book. Ah even heard that he booked an auld wumman, who was pullin' a heavy basket of washin', for obstrucin' the pavement. Noo, that is crass, that is, definitely crass!"

Annie shook her head in disbelief.

"Whit a shame for that auld wumman!" she said. "Who was she?"

"His maw," Rita said sharply.

Annie gasped and her hand came up to her mouth. Wullie was stunned.

"Surely no'?" he muttered incredulously. Rita nodded.

"No' only that," she said, "He booked Wee Senga McLaughlin wan night...for loiterin'."

Wullie shook his head.

"Is that a fact?" he said, "Nice wee lassie, Senga, tae! Was she loiterin'? Ah mean if ye think somebody's loiterin' wi' intent, then Ah suppose it's fair enough tae book them....although Ah canny imagine Wee Senga intendin' a robbery or anythin' like that."

"The only thing Senga was intendin' stealin' were a few kisses, Uncle Wullie," Rita said. "She was staunin' up a close....WINCHIN."

"And she got booked for that?" Annie said with disbelief, her mind suddenly flashing back for an instant to her own courting days, 'up the close'.

Rita nodded.

"It's a fact, Mammy!"

"Who was she staunin'winchin up the close?"Annie asked curiously.

"HIM," Rita said, "Erchie McPherson."

Wullie threw up his arms.

"Huh!" he said sourly, "He's just another Ina McLatchie wi' troosers and a tin hat."

Annie scowled at him. "YOU should be flattered that Ina's got her eyes on you," she snapped.

"Her eyes oan me, Ah don't mind," Wullie said, "it's her haun's Ah don't like!"

Annie glanced at Rita.

"Listen tae Fusspots, here," she said." Ye're nae Errol Flynn yersel', Wullie.We don't a' get whit we want in this world, y'know!"

Wullie agreed.

"True enough!" he said, "Look at your Sammy." Annie turned on him.

"Jist you leave Sammy oot o' it," she said angrily. "Ah jist worry aboot him a' the time. Where is he? Whit's he daein'? Is he a'right? It's nothin' but worry, worry and mair worry in this rotten world, so it is."

Wullie felt a twinge of pity for sister. He knew she worried and he knew, too, that she was 'a wee brick'.

"Sammy'll be a'right," he said reassuringly. Annie's brows knitted.

"Whit if he's been captured on some dangerous mission?" she said, wringing her hands. "Dae ye think he could staun' up tae they Gestapo?"

Annie looked pleadingly at her brother.

"Forget the Gestapo," Wullie said, "Ah'll be surprised if he can just staun' up, period."

Annie let out a howl and Rita stepped in immediately to cool things.

"Don't you worry, mammy," she said reassuringly. "Wait till you see, ma da' will come back frae the war before ye know it....and he'll have a V.C. in his haun."

"A V.P. ye mean," Wullie rasped, referring to one of Glasgow's favourite wines.

Annie put her arm around Rita's shoulders and gave an affectionate squeeze. Wullie's caustic remarks were less worrying than the problems in hand.

"Let's try and no' think aboot yer da' the noo," she said. "we've got other things tae worry aboot at this particular moment in time! Ma wee lassie's engagement party comin' up and no' a pun a links between us. It's YOU Ah'm thinkin' aboot, hen," she said, giving Rita another squeeze .

Rita sighed.

"Don't worry, mammy," she said softly, "Ah'll pop intae the chapel and pey for a caun'le...would ye like that, eh?"

Wullie screwed up his nose.

"We're no relegated tae eatin' bloody caun'les, are we?" he grumbled.

Annie smiled:

"A wee prayer gets ye there," she said philosophically.

Then putting her hands together and looking up, she added:

"PLEASE!"

CHAPTER SEVEN

Annie found no rest that night. She tossed and turned in bed, her thoughts on the morrow and Rita's big day. She cursed the bomb that had flattened Auld McPhee's shop and she prayed that 'something will turn up'.

Wullie had been unable to contact Fingers McGeachie to inform him about the catastrophe of the vanishing pig. He had left word at all drinking hostelries in the surrounding district for the Big Man to communicate with him immediately he turned up. He knew that Fingers would pull out all the stops to replenish the missing grub. As for 'Caun'les', the only good they would do, he had told Annie, was save electricity.

"Nae sign of Fingers!" she said turning away from the window, despair in her voice.

Wullie looked up.

"Ah've left messages a' ower the place. He'll BE here, believe me," he said confidently.

Annie wrung her hands.

"Ah just hope ye're right, Wullie, so Ah dae," she said, biting her lip and tidying the top of the sideboard for the fifth time.

Wullie snorted and went back to his paper. Annie switched on the wireless and, for the third time, re-spread the flowered oil cloth on the table top.

"Germany Calling....Germany Calling," the drone of Lord Haw-Haw's voice crackled. "Hello England. We will be visiting you tonight. Yes, our pilots are giving up their Saturday night just to pay you a little call. So, stay awake if you want to"

Annie angrily switched him off.

"That's a' we need!" she said bitterly, "a bloomin' air-raid," she flopped on to the chair,sighed deeply and closed her eyes.

Wullie shrugged.

"Ah widnae bother wi' anythin' HE says," he said, turning his paper,"Besides he said 'Hello ENGLAND... .that definitely disnae take in Glesca."

Annie glared.

"Ye know fine that when they say 'England' they're takin' in Scotland as well!"

116

A gasp from Rita made Wullie turn quickly. Rita, her hand to her mouth, turned away from the window.

She paled and was agitated.

Annie jumped up.

"Whit's up...whit's up?" she said, grasping her daughter's arm tightly. "Whit is it?"

Wullie had put his paper down and hurried over to the window. He could see nothing.

"Whit is it, eh?" he demanded.

There was a sudden, authoritative rap on the door and all three stood still for a moment

"It...it's a telegram boy, mammy!" Rita said quietly. "Ah saw him cyclin' up tae oor close." There was fear in her voice.

Annie's hand went to her mouth and she drew in her breath sharply.

Telegram boys were not welcome. Their appearance in a street had frightened women throwing up their windows and leaning out to see which close the messenger would enter....and sigh when he passed theirs by.

Men standing at corners became silent and, with their eyes, followed the post office messengers the minute they saw those creaking red bikes turn into the street.

Gossiping women at closemouths suddenly stopped and, as the boy with the buff envelope entered a close, the speculation began as to who was receiving bad news – for it was always sure to be!

Annie was frozen to the floor and it was Wullie who hurried to the door. Annie, still clutching nervously to Rita's arm, heard his muffled conversation and then she heard the outside door close quietly.

It seemed an eternity before Wullie finally entered, walking slowly and carrying the unwanted communication.

He put his hand on Annie's shoulder and, holding out the envelope, said softly:

"It's addressed tae you, Annie."

Annie did not move. She was rooted to the spot. She stared at the envelope. Her arm seemed paralysed. Rita gave her mother a squeeze, as though trying to drive some strength into her.

"Ah...Ah canny read it, Ah canny touch it," Annie said, shaking. She sat down and, looking up at Wullie, said quietly:

"You read it, Wullie...please!"

Wullie took the envelope and Annie dabbed her eyes with the corner of her apron. Rita sat on the arm of the chair and clutched her mother's hand tightly. Wullie tore open the envelope and slowly read the message to himself. Annie closed her eyes, too afraid to look up.

Wullie finished reading the note, let his arm clutching it fall to his side and, putting his hand under Annie's chin, brought her head up. Slowly she raised her eyes and saw the downcast look on her brother's face. She thrust her knuckle into her mouth and gasped.

Wullie's eyes suddenly brightened. With a whoop he threw the telegram into the air and let out a cry of joy. Pulling Annie out of the chair, he twirled her round and round in a carousel of glee.

"Sammy, that Big, Bloody Eejit," he cried, "is a Prisoner of War, in France...he's a'right...d'ye hear me....he's safe...unhurt...jist CAUGHT, that's a'...CAUGHT!"

Rita let out a scream of delight. Annie danced and dabbed her eyes with her apron as they danced, whooped, yelled and waltzed around the floor.

"Ah think we'll have a wee drink oot that boattle right this minute," Annie said, brushing away happy tears and retrieving the whisky from the sideboard.

"And why not!" Wullie agreed, rubbing his hands.

Rita hurried and collected three glasses from the sink and Annie poured.

"Tae ma Sammy," she said proudly, raising her glass, "God Bless him!"

"And God help the Jerries!"Wullie added, taking a gulp and smacking his lips.

Everybody laughed! There was a knock on the door and Ina put her head round.

"Yoo-hoo," she cried, "can Ah come in?" "Of course ye can," Annie called.

Ina entered and was surprised to see them laughing loudly and with glasses in their hands.

"Here," Rita said, fetching another glass from the sink and pouring out a drink, "have a dram."

Ina took the glass, sniffed it and said:

"Ah don't usually partake of strong liquor, you know!"

"Partakin grub's mair in your line!" Wullie said, looking over the top of his glass.

Ina ignored the remark, sipped her drink and grimaced.

"Are youse celebratin' something?" she asked, taking another sip. "We have just received word frae the War Oaffice," Annie said proudly, "that Sammy is a P.O.W."

"A pow?" Ina said, puzzled. "Whit's a pow?"

"He is a Prisoner of War, Ina — a P.O.W."

Ina gulped.

"Is...is that good, then?" she stammered. "Whit does it mean?"

"It means he's no' deid, Ina," Rita said, It means he's alive and kickin'!"

"Aw," Ina said happily, kissing Annie's cheek, "is that no' wonderful,eh? A prisoner! Just like bein' in Barlinnie only wi' different accents roon' aboot. They Germans wull no' understaun' a word he's sayin'!"

"Glaswegians don't understaun' a word he's sayin'," Wullie said sarcastically.

"Dae ye think the prison camp will be anythin' like Barlinnie, Uncle Wullie?" Rita asked.

Wullie shook his head.

"Naw, naw," he said with authority. ""Completely different! They'll a' be in big huts. They call them Stalags."

Wullie puffed out his chest, pleased at getting the opportunity to show off his German military knowledge...especially when he saw the look of admiration in Ina's eye.

"Oh, ye're that knowledgeable, Wullie!" Ina purred. "But Ah canny understaun' how the Germans call their jails efter the Russian leader".

Wullie gave her a look of contempt.

"That is Stalin," he said, reiterating, "StaLIN....STA, in German means...er....stay and lags means...er...lags—like the expression, 'he's an auld lag. . .they ur auld lags. . .meanin' auld prisoners. So, the Jerries just say STALAGS....see whit Ah mean?"

Ina thought Wullie was wonderful...and the drink wasn't bad either!

After the initial exuberance of the news of Big Sammy's safe incarceration had died down, Annie began to worry. Would her husband be getting enough to eat? Would he do something stupid and end up in front of a firing squad? Annie's hand came up to her mouth as she gasped at the terrible thought.

"Whit's up, Annie?" Wullie asked, noticing his sister's concern.

Annie looked serious: "Ye..ye don't think Sammy could end up in front o' a firin' squad, dae ye?" she said, biting her lip.

"Only if he sings," Wullie said without a smile."Oaften, on a Setturday night, efter he's visited the Come Inn and started tae belt oot 'Why Did You Make Me Care?' ah've wanted tae put him in front o' a firin' squad!"

Annie smiled, the ice broken.

"Oh, Wullie," she said in mock rebuke. " YOUR tonsils were well oiled tae, if Ah remember correctly!"

Wullie smiled:

"Aye, right enough," he recalled with a twinkle, "many a good night we had....and we wull have them again," he quickly added. "When this damn war's ower we'll have plenty of singin'..AND dancin'. We'll have a a..a..great CLABBER so we wull!"

Rita drew her eyebrows together.

"Whit's a Clabber, Uncle Wullie?" she asked, puzzled. Wullie looked at her with slight disdain.

"A CLABBER, my girl," he said with authority, " is a backcourt party where ye hiv bonfires and singin' an' dancin' and a rerr terr. There's laughin' and great camaraderie ...and everybody loves everybody!"

Ina raised her eyebrows with interest.

Glancing over at Annie she said: " Is that a fact?"

"Oh, it's a fact, right enough, Ina", Annie said with a smile. Ina turned to Wullie.

"Will you gie me a dance, Wullie?"

Wullie ran his finger under his collar and gave a slight, nervous cough.

"Mmm" he growled, "if you jump up an' doon in the street, everybody'll run tae the air-raid shelter oot o' force of habit! They'll think the bombs are still drappin'."

"Whit if we DON'T win the war!" Annie exclaimed, with alarm.

Such a thought had never crossed anybody's mind and Annie's suggestion was dismissed immediately by Rita.

"That IS impossible!" she said cheerily. "Oh, and how dae you know?" Annie asked. "Well," Rita laughed, "MA Raspy will soon be in uniform, did ye forget that, eh? "

Wullie nodded.

"Oh, aye!" he said "The Jerries wull be shakin' in their jackboots right noo just thinkin' aboot it — 'Mein Gott, Wee Rasputin Plunkett is on ze warpath," he said mockingly, 'VE IS DOOMED...DOOMED..!" Everybody laughed..except Rita, who turned away hurt by her uncle's snide remarks.

Wullie noticed his niece's wounded expression and put his arm around her shoulder.

"Only kiddin', hen, only kiddin'," he said, giving her an affectionate squeeze.

Rita smiled and Annie, whose mind had gone back to memory lane, said, with a faraway look:

"Ah remember the last time we whooped it up at a Clabber....an' it disnae seem a' that long ago!" she said. Turning to Rita, she went on:

"Ah danced wi' yer faither up and doon, up an' doon...aw, it was great so it was!"

"When was that?" Rita asked quizzically.

Annie puckered her brows and took her mind back.

"It was the night clatty Charlie got released frae Barlinnie.

"You were there, Rita. You were just young at the time... dae ye no' mind?"

Rita nodded.

"Aye, Ah remember that," she said, "but Ah didnae know ye called it a clabber!"

"Ah always thought a clabber was a dod o' dirt," Ina said. "You would think that!" Wullie scowled.

Annie's eyes glowed as she reminisced.

"Aw, it was a lovely night!" she said, her mind re-living the past. "There was a big bonfire. And there was Wee Plooky Paterson playin' his accordion...he belted oot 'The Sash' and 'Faith of Our Fathers'..Plooky wisnae a bigot!"

"He was rotten!" Wullie grunted. Annie ignored the interruption.

"Then somebody brought doon an auld gramophone," she went on, her eyes shining, "and we danced tae Henry Hall and Ambrose an' a' the top baun's. And, Ah remember, there was a big, big yella moon...and Sammy said it was mine....and that he was gonny gie it tae me." Annie sighed.

Wullie gave an incredulous glance towards heaven.

"It was moonshine that Sammy was gonny gie ye," he said.

Rita glared at him.

"Don't you mind him, mammy," she said. Wullie shrugged.

"A'right, a'right," he said, "we now know that the moon belangs tae yer mammy," Ina sighed.

"Ah think it's very romantic!" she said. "Ah never thought that Big Sammy was so poetic....did you look oan him as the romantic type, Wullie?"

Wullie shook his head.

"Naw," he said, "Ah looked oan him as the drunken type. Mind ye, if he telt Annie he was gonny gie her the moon, Ah could well believe him. He was as high as a bloody kite every time ye met him."

Annie scowled and dabbed her eyes.

"He's a good man, ma Sammy," she whimpered, "although he does have his wee odd eccentricity."

Wullie held up his hand: "Well, you'll be the only wan that knows aboot that particular physical deformity," he said.

Rita, over at the window, turned and groaned.

"Ah canny staun' here a' day at the windae wi' these curlers in," she complained. "Raspy could turn up any minute."

Annie hurried over and steered her towards the bedroom door:

"Aye, away you go, hen," she said, "You get ready....and say a wee prayer while ye're in there. Better still, nip doon tae the chapel and light hauf-a-dozen caun'les."

Rita, getting excited, said:

"Aw, Ah've nae time, mammy. "HE wull hear me just as well frae the room. Ah really don't think ye need caun'les tae catch his eye."

"Ah'm only kiddin', hen," Annie said, "away ye go."

Before entering the room, Rita stood up on tip-toe and attempted a last, hopeful glance out of the window. She sighed, turned and hurried into the bedroom, praying quietly that all would go well. "Poor Rita!" Annie said, a lump in her throat. "Y'know, Ah think hauf the Ruby Street depot's comin' up the night. Ah just don't know how Ah'll face them if Fingers McGeachie "

Wullie held up his hand.

"Everythin' wull be all right," he said reassuringly. "Fingers wull not let us doon!"

"Ah just hope there will be nae air-raids the night!" Ina said. "Dae ye think there is parachutists in they aeroplanes Wullie?"

Wullie knitted his brows.

"Whit dae ye mean?" he said.

"Well, Ah was just thinkin'," Ina went on, "that we could a' be in oor beds and the sirens could go and, a lot of the time, we just ignore them and turn ower....thinkin' that their bombs will no' touch us."

"Aye, we a' dae that at times," Wullie agreed. – "So, whit's yer problem?"

"Well," Ina said, "supposin' that's whit they want us tae dae. Then wan night when we are in oor beds ignoring their air-raid, they don't drap bombs at a'. They drap parachutists ready tae attack us...lyin' there innocently in oor beds. We would have nae chance!"

Wullie looked skywards with despair.

"YOU would have every chance, Ina," he said. "Paras ower the Barras: You would have nothin' tae fear, believe me. In fact the parachutist that would come through your ceilin' would take wan look and immediately start frantically blawin' up his shute again tae balloon proportions....hopin' it would float him back up tae his aeroplane again."

Ina was unperturbed at Wullie's outburst.

"Ye still hivnae answered ma question," she said.

Wullie threw up his arms.

"How the hell should Ah know if there is parachutists in them airies, eh?" he cried. "Hitler does not take me intae his confidence."

"Ah was just wonderin'", Ina said.

Annie had taken her turn at the window. Turning, she said despondently:

"Still nae sign...! Oh, where are ye, Fingers?"

Wullie joined her, took a quick glance out of the window and returned to his chair muttering:

"Ach, where's yer faith?"

Wullie was irritated at his sister's lack of trust. Annie turned and walked towards the sink.

"Aye, well, Ah'll..er..just put oan the kettle," she said. Ina wandered over to the window.

"Can Ah look oot the windae, Wullie?" she asked, feeling that she should be helping...even if only doing the window vigil.

Wullie looked up.

"Ye can jump oot the windae if ye like," he said, picking up his newspaper.

Annie boiled up the kettle and poured out three cups of tea. Wullie would have preferred something stronger, his eyes straying now and again towards the bottle of sherry which Annie had left conspicuously and temptingly on top of the sideboard

All three of them sat round the table sipping in silence.

"Dae ye think Sammy will try tae escape?" Annie said at last. Wullie nodded.

"Oh, aye," he said with conviction. "It is every prisoner's duty to escape... even if it means diggin' yer wey oot wi' yer soup spoon!"

Ina said. "Better Sammy steyin' where he is...just don't rock the boat — know whit Ah mean?"

Annie nodded.

"Ach, it's a terrible cairry-oan, anywey!" she said. "This war... ye don't know if ye're comin' or goin'. When the war was declared, ma Sammy was really uptight, so he was!"

Wullie put his cup down.

"Sammy was always uptight," he said, "because he always went tae bed tight."

Annie scowled.

"Ye know fine well whit Ah mean," she snapped.

"How did it a' start, that's whit Ah would like tae know?" Ina said, taking a sip and looking at Wullie.

Wullie shuffled.

"Aye, well...er.." he began, then, clearing his throat, "it's...er...this bloke Hitler, y'see. He intends tae conquer the world an' that, know whit Ah mean?"

Annie shook her head.

"He'll never dae it," she said knowingly. "He might conquer America an' Poland an' that....but he will never conquer Glesca. The Billy Boys and the San Toi, no' forgettin' the Norman Conks, the Sticket an' the Baltic Fleet an' a' the rest wull forget their differences and wull amalga...amal..er... get the gether. It's in times like these that they patch up their differences."

"Instead o' their faces," Wullie added.

Annie had elevated the Glasgow gangs to take on the common enemy. Annie went on, "Hitler hisnae heard o' the Brigton gangs, or the boys frae the Calton and Govan and Possil an a' roon' aboot. Let the Jerries try and march doon Gallygate and they wull have a war oan their haun's!"

"They've GOT a bloody war on their haun,"Wullie snapped. "That's whit it's a' aboot!"

Ina sighed:

"It's a' this rationin',tae," she said. "It gets ye down...queuein' an' queuein' and queuein' for everything! "

Annie nodded.

"Ah know!" she said. "Ah'll bet this yin Hitler's got nae problems gettin' some grub for his daughter's engagement party."

Annie was bitter.

"He isnae merried!" Wullie said. "He is devoted tae the party."

"Well," Annie said, "at least he's got a party. It's mair than we're gonny have by the looks o' it."

All fell silent again and sipped their tea.

"Ah just wish ma Sammy was here," Annie said finally. "HE can get oot o' anythin'...any tricky situation." There was pride in Annie's voice.

Wullie said nothing.

"Ah wonder whereaboots in France they've got him?" Ina said, adding, "Ah'll bet Madame Wee Nellie knows."

Wullie's brows shot up.

"Who the Hell's Madame Wee Nellie?" he said, intrigued.

"Madame Wee Nellie is the wonderful internationally renowned hairdresser who has an establishment in London Road, She did ma hair," Ina said proudly.

"So, how would a barber know where Sammy is incarcerated, eh?" Wullie said scornfully.

"Well, she's French, int she?" Ina snapped back. "She wull know her wey aroon' her ain country!"

Annie laughed:

"Ina," she said, "Yer Madame Wee Nellie, frae France, is really Bunty McLaughlin, frae Marquis Street, in Brigton. Not only does she not know her wey around France, she finds it hard to find her wey around heids."

Ina was hurt.

"Well, she found her wey aroon' mine well enough," she said, smoothing her hair at the back with the palm of her hand.

"Aye, well maybe simple heids are a'right," Wullie said.

Annie glowered at her brother.

"She did dae a good joab on you, Ina," Annie said. "Ye must've got her on wan of her good days. Skinny Sadie, frae up the pend, got her hair done by Wee Madame Nellie for a weddin' she was goin' tae and the bride did a better joab cuttin' the cake than Nellie did cuttin' Sadie's hair!"

"Is that a fact?" Ina said nonchalantly, "and Skinny Sadie wi' such lovely red hair!"

"It's a fact!" Annie said. "Nellie nearly scalped her.Right intae the wid, she went. Skinny Sadie turned up lookin' like a five-foot tall Swan Vesta."

The two women burst out laughing.

"Oh, Ah shouldnae be laughin'," Annie said, hurrying over to the window.

Darkness was approaching and soon it would be time to close up the blackout blinds.

There was a sudden rapping at the outside door and Rasputin entered smiling broadly.

"It's only me," he said.

Annie hurried over and steered him towards the table.

"Come in, come in, son," she said, pushing him into a chair. "Rita's just gettin' ready, she'll no' be long."

Rasputin nodded to Wullie and Ina, who smiled sweetly.

"Would ye like a wee cup of tea? Raspy," Annie asked, making towards the teapot.

Rasputin shook his head.

"Naw, thanks, " he said. "Maybe..er..youse would like something a wee bit stronger, eh....seein' this is a special night?"

Rasp pulled out a full bottle of Johnny Walker Red Label. Wullie's eyes popped.

"Noo, there's a man efter ma ain heart," Wullie said, making for the sink and some clean glassses.

Putting the glasses on the table with a flourish, Wullie took command of the bottle and poured out four drams, three small ones and one large one.

"Where did ye manage tae get yer haun's on this?" Wullie said with admiration.

Rasputin smiled.

"Ah met Fingers McGeachie and he and I did a wee deal. He gave me the whisky and Ah gave him the money."

Wullie spluttered on his drink and Annie went into a fit of coughing, her whisky going down the wrong way at the news that Fingers McGeachie had surfaced.

Wullie gave Annie's back a good thump and, turning to Rasputin, stammered:

"You have seen Fingers?"

Rasputin nodded.

"Aye, Ah met him in London Road."

"We've been tryin' tae contact him a' day," Wullie said, relief in his voice.

"He knows yer problem," Rasp said. "Jimmy in the pub telt him and he says you've no' tae worry. He's got everything in hand and he'll be up in plenty of time."

Annie fell back on the chair, sighed and smiled broadly.

"See, Ah telt ye Fingers would not let us doon," Wullie said smugly.

"Thank God!" Annie said, fanning herself.

Annie rose and closed the blackout blinds, taking a quick look down into the street.

"He had two big boaxes wi' him when Ah saw him," Rasp said. "And he said he said he was lookin' forward tae the party."

"Ah'm that pleased for ye, Annie," Ina said, taking a sip from her glass.

Wullie replenished the glasses and felt more content with the world. Sitting opposite Rasputin, he raised his glass.

"To Fingers McGeachie," he said.

All raised their glasses and toasted the Big Man.

"So," Wullie said, smacking his lips, "still on the Swahili dictionary, Rasp, eh?"

Rasputin shook his head:

"Naw, naw," he said, "Ah've finished wi' that. Ah started a new ninety-day course this moarnin'."

"Oh, that's interestin'," Annie said, a surge of pride shooting through her body. This super intellectual was to be her Rita's man...and not many of his brilliance pervaded the streets of Calton!

"How...er..can ye possibly begin a ninety-day course if ye're goin' away intae the army on Monday?" Wullie asked pertinently.

Rasputin shrugged.

"Och, Ah'll have finished it by then," he said casually.

Ina was very impressed. Rita was a lucky girl to have captured such an outstanding mastermind, she thought. She would be content with Wullie McSorley.

"It must be wonderful tae be such a genius," Ina said. "Have ye got a photographic memory, Raspy? "

Rasputin looked over the top of his glass.

"Ah widnae say that exactly," he said, putting the glass down and puckering his brows, "but at school they called me Kodak."

Annie's heart swelled just a little larger.

"Yer maw must be awfu' proud o' ye, son," she said with some awe. "When did she first notice yer geniusity...if that's the right word?"

Rasputin tapped the side of his cheek with his forefinger and thought deeply.

"She noticed the day she walked intae the room and Ah had completely dismantled oor Marconi wireless set. Ah had a' the parts laid oot neatly in wee rows on top of the table....and Ah was only three at the time."

Ina clapped her hands together.

"Oh, that's wonderful!" she cooed. "Then did ye put them a' together again?"

"Naw, we had tae throw the wireless oot," Raspy said. There was an uneasy pause.

Annie gave an embarrassed little cough.

"Ach, well, ye were learnin', son," she said and took another good swig of her drink.

Rasputin nodded.

"True enough!" he said. "It was the first hint she had that Ah was a prodigy."

Ina was stunned.

"Imagine that!" she exclaimed. "Yer ain mammy didnae know whit religion ye were!"

Wullie glared over at Ina.

"Whit the hell's that got tae dae wi' his religious affiliations?" he groaned. Ina flushed.

"Well, you would think that yer ain maw would know whit church ye attend, wouldn't ye? And Ah canny see the logic oan her walkin' intae the room, seein' her wean with the wireless a' broke to bits and immediately sayin' tae hersel'..'that yin's a Wee Proddy'. Ah just canny see how she came tae that conclusion....unless the Pope happened tae be broadcastin' at the time."

Wullie threw up his hands in despair.

"Ina," he said deliberately, "Prodigies are geniuses." Ina shook her head.

"No' them a'," she said. "Some o' them are as thick as two planks. Ma ain minister, The Reverend Hector McFungas, studied every night o' the week for a full two years before he was accepted intae the church and ordained, so he was!"

Wullie shrugged.

"Two years isnae bad goin'," he said in admiration. "He must've been pretty smart, it usually takes aboot five or six years. He must've been quite surprised that efter only two years he was made a minister of the church, eh?"

Ina nodded.

"He was right enough. He was studyin' tae be a plumber."

There was a stunned silence and then they all burst out laughing.

"Ah, ye were havin' me on there," Wullie said, flushing slightly. Ina giggled! "How is yer mammy, anywey?" Annie asked. "She'll be comin' up the night, Ah take it?" Rasputin shrugged. "Ah don't think so," he said."When Ah left the hoose, she was lyin' doon." "Oh, is she no' well?" Annie asked with some concern "Naw, she was plastered," Rasputin said, taking a sip. "It'll be a' the excitement o' the engagement," Ina said in way of mitigation. "And you goin' away tae war. Is yer da' comin' up, Raspy, or is he stoned as well?"

Rasputin shook his head.

"Naw," he said sadly. "He is deid and it was the boattle that killed him! Ah was just four at the time...."

"Just a year efter ye dismantled the wireless?" Wullie said.

Rasputin ignored the remark.

"Him and six of his pals...drink was the cause of their demises."

Annie sighed and shook her head at the sad narrative.

"Whit happened, son?" she asked in a hushed voice.

"Well," Rasputin began," as faur as Ah've heard, ma auld man would have done anythin' for a gargle...."

"Did he have a sore throat?" Ina asked innocently.

"A gargle...a drink," Rasputin said coldly.

Ina blushed.

Rasputin took a quick swig from his glass,wiped his mouth with his cuff and continued.

"He'd drink anythin, and did. He could drink anybody under the table. Then, in the builders' yard where he worked as a watchman,he took an unquenchable urge. His sharp eye spotted a whisky boattle on a shelf in the storeroom and he couldnae resist. He knocked back the lot in wan gulp. That was it!"

Rasputin took another long swallow from his glass. Ina tut-tutted and Annie gave a reverent silence.

""Well,"Wullie sighed, "a full boattle o' whisky would kill anybody....even the hardenist of drinkers....especially in wan gulp!"

He quickly replenished Rasputin's glass...and his own. Rasputin shook his head.

" THAT was the problem," he said earnestly, "it wisnae whisky that was in the boattle. It was a lovely golden coloured nitro'glycerine." Wullie's jaw dropped.

"Is that whit they use for sore throats, that glycerine?" Ina asked, adding, "Ye widnae think that would kill him. If it did, hauf the weans in Glesca would be deid."

Wullie shut her up quickly.

"It's no' the same stuff, Ina. "

"Oh!" Ina exclaimed, bringing her hand up to her lips.

Annie patted Rasputin on the shoulder.

"Poor boy!" she said softly. "And you just four-years-auld tae...just the age when a boy needs his faither."

Rasputin sighed.

"Aye, Ah was just a wean," he said. "Ah could never in a' honesty say that Ah ever looked up tae ma faither."

Ina puckered her brows.

"Aw, naw, ye canny say that, Raspy," she said rebuking him. "He was still yer faither...you should always look up tae yer faither!"

Rasputin shook his head.

"It was hard tae dae when he was always lyin' flat oot oan the flair pie-eyed!" he said flatly.

Annie and Ina both tut-tutted and Wullie looked at the ceiling and whistled softly.

"Where did he get the money for a' his booze?" Annie, being the practical one, asked.

"Oh, he was never shoart o' cash," Rasputin said. "He used tae go up closes and take money frae the bookies."

Wullie clicked his teeth in admiration.

"He was a winner on the hoarses, eh." he said.

"Naw, he just took their money," Rasputin said. Annie folded her arms and stiffened up.

"Aye, well if ye ask me, he just got whit was comin' tae him," she said coldly. "And if him and his six pals were daft enough tae drink that glycerine stuff, they a' got whit they deserved!"

Ina nodded in agreement. But Wullie was puzzled.

"How come," he said, "his six pals snuffed it as well? If your da' gulped the lot doon in wan gulp, how did they meet their maker? Did they have a wee sneaky swig when yer auld man wisnae lookin'?"

Rasputin shook his head.

"Naw, naw," he said, "ma da' emptied the lot....and that's whit killed him."

"Ah always thought glycerine was good for ye!" Ina said.

Wullie threw her a contemptuous glance. Annie cleared her throat.

"So, how can ye say that it was drink that killed yer faither's six pals?" she asked pointedly.

"Well," Rasputin said, "they had a good few bevvies before the funeral and when they were staggerin' doon the aisle in the church wi' the coaffin, wan o' them slipped and fell and brought them a' doon wi' him....coaffin an' a'!"

Ina tutted once more.

"Did they have to get a new coaffin?" she asked innocently.

"They had tae get a new church," Rasputin said, shaking his head. All fell silent as they digested this terrible narrative.

Annie was first to speak.

"Seven widows...a' in a flash!" she said, sadly shaking her head.

Ina nodded in agreement.

"He would've been better drinkin' Syrup of Figs," she said

Rasputin nodded in agreement.

"Aye," he said, "it was seven new customers for Dalbeth Cemetery...and Sandymount...and Daldowie...and Kilbowie, in Clydebank. "

Ina dabbed her eyes with her handkerchief.

"Is that where they were a' buried?" she asked through a slight whimper.

"That's where they a' LANDED," Rasputin said, taking another sip. Wullie immediately refilled the glasses . The conversation had put a damper on the gathering...after Annie had done mental cartwheels at the good news of Fingers's message.

"It says a loat for you, Raspy," Annie said, "everything against ye and you turnin' oot tae be the genius ye are! It looks like there's a wee bit o' yer faither in ye!"

"There's a wee bit o' his faither a' ower Glesca!" Wullie said with a wry smile.

The bedroom door swung open and Rita, resplendent in a dazzling new frock, purchased from Fat Fanny Ferguson, a fellow clippie who was fortunate enough to run one of the few menages still in existence, swept in. She beamed broadly and did a pirouette in the middle of the floor.

Rasputin spluttered on his drink as his eyes took in this picture of his bride-to-be.

"How dae Ah look?" Rita asked, her gaze on Raspy.

He put his fingers to his lips and blew a kiss towards her.

"Aw, Rita," he dribbled,"ye look like ye just stepped oot o' a Goldberg's catalogue!"

Ina sighed and once more made use of her handkerchief.

"Aw, Rita, ye remind me o' masel' when Ah was your age," she said, dabbing her eyes. "ma mammy used tae say that Ah was her crownin' glory. She called me her 'Wee Laurel'."

Wullie eyed Ina and threw a cynical look at the ceiling. "If she saw ye noo she would be callin' you her 'Big Hardy'," he said.

Annie glowered at him as she hurried over and gave Rita an affectionate peck on the cheek.

"You ur lovely, hen!" she said, pride in her eyes. "Aye, ye are that," Wullie said with a nod.

Annie, at the window, pulled back the curtain just enough to allow her to see down into the street.

"Nae sign o' Fingers yet, mammy?" Rita asked nervously.

Annie turned away from the window. "No' yet, hen," she said, "but there's nae problem. Raspy met him in London Road and he says he's got mair stuff and he'll be up in plenty of time, so there!"

Annie could not hide her joy.

Rita did a jig.

"Aw. that is wonderful!" she cried. "Good auld Fingers!

131

Wullie clapped his hands together and rubbed them vigorously.

"Never mind, hen," he laughed. "Even if Fingers hadnae said he'd be up wi' the grub, YOU would've been sure o' a bite, eh?"

Rita's eyes narrowed.

"Whit dae ye mean?" she said.

Wullie patted her cheek. "A Love Bite, hen," he said and laughed loudly.

"Hmm! " Annie said, " ye canny live oan love bites!"

"Oh, Ah widnae say that, " Ina chirped.

Wullie grunted and Annie proceeded to poke up the fire. She looked over at Rita, now sitting happily on Rasputin's lap and her thoughts went to Big Sammy and the night of her own engagement.

Of how Big Sammy slipped his hand into hers. Of how they splashed out and went to The Geggie, in Kilpatrick Street, off London Road. The Premier was the official title of the Bridgeton cinema, but it was affectionately known as 'The Geggie'.

She remembered how they sat in the back row, on the long wooden bench, crushed up against other 'winchers' at each side of them. Yes, she recalled those splintered wooden benches where not only did you get skelfs on you backside, you got woodworm and fleas as well! She sighed at the thought.

Wullie's voice interrupted Annie's thoughts.

"Have ye thought aboot whit ye're gonny dae efter the war, Rasputin?" he was saying.

Raspy had no hesitation in answering.

"Ah've been thinkin' a lot aboot that," he said, "and, seein' that Rita is a very religious lassie, Ah thought Ah might join the church. "

Annie jumped up.

"Ye canny dae that," she cried, "Rita's a catholic."

Ina nodded.

"It's true enough," she said, "ye canny be a priest and get married, so ye canny."

Rasputin dismissed the protests with a wave of his hand.

"That'll be nae problem," he said, "Ah wull personally chinge the rules when Ah become the Pope."

Wullie lighted up his pipe.

"Ah should've guessed," he said, blowing out his smoke, "that there is nae wey that you would just be an ordinary priest."

Rita leapt from Rasputin's lap and stood in front of him, hands on hips and mock anger in her eyes.

"Stoap talkin' nonesense," she said. "You ur away in a dream world, Raspy. Ah do not want ye tae be the Pope. It would mean me bein' doon on ma knees a' day, so it would!"

Rasputin shook his head.

"Naw, naw," he said. "It would be ME that would be daein' a' the prayin'....you could look efter the Bingo."

"Who says anythin' aboot prayin'?" Rita chuckled. "Ah'm talkin' aboot doon oan ma knees scrubbin' they flairs. Have ye seen how many rooms that Vatican's got, eh?"

Wullie nodded.

"Aye, ye're right there, Rita," he said blowing out a cloud of smoke. "Ye'd be at it a' day. Ye're better becomin' a Mullah, Raspy, then she'd only have a wee bit carpet tae clean."

Everybody burst out laughing. Rasputin finished his drink, smacked his lips and said:

"Youse were a' worried, there eh?"

Rita gave him a playful slap.

"Never mind," Annie said, "just let's get the war ower first and then we can a' decide whit we're gonny dae. This man Hitler has a loat tae answer for. He has turned a' oor lives upside doon."

Annie was bitter.

"Ye know," Rasputin said incredulously, "Hitler was an artist."

"Aye, a con artist," Wullie said.

Rasputin shook his head.

"Naw, naw," he said seriously, "an artist...a painter — and Hitler isnae his real name either. He chinged his name"

"Ah wish Ah could chinge mine," Ina said, glancing at Wullie.

"His real name is Shicklegruber," Raspy went on.

"Nae wonder he chinged it!" Wullie said, screwing up his face, "Who would want tae go through life wi' a moniker like that, eh?"

Ina looked up.

"Ah would," she said, "if your name was Wullie Shicklegruber."

Wullie gave an embarrassed cough and struck a match to light his already well alight pipe.

"He thinks he's gonny conquer the world," Raspy said, "but we'll stoap him, aye, we'll stoap him," Rasputin was deadly serious.

The sombre moment was suddenly interrupted by a loud rapping at the door. Rita leapt up.

"Ah'll get it", she cried excitedly, hurrying to the door. "It might be Fingers!"

Annie went over to the window, pulled the blind back a fraction and peered down into the street. The shaded street light, on the pavement by the baffle wall at the closemouth, was already switched on. The street was quiet with no sign of activity....not even a warden's whistle blast! Only the rumble of the trams at the top of the street, in London Road, told Annie that life was still going on. Turning back, she saw Rita ushering a shy young lad into the room.

Curdy McVey,the undertaker's apprentice, clutched a brown paper bag tightly in his hand.

"It's somebody for you, Uncle Wullie," Rita said, disappointment in her face.

Wullie rose and greeted Curdy with outstretched hand.

"Ah might be lookin' a wee bit pale," he said,a twinkle in his eye, "but Ah'm still no' ready for you yet, son!"

Curdy gave an embarrassed laugh.

"Ah..er..just thought Ah'd come up and apologise for that wee mixup...know whit Ah mean?" he stammered.

Curdy handed Wullie the parcel.

"Jist a wee somethin'," he said.

Wullie peered into the bag and a wide grin crossed his face as he drew out a bottle of Rich Red Ruby Wine.

"Ah...er...got it at a fancy funeral that Ah officiated at the other day," Curdy said, shuffling his feet, "and Ah wanted you tae hiv it."

Wullie was delighted! He put his arm around Curdy's shoulder and steered him into the room.

"Ma boy," he said, "that was a very kind thought. You'll stey and help us tae finish it aff!"

Curdy started to protest but was silenced by a gesture from a grateful Wullie.

"It's ma niece's engagement party the night," Wullie explained, "and we're gonny have a wee celebration."

Curdy murmered his thanks and Wullie poured him a drink from Ina's bottle.

"Make yersel' at hame, son," Annie said, pushing a chair towards him.

Curdy nodded.

"Thanks missus," he said.

Curdy walked over to Ina, who was sitting at the table, and raised his glass.

"Ah wish ye a' the best on yer engagement," he said, taking a sip .

Ina blushed.

"Ye've got the wrang wan, son," Ina twittered, adding...."unfortunately!"

Wullie laughed.

"No' half," he said. "You've been dealin' wi' too many corpses, son." Then, as an afterthought, added: "Mind ye, yer mistake is understandable!"

Wullie guided Curdy around the room, introducing him to those present.

"This is ma niece, Rita..this is ma sister, Annie... the wan you have just toasted is Ina, oor next door neighbour – and whose faither ye also toasted... and that... er... this is Rasputin, or Pope Rasputin, the First... Rita's boyfriend... This is Curdy, everybody... apprentice undertaker tae the rich...the dead rich." There was a chorus of 'Hellos' and 'Nice tae meet ye's."

Curdy nodded and sat down beside Ina.

"Ye're no' in the army, then?" Ina said, making conversation. Curdy shook his head.

"No' yet," he said, "but Ah'm hopin' tae be a gunner!" Wullie's brows shot up.

"That's whit Annie's man is," he said.

"A gunner?" Curdy said, showing interest.

"Oh, Ah thought ye said 'a gonner'," Wullie chuckled.

"Ma Sammy is NOT a gonner," Annie snapped. "He is just temporarily oot o' commission."

Turning to Curdy, she said:

"Is your faither in the army, son?" Curdy shook his head.

"Naw," he said, "ma faither snuffed it a couple of years ago. It was a terrible tragedy!"

Ina's arm froze halfway to her mouth. She looked at Curdy with some pity.

"Aw! Was it sudden, son?," she asked.

"It was tae him," Curdy said. "We had been waitin' a' day for the coalman and ma maw asked ma da' tae go doon tae the street tae see if there was any sign o' him comin'. Then ma maw heard him shoutin' up tae the windae that he could hear the clippityclop of the coalman's hoarse and, then, that he could see it comin' doon the street. That was the last we ever heard his voice!"

Curdy took a good swig at his drink and all in the room fell silent.

"Did he have a heart attack, son?" Annie said finally. Curdy shook his head.

"Naw, he got knocked doon by the hoarse," he said. "A big Clydesdale..a lovely big hoarse, like a big pet, it was. It stamped a' ower ma da's face. It was called Dainty.Then it ran away an'disappeared roon' the coarner."

Ina tut-tutted and sadly shook her head.

"Whit did yer maw dae?" Annie asked softly.

"Luckily she had some briquettes," Curdy said.

Nobody said a word for at least two minutes. Wullie finally rose, coughed and poured himself another drink.

"Well," he said, by way of consolation, "at least it got him oot o' bein' called up for the army,"

"It got him oot of everythin", Curdy said.

"Aye, well..er..so noo you're goin' intae the army, eh?" Annie said, changing the topic of conversation.

Curdy nodded.

"Ah am," he said proudly.

"And whit aboot yer maw?" Annie asked with concern. "Naw, she's got nae notion tae go in," Curdy said.

Ina giggled.

"Naw," Annie said, "ah meant is yer maw gled you're goin' in tae the army...leavin' that morbid profession ye've got yersel' intae?"

Curdy was hurt at this snub against his chosen occupation.

"There is nothin' wrang wi' the work Ah do," he said huffily. "Somebody's got tae dae it or every hoose in Glesca would be jammed packed wi' deid boadies."

Wullie nodded.

"You tell them, son," he cried. "You are not just a Bampot...you are an EMBALMPOT." Wullie winked... "Only kiddin', son, onlv kiddin'!"

Rasputin stood up and pulled his shoulders back.

"Ah'm goin' away intae the army on Monday," he said proudly.

"Aw, that's great!" Curdy exclaimed. "Whit regiment are ye goin' intae?"

Rasputin stuck out his chest.

"The only regiment that wull clean up this whole sorry mess," he said, "The Pioneer Corps....but Ah hope tae have a pow-wow wi' the generals tae present ma brilliant idea that wull shorten this war....it involves elephants."

Rita gave his arm a squeeze.

"That's ma Raspy!" she said proudly.

Curdy gave Rasputin the thumbs up sign.

"Great animals, elephants! " Curdy said. "But personally Ah prefer dugs."

Annie indicated to Rita that she would like a quiet word with her. She went into the bedroom, followed by Rita, who made her excuses.

"He's a nice boy, Curdy...but he's wan mair mooth tae feed!" A worried expression crossed Annie's face.

"Look, mammy," Rita said, "ye heard whit Raspy said, didn't ye? Fingers has got it all in hand...there's nothin' tae worry aboot!"

Annie was not so sure.

"How many freen's have ye asked up the night?" she asked.

Rita saw the worry was still on her mother's face. She shrugged and decided to chop off a few from the invited list.

"Aboot twenty-two, Ah think," she lied.

Annie threw up her arms.

"TWENTY-TWO?" she cried, "TWENTY-TWO?...we're gonny need a miracle like the loaves an' the fishes here....TWENTY-TWO!" Annie shook her head in despair.

Rita sighed and put an arm around her mother's shoulder.

"Listen mammy," she said, "even if they just get a wee cuppa tea...that'll dae just fine."

A cup of tea!? The very idea! Annie thought.

"Naw, naw," she said, "we've still got a tin o' coarned mutton. We'll just bless it and, who knows, it might turn intae five pun' of lorne sausages eh?"

They both laughed loudly.

"Right, cummon," Annie said, "let's get back tae the fray."

The two women entered the room to find Ina in the middle of the floor.

"Right you two," Ina said, "come on. Ah've just been sayin' that we should have a sing-song on this happy occasion."

Rasputin jumped up.

"How aboot Roll Out The Barrel?" he cried.

"You just leave Ina oot o' this," Wullie said with sarcasm. Ina turned on him.

"Are you suggestin' Ah'm fat or somethin'?" she snapped.

"Ah am sayin' nothin'," Wullie replied, "but you're the only wumman in the street that can staun' behind a baffle wa' and still be seen at either side."

Ina noted the impish sparkle in Wullie's eye and any umbrage she felt fell away.

"Well, that's a' the mair tae cuddle, int it?" she laughed and gave Wullie a poke in the ribs with her elbow.

Wullie could only laugh.

"Ah'll sing youse a song," he said, stepping in to the centre of the room and clearing his throat. "This is wan a man an' wumman sang roon' the backcourt last week."

The Depression of the 'Thirties' had nurtured the birth of the backcourt singers and Glasgow had a large contingent . They came and they sang, sometimes a man alone, a tenor or a gruff baritone. Or, perhaps a woman, with a sweet soprano voice or the guttural, grating echo of every bad inflection of the 'Glesca' accent. Sometimes 'The Wean' came too, snottery and malnourished and always good for the sound of an extra copper clattering on to the ground from a hanging granny at a third-storey window.

The backcourt serenaders were still touring when the war broke out and, when darkness fell, there was always the picture queue at The Kings, in James' Street, and the Arcadia in London Road,and the Orient, in Gallowgate and all the other backstreet picture halls and the countless pub doors..

Wullie burst into 'If You Were The Only Girl In The World' and was warmly applauded at the end of the song...especially by Ina.

"Aw, that was lovely," she said, "it put me in mind o' ma faither. He used tae sing that when Ah was a wee lassie."

"Ah'll bet he wishes he was here the night'" Wullie said. "Whit makes ye think that?" Ina asked.

"'Cos he's deid, int he?" Wullie replied. Ina let the snide remark pass.

"He was the life and soul o' the party, ma faither was," Ina said happily. "He used tae have everybody dancin'."

"Aye," Wullie said, "nae wonder he had them a' dancin'. They were a' probably queuein' up waitin' tae get intae the lavvy. He used tae have ME bloody dancin', tae ,oan that landin' oot there."

He nodded towards the outside door.

Ina dabbed her eyes. Wullie's facetious remarks hit a soft spot and Annie, sizing up the situation and wanting to avoid an unpleasant atmosphere creeping in, hurried over and switched on the wireless.

Joe Loss and his dance band were well into a Quick Step.

"Right, let's a' have a dance," Annie cried. "Raspy, you and Curdy move that table oot the road. Let's let oor hair doon and tae Hell wi' the war!" Annie laughed loudly but it was a pretence. This was to be the night when trouble took a back seat, when she could enjoy some of Rita's happiness.

She had tried to contact Auld McPhee but he had gone away. The other stores in the area had sympathised, Galbraiths, Cochrane's, the Co-op, but could not help out.

The dancers took the floor - Rita and her beau and Wullie, who had made a determined effort to flee to the little room on the stair landing, was blocked at the door by an equally determined Ina and almost spun off his feet.

Annie drew back the blackout blind and looked down into Well Street. A large, tawny moon shone, A "Bomber's Moon" that bathed the city in a soft, dangerous light.

Up to her right she could see the shadowy tramcars passing to and fro, warning bells clanging. Warnings, too, echoing in the distance from angry wardens' whistle blasts. An escaping chink of light was showing from somebody's window..She could see down the street and could hear the echo of loud conversation and clinking of glasses coming from the Come Inn pub. From Peter Rossi's cafe, at the other end, soft music floated out and somewhere in the night a dog howled at the moon.

At the corner of Well Street, in the Social Club next to Mary Welsh's shop, they would be preparing for the Saturday night dance! And Mrs Cominsky, up the Paddy close, would be at her old Singers sewing machine creating an artwork of coloured silk and cotton patches that would grace the hole-in-the-wall bed of the lucky purchaser.

The Salvation Army and The Red Cross and The Women's Institute and others would be getting mobile canteens organised in case the Luftwaffe should come to call.

The lenses of the searchlights would have been repolished and the Ack-Ack guns would be well greased, ready for the unwelcome visitors.

At the North British Locomotive Works, in Queens Park, they would be turning out battle tanks during two twelve-hour shifts and down on the River Clyde busy shipyards would be working flat out with welding torches getting no chance to cool.

Life was going on in this no mean city!

The ladies labouring on the Cathcart railway track were probably on their tea break....sitting at the side of the line and sipping strong, sweet tea from tin mugs. Miss Cranston's would have to wait!

And the women porters at the College Goods Station had found a strength they never knew before. The city's pulse had quickened...as Annie's had. And she still worried!

Joe Loss Band swung into 'Don't Sit Under The Apple Tree' and Ina and

Rita were in full stride along with Curdy and Rasputin.

Annie came back from the window, put on a brave smile and pulled Wullie up from his chair.

"C'mon, Wullie," she cried, "get the legs movin'."

Wullie joined in and took to the floor. Immediately Ina saw Wullie on his feet, she left Curdy and grabbed him.

"Come on," she laughed, "we're gonny have a whale of a time!"

Wullie grunted.

"Aye," he gasped breathlessly," dancin' wi' you is like goin' roon' the flair wi' Moby Dick!"

The fast music ended and the quiet sound of muted trombones struck up 'My Blue Heaven'. Wullie flopped on to his chair, puffing, panting and cursing. Ina, too, dropped into her chair, happy and smiling and pleased with herself. This had been the closest she had ever managed to get to the elusive, hostile Wullie McSorley.

Rasputin and Rita stayed on the floor and were cheek-to-cheek in their own dream world!

"Ye canny half move yersel, Ina!" Annie said by way of a compliment. "ye're that light oan yer feet!"

Ina flushed and puffed out her generous chest.

"Ah trained at the Alex Warren Dance School, up the toon," she said proudly. "They were really brilliant, so they were!"

"They must've been tae make you light oan yer feet," Wullie sniped.

Ina frowned.

"Ma faither," she said sharply, "was a great actor....a man of the theatre and he said he wisnae surprised that Ah was a star pupil at the Warren School o' Dancin'.He said that Ah had the smell of the theatre comin' off me, so he did!"

Wullie nodded.

"There's definitely the smell of somethin ' comin aff ye," he said, screwing up his nose.

Annie glowered over at Wullie.

"Don't you listen tae him, Ina," Annie said, throwing another dagger glance at her brother, "Ah could imagine you bein' a smashin' dancer...ye've still got that poise!"

"That pong ye mean," Wullie said, disregarding Annie's anger.

Ina was now away on a nostalgic trip as the happy days of Warren's Dance School came back to her.

"The tango was ma dance," she said with a faraway look. "Ah wance entered a tango contest at the Plaza. It was wonderful, so it was...."

Wullie sighed and threw a weary glance towards heaven. Did he have to listen to this?

"Ah wore this black silk dress," Ina went on, "with a lace mantilla tae match. And, when Ah took the floor, Ah had a red rose between ma teeth."

"Oh, did ye have teeth then?" Wullie said. "Ah thought ye just got them recently."

Ina ignored him and carried on with her nostalgic narrative.

"Ma greatest ambition was tae dance the tango wi' Rudolph Valentino?" she said, referring to the silent film heart-throb. "Ah knew he was deid...but Ah could dream".

Rasputin stopped in mid-stride as his ears picked up Ina's commentary.

"Ah invented a dance wance," he said, In the same lines as the Spanish...the Tango, an' that. It was called The Rasp but it never took on." He sounded disappointed.

"Whit kind o' dance was it, Raspy?" Annie asked, interested in anything that Rasputin did.

"Ah called it The Rasp, efter masel'," he said. "Everybody went intae the middle o' the flair, faced each other and stuck their tongues oot."

Wullie threw up another fatigued glance.

Turning to Ina, he said:

"It's a good joab that wisnae your speciality. The bloke facin' you would've found himsel' flyin' across the room and gettin' pinned against the opposite wa'."

Ina brushed Wullie's rudeness aside.

"Are ye musically inclined, Raspy?" she asked Rita's intended.

"Depends whit wey Ah'm sittin'," Raspy replied, turning once more to take Rita in his arms and whirl around the floor, leaving Ina to think.

The conversation made Annie, too, think of her dancing days when she and Big Sammy tripped the light fantastic.

"Ah met Sammy in Barraland," she said to Ina with a sigh."Ah didnae like him at first 'cos he was too smooth, if ye know whit Ah mean.."

Ina nodded.

"He gave me a couple of dances,"Annie went on, "until he got chucked oot for jitterbuggin'."

Ina was taken aback.

"They didnae dae Jitterbuggin in they days, Annie," she said.

"Sammy did," Annie said adamantly.

Ina pursed her lips.

"They definitely didnae allow jitterbuggin in the Denistoun Palais!" she exclaimed.

Rita, still in a shuffling embrace with Rasputin, overheard Ina's remark.

"That's right," she said, without breaking her rhythm. "they still don't....but they allow it at Barraland in a coarner so ma da' couldnae have been chucked oot o' Barraland for jitterbuggin, 'cos they allow ye tae jitterbug!"

"No' oan tap o' the manager's desk, they don't," Annie said. Wullie raised his voice.

"Ah don't ever remember Big Sammy bein' cognizant wi' dancin'," he said. Annie frowned.

"Ah'll tell ye this, Wullie, ma Sammy was a brilliant jitterbugger. He used tae throw me up in the air and chuck me ower his shoulder an' everythin'!" Wullie shrugged.

"He did that tae ye when he came in plastered on a Setturday night and he wisnae dancin'!"

"Aye, well," Rita said, still dancing, "jitterbuggin's the big thing noo. Barraland is full o' Yanks...and can they jive or can they jive!" Rita was ecstatic!

"Wan o' them actually mistook me for Betty Grable the other night," she sighed.

"Aye, he was just lonely," Raspy said, feeling a little resentful.

"Ah wance got took for a film star," Ina said.

"Who? Charles Laughton?" Wullie said snidely.

Annie drew Wullie an angry look. Ina was on her nostalgic travels once more and Wullie sighed deeply. "Ah was just a wee lassie at the time," Ina reminisced, "and ma faither took me wi' him wan day when he was goin' up tae see his agent in West Nile Street. Well, the agent took wan look at me...and then another..."

"A loat o' people dae that!" Wullie said.

Ina gave him a scornful look.

"Anywey," she went on, "he looked again and rubbed his eyes."

"They dae that as well," Wullie said.

Ina ignored him this time.

"Then the man said tae ma da', 'She looks like a child film star Ah just canny put a name tae'."

"He was probably thinkin' o' Mickey Rooney," Wullie said.

"It was not Mickey Rooney," Ina snapped. "It was Shirley Temple..."

Annie's cool snapped.

"That's enough o' that, Wullie," she said angrily. "Enough's enough.

Ah'm fed up wi' your snide remarks tae Ina. It's a wonder she comes near us at a'!"

Wullie shuffled his feet.

"Ach," he murmered, "Ah don't mean..er...well, Ah mean..."

His shame was cut short by a cry from Rita, now looking out of the window.

Rita was dancing a jig and excitedly clapping her hands:

"He's here! He's here!" she shrieked "LOOK!"

Everyone hurried to the window, Annie making sure the room lights were switched off.

Wullie had opened the blackout blinds and all stood gazing down into the street. Rita had thrown her arms around Raspy's neck and was hugging him tightly. Annie was beside herself with joy.

"Telt ye, didn't Ah!" Wullie said, slapping his thigh.

Fingers McGeachie was pushing a hand barrow and stopped at the baffle wall at Annie's close.

"Oh look, mammy," Rita cried, "he's got two boaxes...TWO boaxes!"

"TWO!" Annie repeated and did a quick skip.

Ina gave Annie an affectionate peck on the cheek.

"Ah'm that pleased for ye,Annie?" she said, "and you, tae, Rita."

Fingers slid one of the boxes to the edge of the barrow and, with some difficulty, lifted it off and staggered across the pavement, disappearing up the close.

"Geez, did ye see how heavy that was, mammy!" Rita exclaimed.

"He must have a coo and a couple o' bags o' totties in there at least!" Wullie said.

Annie pulled the blinds back, switched the lights back on and hurried to the door where she threw it open widely and waited with a thankful prayer for her 'messenger from Heaven'.

"Bring them noo, bring the whole lot o' them and they'll have a night they'll never forget," she said softly to herself. Her Rita would have a proper engagement as is her right!

Annie could hear Fingers' grunts and his heavy footsteps as he climbed the newly pipe-clayed stairs...done by Annie for the benefit of the expected guests.

The Big Man arrived at the door, clutching the large box, heaving and gasping for breath.

"Aw, ye're oot o' condition, Fingers," Annie said.

Fingers was too breathless to respond. To a chorus of cheers and applause he wobbled into the kitchen and, with a thankful groan, dumped the box on top of the table.

"Sorry Ah was delayed," Fingers said, wiping his brow. "It was a' due tae some important business that Ah'm conductin' for the War Department....know whit Ah mean?" He tapped the side of his nose. "You're here noo and that's a' that matters," Annie said.

"Ah was sorry tae hear aboot the pig!" Fingers said shaking his head.

"Aye, well the pig might've flew oot the windae, but you have saved the day just the same," Wullie said.

"We were gettin' worried, " Rita said, "but we should've known better. "

Fingers puffed out his chest.

"If ye're gonny have a party, come tae Fingers and you'll eat..er...hearty," Fingers said.

All applauded.

"Right, noo," Fingers went on. "Ah managed tae get ye some tins o' ham, some o' sardines, not forgettin' the good auld coarned mutton. There's even a few tomatoes there, some rolls, courtesy of the Welma Bakery, some ginger..i.e. iron brew and ginger beer...some ...wait for it..wait forit..." Fingers beamed as he was about to announce his piece de resistance, "SALMON FIVE TINS of John West!"

Annie grabbed Rita and they whirled and whooped around the table.

"The siege is ended!" Wullie cried. "Geggies to be fed at the double...Good Old Fingers! Eat your fill, folks."

With a flourish, Fingers swept his hand over the top of the box.

"Your banquet, madame," he said to Rita.

Rita, finger under chin, curtseyed and proceeded to delve into the box of goodies. Her face fell as she pulled out a bicycle pump, then another and another and another, Wullie tore at the box and threw up his arms in despair.

"Are we supposed tae fill oorsel's wi' wind?" he cried.

The box was packed tightly with black bicycle pumps. Annie looked on, stunned as Rita put her arm into the box and produced more and more pumps. She looked pleadingly at Fingers, who flushed slightly.

"Have nae fear," Fingers said, holding up his hand. "A slight error has occurred.. A slight case of mistaken identity. Youse have inadvertently just seen the contents of a top secret boax." Fingers gave an embarrassed cough.

Annie threw up her hands. More snags! Fingers, seeing her distress, put an arm around her shoulder.

"Don't Fred McMurray," Annie," he said. "It's just a matter of goin' doon the stairs and chingin' the boaxes. This wee consignment is for the Home Guard...for special..er..assignments. YOUR wee consignment is for Home Use and a VERY SPECIAL assignment. Noo, haud oan!"

Fingers took the box and hurried downstairs. Annie and Rita went to the window, Annie signalling Wullie to douse the lights. The barrow was still there, beside the baffle wall and easily seen in the glow of the street light. Fingers emerged from the close, slid the box of pumps on and pulled the box of food towards him.

"'Ello, 'Ello! Whit have we got here, then, eh?"

Fingers spun round. Erchie McPherson emerged from the back of the close, his flashlight turned on Fingers' face.

"Whit dae ye mean, 'Whit have we got here?'" Fingers said, a puzzled expression on his face.

"The barra," Erchie said, nodding towards Fingers' transport system.

"Whit barra?" Fingers asked, his brows knitted.

"THAT barra," Erchie replied impatiently,nodding towards the wheel-barrow.

"Aw, ye mean THAT barra?" Fingers said, his face lighting up.

"Ah don't see any other bloody barras at the foot of this close!" Erchie snapped.

"Oh my God!" Annie bawled out, her heart leaping up to her mouth at the sight of Erchie coming out of the closemouth. Clutching her chest, she swayed and was caught by Rita, who also swayed but was steadied by Wullie who stepped quickly in at Annie's first tortured exclamation.

"It's Erchie!" Annie moaned. "Erchie, the last wan we want tae see."

Rita felt a tear come to her eye.

"Everything was goin' that well, tae!" she said. Wullie shook his head.

"Ah must admit," he said, "that anybody else, any other polis,might have turned a blind eye, on compassionate grounds, tae this particular wee errand of mercy taken on by Fingers. But no' Erchie! He sees every arrest as the door opening a wee bit wider for that permanent joab he's efter."

Annie could watch no longer. She turned away and sat on the chair, comforted by Ina.

Down at the closemouth Fingers was trying to extract himself from the situation in hand.

"See that barra," Fingers was saying, "that barra shouldnae be there."

"YOU are tellin' ME that it shouldnae be there?" Erchie blurted. "Ah am tellin' YOU that it shouldnae be there. And Ah'm waitin' for an explanation."

"And so ye should," Fingers said.

"Whit dae ye mean, 'so Ah should'?" Erchie said, his eyes narrowing.

"'Cos that was exactly ma first thought as Ah was walkin' doon the street," Fingers said. "As soon as a clapped ma eyes oan that barra sittin' there unattended, Ah said tae masel, "That barra shouldnae be there."

"Mmm!" Erchie grunted, "Did ye noo?"

"Ah did!" Fingers said. "And just at that, Ah saw two wee boys runnin' away frae the barra as Ah approached. 'Hello' Ah said tae mael', whit are they two wee boys runnin' away for when they saw me approachin'? Maybe they think Ah'm the polis and maybe this barra that they were staunin' beside contains stolen goods. 'Ah wull just investigate'. Ah said tae masel', 'and if, by crickey, they ARE stolen goods, Ah will immediately inform the law." Erchie's eyes got even narrower.

"Hm'ph!" he murmered, "so let's see if you were right, eh?"

Erchie began to rummage in both boxes, watched by Fingers standing beside him and Rita and Wullie from behind the blackout blind.

"Ah-Ha," Erchie cried in triumph, pulling out a bicycle pump in one hand and a large, cooked ham in the other." "Oh!" Rita cried, turning away and hurrying over to her mother. "He's found the ham, mammy!" Their eyes met and they fell into each others' arms wailing loudly.

Fingers gave Erchie a hearty slap on the back:

"Good for you, Constable McPherson!" he said, shrewdly knowing that Erchie's chest inflates to double its size when he is addressed as 'constable'.

"Aye, well..er..just goes tae show, eh!"

"You are holding a symbol in yer hand there, dae ye know that?" Fingers said.

Erchie shook his head.

"Naw, Ah am not musically inclined," he said. "This is a bicycle pump," he went on, holding up the appliance.

"Naw, Ah did not mean that that was a musical instrument," Fingers said. " THAT combined wi'the ham you've got there,symbolises that the price of ham has went up because of inflation..get it?"

The penny dropped and Erchie was not amused.

"Aw, very funny, Fingers, very funny!" he said. "And if Ah wisnae in a perticularly good mood the night, Ah would think that you've got somethin' tae dae wi' a' this!"

Fingers fell back.

"Who? ME?" he cried, with a hurt expression. Erchie nodded.

"Aye, YOU," he said. "Noo, you just grab haud o' they two shafts an' start pullin' this barra doon that street."

Fingers stepped back:

"And why should Ah dae that?" he said defiantly. "Ah have got a bad back and pullin' barras protrudes the umbrex cord tae very painful proportions. If Ah should perchance end up in the Royal Infirmary on traction, Ah wull be compelled for tae sue the Glesca Police Department."

Erchie McPherson had never heard of an 'Umbrex Cord' but would do nothing that would bring down the wrath of the Chief Constable.

Fingers McGeachie reckoned on this and was glad that he had invented a new medical condition.

"A'right," Erchie said, "Ah wull pull the barra....you follow me."

"Hey wait a minute," Fingers cried, "you are not suggestin' that Ah should accompany you doon tae Tobago Street, are ye?"

"That's where the polis station is, "Erchie said, "and that's where Ah'm goin' wi' this load of contraband."

Fingers nodded.

"Aye, maybe YOU'RE goin'," he said, "but AH'M no' goin'....Ah've ma reputation tae think aboot, ma image!"

Fingers felt that his persona would be tarnished if it were ever known that he had set foot inside the precincts of the, to his mind, sub-station, he considered Tobago Street to be. Central Headquarters, he didn't mind, although he preferred to steer clear of all spheres of police activity.

Fingers was beginning to irritate Erchie. "Look," Erchie snapped, "Ah am not totally convinced of your innocence in a' this. For example Ah am sure that Ah saw you cairryin' this boax and puttin' it oan this barra."

Fingers put a finger to his mouth.

"Ah would be careful of whit Ah am sayin' if Ah was you," he said in a whisper.

"Oh, and how is that," Erchie said, drawing his brows.

"Because," Fingers said, "you could easily misconstrue what you saw. "

Erchie folded his arms. "Oh, and how Ah could Ah possible dae that?" he asked quizzically.

"Because, you did indeed see me cairryin' that boax of bicycle pumps," Fingers said. "And you DID see me puttin' it oan this barra but that was because ma War Department driver had just drapped me aff wi' this consignment of bike pumps that are required by a certain Home Guard unit...for special operations."

Erchie's brows went up.

"Yer War Department driver?" he said with some surprise. Fingers nodded.

"He drapped ye aff here wi' a big boax o' bike pumps...HERE? Why did he no' take ye tae where the pumps were intended for?"

"Because," Fingers said, "Ah telt ye...they're intended for a special mission and naebody, but NAEBODY must know who was gettin' them. Ah was tae secretly take them the last part of the journey masel'."

"Oh! And so ye were gonny cairry this big boax oan the last lap o' yer journey, is that it?" Erchie said sarcastically.

Fingers shook his head.

"Naw, Ah was supposed tae get picked up here in an unmarked car," he said. "But when it wisnae here waitin' and Ah saw the barra just sittin' there, Ah decided tae use ma initiative. Ah didnae want these very special and expensive instruments exposed unnecessarily."

Fingers wiped his brow.

"Aye, a'right, be that as it may," Erchie said, "but you are the wan that came across this barra and you are the wan that's comin' wi' me tae the station tae gie a statement. And if the Home Guard want tae get oan their bikes withoot their pumps, they can go wi' flat tyres for a' Ah care. Ye must think ma heid buttons up the back!"

Erchie took hold of the shafts and pushed the barrow on to the street.

"Come on," he snapped, "this wey."

Fingers shrugged, gave a discreet quick glance up at the window and followed Erchie up Well Street where, after turning into Stevenston Street, they headed for the 'Polis Oaffice'.

Wullie let the blackout blind fall back into place, walked across the room and switched the lights back on.

"Well," he sighed, "there's an auld sayin' – that is the hollow sphere containing a full pressure of air now elevated up to the metamorphic rocks....in other words...that's the ba' up oan the slates."

Wullie was shaking his head. He saw all his endeavour going to waste.

"Ye know somethin'," he said, "Ah've just seen somethin' that Ah never thought Ah'd live tae see!"

"Oh! And whit's that, Uncle Wullie?" Rita asked, rising from the arm of the chair.

"Erchie McPherson pushin' the barra oot," Wullie said, not attempting to hide the wry grin.

Annie rose from her chair, wiped her eyes and put the kettle on.

"Put that wireless aff," she ordered, as the band played 'I'll Get By'

Curdy McVey felt embarrassment flush over him. He felt that he should not be here in this moment of family crisis.

"Will er Ah just go then, eh? Ah'm awfu' sorry Missus."

"You just stey where ye are, son," Annie said kindly. "There's tae be an engagement here the night and Erchie McPherson isnae gonny spoil it."

Wullie slapped Curdy on the back.

"Besides," Wullie said, "if by any chance Erchie McPherson should show up at this door the night, we just might be in need of your professional services, Curdy."

Everybody laughed and the ice was broken.

"And another thing," Wullie said, "whit aboot a' they caun'les ye've been lightin', eh? Surely that's no' effort a' wasted!"

"Maybe we'd have been better eatin' them right enough!" Rita smiled.

"Things could be worse, Ah suppose," Wullie said finally. "We could have nae drink left."

Ina sat up, smoothed her dress and decided to change the conversation.

"Ah hivnae seen yer engagement ring yet, Rita," she said perkily. Everybody sat up.

"True enough!" Annie said, clapping her hands together."Come on, oot wi' it."

Rasputin shuffled his feet and grinned impishly.

"Ah hivnae seen it either," Rita cried. "He hisnae gied me it yet!"

"Come on, dae the necessary, Raspy, or ye'll never hear the end o' it," Wullie said, "Produce the H. Samuels dazzlin' special and gie us a' a treat."

The reference to Glasgow's popular jeweller's shop made Rasputin's face flush. He had never been there. Rita's boyfriend had done his shopping elsewhere.

He tried to avoid Rita's eyes but she took his hand and squeezed it tightly, showing her affection and also giving him courage.

"Don't be shy, Raspy," she said, giving his hand an extra squeeze.

"Well, Ah was hopin' we could dae this when we were..er..by oorselves, if ye know whit Ah mean?" he said sheepishly.

Ina tutted impatiently:

"Och, go on," she urged,"put us oot oor misery. Who knows, maybe this magical romantic moment might be catchin'," she smiled, looking over at Wullie, who immediately averted his eyes.

Annie stood up and began to arrange the chairs in a single row.

"Right," she said, "everybody take their seats for the big show." Saying that, she took Rasputin and Rita by their wrists and led them to the centre of the floor. Then, returning to her seat, she joined the rest, coughed slightly and was quiet.

"On youse go," she finally said, seeing some prompting was required.

"Dae you no' mind us getting engaged in front o' an audience, Rita", Rasputin asked reticently.

Rita shrugged.

"Ah don't mind. Ah mean it's a' family and freen's, int it? But if you would rather we went oot tae the landin' or intae the room, well, Ah don't mind we'll still be engaged —OFFICIALLY." Rita smiled happily!

Rasputin began to look through his pockets.

"Aye, Ah suppose ye're right," he said, "oor love wull be hidden from naebody."

Everybody edged forward in their seats...especially Ina.

Rasputin patted his inside pocket and, finding what he wanted, his eyes lit up.

"Before we go through this very important ritual," he said, "there's somethin' Ah must say."

All moved forward a little closer with eyes a little wider. Rasputin turned and took Rita's hand in his. "Ma intentions, Rita," he said, "was for to gie ye ma mother's ring. It's got a beautiful stone in the middle and ma maw always said that it had great sentimental value and that she treasured it as it was her mother's before her." Rita sighed. "Aw, whit a lovely story, Raspy!" She squeezed his hand. "Alas!" Rasputin went on, "Ah find that Ah canny gie ye it...as much as Ah want tae." Rita affectionately patted his cheek. "Ah understaun'," ma wee lamb," she said. "Is it because it's a family heirloom?"

"Naw, it's no' that," Rasputin said. "Whit is it, then?" Rita asked, knitting her brows. "Ma maw wull no' gie me it," he moaned. Rita stepped back and, hands on hips, snapped. "Does that mean you've come here the night...RINGLESS?"

"Gormless is mair like it," Wullie said.

Annie stood up. "Noo, gie the boy a chance," she said with some pity. Rasputin put up his hands as though in surrendering. "Naw, naw," he said in an urgent tone, "Ah would not dae that. Ah have here, in ma poacket, the perfect symbol of oor love...of us being joined together as wan."

Ina dabbed her eyes and turned to Annie. "He's that romantic, int he?" she said.

Rasputin dug deeply into his inside pocket and fumbled about before bringing his clenched fist out.

"Close yer eyes, darlin', " he said softly.

Rita smiled and closed her eyes. Ina dug Annie in the ribs and sighed and Wullie watched closely. Curdy McVey yawned.

Taking Rita's left hand in his, Rasputin said, "This is the bond, the bond of love between us. It is a symbol of oor togetherness. . .of oor joining together ... FOREVER".

Rita's naked finger began doing palpitations, like a dancing fish hook desperate to catch its prey. She sighed as she felt the touch of the metal entwine her finger and her engagement, at last, was ratified.

"Ye can open yer eyes noo," Rasputin said.

Rita held her arm out, tilted up her hand and opened her eyes....which got wider and wider as she surveyed her engagement finger. Placed on it was a nail, bent in a circle by a pair of strong pliers with the point and the flat head meeting in a 'V' shape.

"Ah know it's no' worth much, but it's the thought that counts," Rasputin said.

Rita, stunned for a moment, suddenly found her voice.

"Well," she bawled, "ye can keep yer thoughts tae yersel."

Rasputin's jaw dropped: "Ye..ye..mean ye don't like it....ye don't see the symbolism in it? The uniting, the merging, the combining..".he stammered, hurt by Rita's reaction. Rita stuck her outstretched hand under his nose. "Look at that...just look at it," she cried.

"The lassies at the depot are dyin' tae see ma engagement ring. They're comin' up here the night. Ah canny use that as an engagement ring, so Ah canny!"

Wullie peered over Rita's shoulder. "Ye couldnae even use it as a nail," he commented dryly.

"THEY might see the symbolism!" Rasputin said pleadingly.

Rita looked at Wullie, a plea in her eye.

"You could say ye got yer haun' caught in a door," he said. Ina McLatchie came over, took Rita's hand and studied the romantic symbol.

"It's definitely different!" she exclaimed. "AH would wear it. "You would wear an elastic band if somebody was daft enough tae gie ye wan," Wullie sniped.

Annie sighed.

"Ah'd love tae lend ye MA engagement ring," she said.

"Why don't ye, then?" Wullie said. "'Cos Ah hivnae got wan," Annie said, with some sadness.

"Was youse too poor?" Ina asked, feeling a little sorry for Annie.

Annie shook her head.

"It wisnae that exactly," she said. "Naw, Big Sammy thought that seein' we would only be engaged for wan week before the weddin', it would be a waste o' money buyin' a ring. So he bought me somethin' he knew fine would bring a smile oan ma face."

Ina was all ears.

"Aw, whit did he buy ye?" she purred.

"A new set o' teeth," Annie said.

Ina's face fell and Wullie nodded.

"That's Big Sammy a' ower," he said, "nothin' for nothin', that's him. Gie him a big smile and ye're daein' it wi' his ain teeth..typical!"

"Well, Ah'm no' smilin'," Rita wailed, "nae food, nae drink and noo nae ring.

"There's still they two planked boattles o' Johnny Walker", Wullie said quickly.

Rita flopped on to the easy chair and buried her head in her hands. Annie and Ina comforted her as best they could and Curdy McVey walked over to the window and stared at the blackout blind.

"Ah wanted tae gie Rita a surprise," Rasputin said to Wullie.

"Aye, well ye did that, son," Wullie nodded. "Maist fellas when they're gettin' engaged, go tae H. Samuels, The Jewellers, in Argyle Street, tae buy the ring. There's no' many go tae Crocket's, The Ironmongers, in Coocaddens!"

Rita, overhearing Wullie's remarks, wailed louder.

Rasputin hurried over and fell down on bended knee.

Taking Rita's hand, Rasputin gazed into her tearful eyes:

"Trust me, hen," he murmered, "just trust me!" Annie looked up.

"How, are ye gonny open up a diamond mine or somethin'?"

"Ah could consider it," Rasputin said. "South Africa," he added, "that's the place for diamonds...."

"You could get yer elephants there, tae," Wullie said dryly.

Curdy McVey, who had pulled the blackout blind back a sliver, let out a cry:

Oh!" he shouted, "there's a big gang o' folk a' comin' up this close...!"

Annie jumped up in panic. Wringing her hands she began to pace the floor:

"Aw, naw! It's them, Ah know it is...it's them, int it? Aw, God, whit a red face....Dae they look like they're oan the caurs, son?" Annie cried.

"Naw, they're a' walkin', missus," Curdy said.

"Naw, Ah meant dae they look like they're clippies...conductresses...?" Annie yelled.

Curdy shrugged.

"Ah widnae know," he said. "Ah dae maist o' ma travellin' in hearses."

Distressed, Annie, hand to her mouth, hurried out of the room.

"Ye'd better go and see tae yer mammy," Wullie said, nodding towards the door.

Rita wiped her eyes and, followed by Ina, left the room. They found Annie sitting at the edge of the bed, her head in her hands.

"Mammy!" Rita said lovingly, sitting beside her and putting an arm around her mother's shoulders.

Annie looked up, sniffled and took a deep breath.

"Ah'm that ashamed," she said. "Ma only wean's engagement and Ah couldnae even provide for her!"

Ina sat down and took Annie's trembling hand in hers;.

"Ye did yer best, Annie," she said softly. "It wisnae your fault that things turned oot the wey they did. In fact, things oaften don't turn oot the wey ye hope they will." Ina had a faraway look in in her eye.

"Ye're a good soul, Ina," Annie said, taking her neighbour's hand and squeezing it. "Ah realise whit ye're meanin'."

The women heard the banging at the door and Wullie's voice as he answered it. The crowd had arrived, boisterous and happy and yelling for the bride-to-be.

Rita stood up.

"Well," she said, drying her eyes and smoothing down her dress, "might as well go and face them, eh?"

Annie and Ina got to their feet and Annie preened herself at the dressing-table mirror. Ina, looking over her shoulder, gave her face a quick dab of powder.

"Well, we'll just have tae dae!" Annie said, taking a quick, last look.

Know somethin', Mammy?" Rita said, "Ah wonder where a' they prayers went tae that we sent up...whit happened tae a' that caun'le power?"

"Maybe HE was too busy," Annie said thoughtfully."

"He DOES have a terrible war goin' on doon here," Ina offered. Annie nodded.

"True enough!" she said. "Ye must get yer priorities right. Maybe a wee thing like an engagement party is..well...no' even worth takin' intae consideration in the scheme o' things."

Rita nodded.

"Only tae them that's involved," she murmured.

The three women went to the door. Annie put her hand on the knob and turned, saying:

"Are we a' ready, then?"

Ina rolled up her sleeves and, in mock agression, said: "Bring 'em on!"

Annie smiled a weak smile and looked at Rita, a softness in her eyes.

"Rita?"

Rita nodded.

"Ah'm a'right, Mammy."

"Right, let's go," Annie said firmly and turned the knob.

The room was bustling when they entered. Cries of 'Congratulations' and 'Hard Up' echoed round and Wullie was busy trying to put equal thimble size amounts of Curdy's Red Ruby round.

Rita was set upon immediately by the girls in the crowd with demands to see her engagement ring.She had already discarded the home-made 'symbol'and was busy explaining that she had still to receive her precious bond band.

"Rasputin is shy," she announced, and would be placing the ring on her finger at the proper moment.

There was a round of applause with calls for Rasputin to do the deed 'here and now!'

Annie pulled Wullie into a corner.

"Ah suppose Ah should make an announcement aboot oor unfortunate lack of party fare," she said.

"Ah'll tell them if ye like?" Wullie said, giving her arm a squeeze.

Annie shook her head.

"Naw, it's ma problem. Ah feel that sorry for Rita, so Ah dae, but we canny keep them here a' night and no' offer them SOMETHING!"

Wullie nodded and Annie pulled a dining chair into the middle of the room.

Standing on the seat, she called for attention.

Annie had to bawl and clap her hands before the babble died down and all ears turned towards her makeshift podium.

"Ah..er..have somethin' Ah must tell..er..say," she stammered. "Due to cir-cumstances beyond... er..."

She was cut short by the sudden wail of the air-raid sirens. Its banshee screaming and panic shrieks from some of the less hardened clippies made her inaudible.

"Don't panic" Wullie cried, "the Luftwaffe wull no' even be at Glesca Croass yet...c'mon, noo, everybody doon tae the shelter...across the road and up the pend c'mon."

Annie climbed down as Wullie ushered the guests out of the door and down the stairs.

"At least he's no' had time tae cart they wally dugs doon wi' him!" Annie said, throwing on a coat and making sure that Rita and Curdy were safely away. Ina had grabbed her bag and was following as near to Wullie as she could and Rasputin had Rita firmly by the hand.

The shelter was filling up with some folk already there, sitting on the hard benches that faced each other along the walls.

The noisy party guests were dispersing around the small, brick building and were gabbing and laughing happily, still filled with the soiree spirit that was to come.

Annie sat down beside a young mum who was cradling a baby in a grey, woollen shawl .. She was pacifying her child with 'cooing' and baby talk. Ina had made sure that she was seated beside Wullie, who was busy lighting up his pipe. Curdy McVey had been jostled along by the crowd down the aisle and had vanished at the far end of the shelter

Raspy had taken Rita by the arm and had found a secluded corner, near the entrance where they could stand in the shadows.

"Is the wean aright?" Annie asked the young mum, leaning over to get a look.

"Och, to be sure!" she replied in a thick, Irish accent."She's used to the wailing and the noise by now and this is just a wee protest at being woken up and carted outside into the cold air."

"Aye, well that's how it affects us a'!" Annie said.

"It doesn't seem to be botherin' that crowd of revellers, anyway!" the young mum said, nodding down towards the end of the shelter.

"Oh them!" Annie said. "Ye know somethin', this is the first time that Ah have been saved by the Luftwaffe."

The Irishwoman raised her brows.

"Oh, now how could that be?" she said, surprised.

Annie went on to tell her the tale of the engagement party and how Auld McPhee's shop was bombed and how she had tried to get new supplies without success —omitting any part played by Fingers McGeachie, of course!

The Irish lady shook her head sadly:

"Aw, I can understand yer dilemma!" she said. "To be standin' there wi' all all these people waitin' to be wined and dined...and you, wit' a red face and nothin' in the cupboard. Aw, yes, it's a terrible t'ing!"

Annie sighed. The woman suddenly turned and, grasping Annie's wrist, said :

"Are ye a prayin' woman at all, at all?" Annie nodded.

"Ah try tae be, so Ah dae."

"Prayers definitely work," the woman said, "I know for a fact. Know what happened to me?" she looked about to make sure she was not overheard. "My man, Barney, had a terrible hankerin' for a bit of ham — he's from County Cork y'see," she whispered. "And I went into St Alphonsus' chapel and lit a candle to the Holy Mother and asked her if she could find her holy way to send a wee bit extra bacon along...'cos Barney's a hard workin' wee fella and deserves a wee bit spoilin' now and again. Well, ye'll never know what happened! Ah had just left the chapel and was walkin' down Well Street when this pig came hurtlin' down from Heaven and landed at me feet... so help me God! It was as quick as that. Ah don't think the Holy Mother could've responded any quicker if Ah had been down on me knees in Lourdes itself...so there!

"That's the power o' prayer for ye!"

Annie's hand went up to her mouth. She did not want Biddy O'Flaherty to see the smile crossing her face.The young mum believed in her miracle....and who was to say that it wasn't supernatural intervention that provided her with the answer to her prayer?

"That's a lovely story," she said at last. "But Ah'm afraid ma prayers have fallin' oan deef ears. Ah've still tae face this crowd when the 'All-Clear' sounds. It'll no' be all clear for me!"

Annie grimaced, bent over and looked down lovingly at baby Marietta who was now sound asleep and had found her escape from the world. Lucky Marietta! Naughty Marietta!

Wullie kept looking down to the far end of the shelter, hoping the mouth organ player had emigrated.

"Ah canny see him," he said to Ina, smiling. "That's a good sign. Wi' any luck he might've choked on it."

Ina sighed.

"Gie the man a break, Wullie," she scolded. "He's just tryin' tae cheer us up, so he is. We canny a' sit doon here wi' long faces! That's whit Hitler wants us tae dae. That's whit them up there in the airyplanes are hopin' we're daein'...a' sittin' here shakin' in oor shoes. We canny let them think that, Wullie. We canny gie in…and Ah'm never wan for gien in…oan any-thin'!"

Wullie was surprised at Ina's outburst.

"That was quite a speech, so it was. Did it come frae wan o' yer faither's scripts?" he said.

Ina turned her ample frame and faced Wullie, who spluttered on his pipe.

"Naw, it didnae come frae wan o' ma faither's scripts, Wullie," she said coldly. "It came frae ma heart. Oh, aye, Ah HAVE got a heart, Wullie, a BIG, BIG HEART, that's jam-packed wi' love. That prompted me tae go intae toon and spend ma money oan a blouse and tae go tae Madame Wee Nellie's and get ma hair done, only tae get a snide remark frae somebody no' hauf-a-mile frae here. Funny things, hearts, Wullie!"

Wullie fell silent. Contrition for all the nasty things he thought and said to Big Ina McLatchie swept over him. But he could never apologise. Wullie could never do that.

Ina sensed what was going through Wullie's mind. She edged closer to him and rummaged in her bag.

"Here," she said, pulling out a paper bag and handing it to him. "Whit's this?" Wullie said hesitantly.

"Open it and see," Ina said.

Slowly, Wullie opened up the bag and looked in. His eyes widened and he turned and smiled broadly at Ina, who smiled back. Putting his hand in he pulled out the delicacy.

"Soday Scones! Soday Scones!" he grinned and took a bite.

"Aw!" he exclaimed ecstatically, "these are smashin', just smashin', even better than Annie's!"

Ina smiled and shuffled closer:

"Ah..er..made them masel'," she said softly. "Ah knew ye liked them efter that time Ah had tea in your hoose. Dae ye really think they're… er…. better than Annie's?"

Wullie was chewing heartily.

"Definitely, but definitely!" he said between mouthfuls. "Aye, ye've opened ma eyes, Ina. They're the best soday scones that Ah have ever tast-ed, so they are!"

Ina shuffled in her seat, happy and just a little embarrassed. Wullie smacked his lips and closed up the bag.

"Ah'll keep the rest for efter," he said.

Ina smiled. Her hand moved across the seat and touched Wullie's drum-ming fingers. She took his hand in hers and turned to him when, out of character,he did not pull his away. She sighed as she felt a slight squeeze on her hand.

But Wullie suddenly pulled his hand away and, taking a handkerchief from his pocket, coughed and gave his nose a good blow.

"Ah...er..Ah think there's somethin' you should know, Ina," he said finding himself unable to look her straight in the eye.

"Oh, aye!" Ina said curiously "And whit's that?"

"It's..er..it's..er..it's aboot yer faither. Y'see..er...that day Ah went tae pick him up, Ah...er...."

He did not get finishing his narrative.

"Oh, aye...ma faither!" Ina interrupted with an impish grin. "Funny thing, Ah got a postcard frae him this mornin'..!"

Wullie's eyebrows shot up and he spluttered: "A postcerd?"

Ina nodded. "Aye," she smiled, "frae Rothesay." Wullie's jaw fell open and Ina chortled. "Ye... ye... know?" he asked shamefacedly. "A wee dug telt me", Ina laughed. Wullie flushed! "Ma da' always liked Rothesay," she said with a twinkle. Ina smiled as she felt Wullie tenderly squeeze her hand.

Rasputin and Rita stood quietly in a small recess near the door. They listened to the drone of the Heinkels and the rapid firing of the ack-ack guns. "Whit a noise!" Rita said, screwing up her face. Rasputin was silent. "Are ye still talkin' tae me?" he said finally. "Of coorse Ah'm talkin' tae ye," Rita said. "We're engaged aren't we?...and Ah've got a nail tae prove it." "Ach, Rita," Rasputin said, "Ah telt ye tae trust me, didn't Ah? Ah just couldnae staun' there and get engaged in front of everybody. Ah wanted you and me tae be alone, by oorsel's...know whit Ah mean?" Rita pecked him on the cheek.

Rasputin patted his top pocket. "See that pocket there?" he said. "Put yer haun' in."

Rita looked quizzically at him and, a little reluctantly, put her hand inside the pocket. She came out with a small, brown envelope. "Open it!" Rasputin said.

Rita tore the paper open and out, into the palm of her hand, fell an eighteen-carat gold ring...with three diamonds that sparkled in the shaft of moonlight flooding through a gap in the door. Rita let out a surprised yelp of delight and threw her arms around Rasputin's neck, kissing his smiling face from every angle. "Aw, Raspy...ye were just kiddin' me on...!" Rita proceeded to smother his face once more with her lips. "Ah telt ye Ah wanted it tae be private," Rasputin said shyly. But the practical side of Rita suddenly surfaced. "How could you afford that beautiful ring?" she asked sternly. "Remember Ah telt ye Ah met Fingers in the street?" Rasputin said eagerly. "Well HE gave it tae me and he says that Ah don't have tae pey him till efter the war!"

Rasputin leaned back, very pleased with himself.

Rita did a jig.

"Aw, whit a man that Fingers is! And noo he's in jail because o' me!"

She suddenly became serious.

"Who's in jail?" the voice at the door said.

Fingers McGeachie stood at the doorway, immaculate as ever. Rita ran over and threw her arms around his neck.

"Aw, Fingers," she cried, "Ah thought they'd loacked ye up...and it was a' ma fault."

Fingers swung her around.

"Lock ME up? Are you kiddin?" he laughed. "Naw, naw," he said, "it'll take mair than a jaunt doon tae Tobago Street to nail me doon."

"Whit happened?" Rasputin said.

"The inspector took wan look at Erchie and took wan look at me and took ma word for it. They're oot lookin' for two wee boys."

He laughed loudly.

"The only thing is," he said, scratching his chin, "is that they've got a' your party grub and a' the bike pumps....but they'll need them."

"Whit for?" Rita asked curiously.

"Tae keep Erchie McPherson's inflated ego goin'" Fingers grinned. "Away you two lovebirds intae that coarner," he went on, "and dae whit newly engaged lovebirds are supposed tae dae."

Before moving on, he pulled Rasputin aside.

"By the way," he said. "Ah've got a very good Bengali contact. I..er..think Ah could get you a good deal on they elephants!"

Raspy's eyes widened and Fingers smiled roguishly as he moved on into the shelter and a rousing welcome.

Annie was now sitting with Biddy O'Flaherty's baby on her knee. It took her back to her younger days when she lovingly nursed Rita. She had promised Rita all the things that she never had. And now here she was, to her own mind, letting her daughter down.

Turning to Biddy, she said:

"Ye know, Ah'm usually dyin' for the All Clear tae sound...but no' the night, no' the night," she emphasised. "It'll mean Ah've got tae face that crowd again."

Biddy tenderly put her hand on Annie's arm.

"Your prayers will get answered, missus, don't you worry. There's always an answer...although it's sometimes not what we expected."

There was a hush in the shelter as the anti-aircraft guns echoed in the distance. Annie handed Biddy back the sleeping little Marietta. She stood up and cleared her throat. She would take advantage of the lull and get this over once and for all.

"Ma freen's," she called, "Could Ah have yer attention for just a wee minute."

All eyes turned to Annie, who stood nervously twisting the wedding ring on her finger.

"As youse all know, this is ma daughter Rita's engagement night..."

She was interrupted by a loud chorus of whistling and happy yelling.

Annie raised her hand for silence. When the noise died down she continued.

"Before the sirens went, Ah was about tae tell youse that...well," she hesitated, "well youse came tae the hoose expectin' a feast. Well Ah've tae tell ye that whit ye're really gonny get is...

"FISH SUPPERS... FISH SUPPERS FOR EVERY-A-BODY?" Annie, stopped in her tracks, spun round.

Mario Valente, carrying a huge clothes basket filled with succulent fish suppers, was standing at the door. The mouth-watering aroma wafted all the way down the shelter and there was a roof-raising chorus of approval.

"Ah've got-a boattles of a-Tizer tae...plenty for-a everybody. Sorry Ah'm-a late, Annie," he winked, "but they a-bloody bombers held-a me up."

Mario came down the aisle and put the basket down on the ground:

"Everybody a-help-a them-a-sel's, eh?" he cried.

Rita hurried down and threw her arms around the big Italian's neck and kissed him profusely. Soon, Annie, too, was hugging and kissing him.

"How did ye know?" Mario, she cried between tears.

"Ah met Fingers goin-a doon the road wi' Erchie Mc-aPherson and Fingers a-telt me aboot your-a bad luck. So, you think Ah'm-a gonny let ma favourite wee-a clippie doon, eh? Ma wee-a Rita, eh. No' on your-a Nellie."

Biddy and Annie's eyes met and Biddy gave Annie the thumbs up and a wink as she jabbed her thumb upwards.

Annie laughed happily.

The wee man at the end of the shelter suddenly produced his mouth organ and immediately burst into a rousing chorus of 'We'll Meet Again'.

Wullie's blood pressure quickly rose until he felt Ina's understanding hand giving him a squeeze. He looked down and Ina smiled and Wullie sudden-ly found himself joining in ... "We'll meet again, don't know where."

Outside, in the darkness, the searchlights continued to stab the night sky and, somewhere in the distance, the sound of the ack-ack guns spat out a dull echo.

Over the Glasgow rooftops the sweet sound of happy laughter mingled, with the sound of music, drifted out of an air-raid shelter near the Barras, ... a song of hope .. the joyful singing, of "We'll meet again in Well Street...."

And somewhere in France, in a prison camp, the stillness of the night was broken only by the quiet scraping of someone digging... with a soup spoon!

The End